D1003732

SLEDGEHAMMER

SLEDGEHAMMER

Paulo J. Reyes

Virtual Word Publishing

SLEDGEHAMMER

Copyright © 2005 by Paulo J. Reyes

Virtual Word Publishing books may be ordered through booksellers or by contacting:

Virtual Word Publishing
P.O. Box 938504
Margate, FL 33093
www.virtualwordpublishing.com

ISBN: 0-977-13870-4 (pbk)

Printed in the United States of America

Special consultant George Saunders

Preface

A WORD OF WARNING

With the advent of the new millennium, the world has been witness to extraordinary and horrific events perpetrated under the name of terrorism. September 11, 2001, marked a watershed event of unparalleled magnitude, wherein the United States, like the sleeping giant it was, awakened to a new kind of warfare. Airplanes used by terrorists to destroy buildings had proven as effective as smart bombs or ICBMS (Intercontinental Ballistic Missiles). The vetted experts within security circles had always acknowledged that commercial airliners, hijacked and skillfully commandeered by well-trained and focused individuals, could prove devastating to civilian populations. Before 9/11, such scenarios were well recognized, the resultant fallout from such theoretical attacks well considered and studied for decades. Following 9/11, the statistical probabilities in favor of such an attack were suddenly moot. The attack(s) was and were fait accompli.

Since September 11, global concern has been focused on a panoply of possible attack scenarios perpetrated by the terrorist element. These scenarios, not surprisingly, revolve around the usual suspect of some kind of nuclear threat, (e.g., radical yet well-organized and committed terrorist factions would somehow obtain small amounts of crude uranium and/or plutonium, smuggle it into the United States or one of its ally nations, and explode a crude device that could do comparable damage to property and population on the level of that of Hiroshima). Other worries look to a chemical threat or nerve agents that could conceivably ravage whole cities with but a few drops of concentrated toxin. The most frightening threat, however, remains one of nightmarish proportions—and the initiation of this form of terrorist attack is admittedly the most potentially devastating compared to all others.

Bioterrorism has been a term of late that has sailed into the forefront of worldwide focus. And the leader of the pack in terms of what *kind* of biological agent might be employed by radical extremists against the United States or its allies generally remains unanimous among experts in the field. The weapon of choice and preference among enemies of America is one, paradoxically, which has technically been absent from the planet, in natural form, for almost three decades. It is a biological monster that is now only kept in laboratory receptacles under tight governmental security—those governments being that of the former Soviet Union and the United States. Before its eradication, it was touted to be responsible for some 500 million deaths in the twentieth century alone (a total greater than the death toll from all warfare during the same century). The biological anomaly in question—in fact, the potential weapon of mass destruction most certainly preferred by terrorist extremists—is none other than smallpox.

Smallpox represents both the zenith and nadir of human achievement. It is the only disease eradicated through a concerted and extensive effort that transcended time, politics, and ideologies. Because of these efforts, not one documented naturally occurring case of this once fatal infection has occurred since October 26, 1977. (The last naturally occurring case was an unvaccinated hospital cook in Somalia). Smallpox officially was declared wiped out by the World Health Organization (WHO) under the stewardship of D. A. Henderson in 1980. Yet it still represents one of the most devastating potential biological weapons ever conceived of in its natural form; and, as a weaponized strain, it is hard to imagine what kind of devastation it would bring to this world.

Historically, smallpox affected political and social agendas. It was thought to be the cause of death of Ramsey V in 1155 BC. A smallpox epidemic struck Athens in 430 BC, killing approximately one-third of the population. This may have played a factor in the defeat of Sparta by the Greeks in the Poleponnesian War. During the Elephant Wars in AD 570, the Abyssinians were decimated by an outbreak of smallpox while they laid siege to Mecca. This preempted a successful conquest of Mecca, again playing a role in the history of man. What affect would an epidemic of smallpox—as a result of an act of bioterrorism—have on the history of this country?

Epidemics plagued the old and new worlds until Edward Jenner developed a vaccine in 1796, when he inoculated intradermally patients with the milder cowpox virus, thus rendering them immune to the variola virus. This was the first and only treatment for smallpox (which remains true today). The incidence of infection in Europe steadily declined from that point onward.

However, in the Americas, smallpox decimated the native population that had no previous exposure to the variola virus or the vaccine (and thus not immune to it), when it was introduced to the native population by the European explorers in the 1500 and 1600s. A state this country finds itself in presently.

The pathophysiology of smallpox breaks down as thus: the disease is caused by variola—a member of the *orthopoxvirus* genus—of which cowpox, monkeypox, and vaccinia are also members. Poxviruses are the largest animal viruses visible with a light microscope and are larger than some bacteria. The virus is acquired from inhalation or ingestion of a variola viron or by inoculation of an open wound. Although naturally, the variola virus cannot survive in the environment outside the human body for more than a short time, the viral particles can remain viable on clothing, bedding, or surfaces for days. There is no specific treatment for the smallpox disease, and the only prevention is vaccination.

The name *smallpox* is derived from the Latin word for "spotted" and refers to the raised bumps that appear on the face and body of the infected person. Exposure to the virus is followed by an incubation period during which people do not have any symptoms and may feel fine. This incubation period averages about twelve to fourteen days, during which time people are not contagious. The first symptoms of smallpox include head and body aches and high fever. People are generally prostrated and too sick to carry on normal activities. This is called the prodrome phase and may last for two to four days. Then a rash emerges, characterized by red spots on the body and oral cavity, with the oral lesions breaking open into sores. At this time, the person becomes most contagious. Around this time also, the rash appears on the skin, beginning on the face and upper extremities and subsequently spreading to the torso and lower extremities. There are two clinical forms of smallpox—variola major (the more severe and most common form of smallpox) and variola minor, a milder form of the disease called alastrim. Historically, it is the variola major that has an overall fatality rate of about thirty percent.

Back when the world was a different place, mass vaccination to smallpox was the most common prevention of the disease utilized and deterrent to its use as a weapon of mass destruction. Smallpox vaccine was given to large numbers of people who had not been exposed to the disease. The mass vaccination strategy helped protect people from smallpox, but it wasn't enough to completely get rid of it. This is because not everyone got vaccinated, and those who didn't could acquire and spread the disease. The consolation, however, was that although vaccination did not eliminate the disease, it did provide protection for the greater community in the presence of the virus.

The Centers for Disease Control and Prevention(CDC) and public health officials' first line of defense in this new world in response to a smallpox outbreak is *ring vaccination*. This requires a surveillance system to identify the first case (*the index case*), then the quarantine of all those exposed, and finally vaccinate those who require vaccination (that is, vaccinating those individuals who were in contact with the index case). In so doing, they believe they can contain an outbreak readily and thus limit the exposure of the American public to the virus...with the notion that, at this juncture, consideration could be given to vaccinating every man, woman, and child in the country.

However, the damning truth for this kind of bioterror deterrent is that there simply may not be adequate time to implement this system.

The variola virus no longer exists outside of a few laboratories around the world. The official virus repositories are at the CDC in Atlanta, Georgia, and the Institute of Viral Preparations in Moscow, Russia. Viral stocks also exist at the Russian State Research Center of Virology and Biotechnology in Koltsovo. While safeguards and adequate security measures are in place with the CDC, it is unknown as to the efficiency of Russian security over its own stockpiles of smallpox. This is, of course, of great concern given the fact that the world has changed since September 11 and the bioterrorist paradigm magnified to gargantuan proportions. And though there is acknowledged concerns that the smallpox virus could be used for bioterrorism, many have put forth the notion that a deliberate release by terrorists is probably pretty low. Many said the same thing about terrorists hijacking commercial jets and using them as missiles to destroy skyscrapers. In fact, the debate continues, and the risks involved for terrorist control and deployment of smallpox is simply unknown.

For the sake of argument in this new world of ours, it is important to consider three important points. First, if a smallpox outbreak occurs, it will be an *unnatural* event. It will not be, as nature would have it, an epidemic spread from person to person, thus slowing the tempo of the epidemic. It will be most likely released from multiple sources, staggered or simultaneously, to infect the maximum number of individuals. Second, the virus released will not be a naturally selected strain as nature would have it, but rather *one specifically selected for its virulence*. Both the United States and the former USSR had (and, arguably, still do) hundreds of naturally occurring strains of the smallpox with varying degrees of virulence. It is important to understand that man did not have to engineer these strains of smallpox. So, we don't have to, in faith, *acknowledge* their existence. In fact, the more virulent strains of smallpox cause what is called hemorrhagic or malignant smallpox with mortality rates as high as one hundred percent in an unvaccinated host. What makes the existence of this strain more plausible lends itself to what took place in Aralsk, Kazakhstan in 1971[1]. In this outbreak, ten individuals were infected; seven survived and three died from hemorrhagic smallpox. The three were not vaccinated. The seven who survived were vaccinated. This would suggest a mortality of *one hundred percent* in the nonvaccinated individuals.

The other alarming point is that many of these patients did not present symptoms *typically*... thus were misdiagnosed initially.

The third and last point is that if the virus is released, it could be *aerosolized*. The resulting horror would be infection of hundreds, if not thousands, of souls if deployed at multiple locations. It is suspected that that is how the Aralsk outbreak began. One does not have to evoke speculation to accept such a possibility. We know from experience that in the hospital setting, the virus was transmitted from floor to floor through air duct systems during outbreaks. So, in this different world, the virus will present itself in an unnatural, different way. To consider further, variola, prior to eradication, carried a mortality rate of thirty percent in unvaccinated persons. Researchers estimate that vaccinated individuals retain immunity approximately five to ten years, although the duration has never been evaluated fully. Vaccination of the general population in the United States ceased after 1980, though vaccination in military personnel was discontinued in 1989 until 2003, when more than 500,000 troops were vaccinated in response to the significant possibility of a terrorist attack using the smallpox virus. The current populace in the United States is considered immuno-naïve to the variola virus, however, forty-two percent of the U.S. population is younger than 30 years old and never vaccinated. As the ease of production and aerosolization of the virus is well documented (researchers estimate that only ten to one hundred virus particles are needed for infection), it is clear and terrifying that smallpox is a potential biological weapon of staggering lethality.

So how does ring vaccination stack up against smallpox in this different world? Success of ring vaccination depends, among other things, on one, the

---

1. "In view of what has been learned in recent years about the former Soviet bioweapons program, it seems that the most likely source of the smallpox outbreak was the test site on Vozrozhdeniye Island. Simply put, the index case and the nine residents of Aralsk who became infected with smallpox in 1971 were in the wrong place at the wrong time. They were unprotected and ill informed about the secret testing of deadly pathogens that was taking place nearby without their consent. By the way, no one has ever apologized to the citizens of Aralsk for those who died in the smallpox outbreak, or to their relatives." Alan P. Zelicoff, M.D., a physician and bioweapons expert at Sandia National Laboratories in Albuquerque, New Mexico, contributed most of the above information.

spread of the smallpox virus from person to person; two, a limited number of primary cases, that is, index cases; and three, of the ability of a surveillance system to identify the index case of smallpox. If an outbreak occurs, the initial spread of the virus will not be from person to person, but rather by a deliberate act to release the virus in an unpredictable way to circumvent attempts to contain it. If it is aerosolized, it will most probably affect hundreds, if not thousands, of individuals over a short period of time, thus inundating the public health system. And if it presents atypically, it may elude detection, thus delaying the recognition of a smallpox outbreak.

In a perfect world, our homeland defense, through the various public health systems, will contain an epidemic. Our surveillance of infectious diseases will identify the smallpox outbreak when it initially presents. Our quarantine of those individuals with smallpox, that is, the index cases, will prevent the spread of the epidemic. And there will be ample time to vaccinate those infected using ring vaccination in a timely way so as to preempt the disease or attenuate the severity of the disease in an individual.

However, in an imperfect world, there may be a *different* scenario; a scenario that would be thousands of times worse than that which transpired on September 11, 2001.

TODAY—FIFTH DAY

It was about 5:00 in the evening, and I felt, to put it bluntly, like a hundred and ninety pounds of condemned veal. The comparison made me involuntarily chuckle. The veal, at least, had the advantage of being already dead…and out of pain. That thought instantly stifled my momentary humor.

The odds at surviving this day were questionable. I gave myself about one chance in ten.

My head pounded. The headaches were unrelenting, the pain so intense it was very difficult to focus or concentrate on anything. Yet my next feeling, commingled with the torment beneath my skull, was one of fury. I was ill today, not because I had contracted cancer or some insidious blood disorder. Nor had I been the victim of some random accident. If these were the reasons for my distress, then I would momentarily rail at God and afterwards accept my predicament—my bad luck, if you will—with clinical resignation that life just plain wasn't fair. As my dad was fond of saying: Sometimes you get door number one and the fifty thousand dollar car, sometimes you get door number two and the can of octopus food. The "loser door," for those in the know, in the great "Let's Make a Deal" experience called human existence.

Hey, that was it. Period. End of story. If you couldn't take the heat, get out of the kitchen…gotta accept the facts…can't shit with the big dogs if you piss with the puppies.

More gentle thoughts from dear old dad…and my voice within.

I closed my eyes and fought for a semblance of mental quiet.

I usually didn't think in terms like this.

I was a doctor, you see…a medical man, a healer, chief defender of life and everything good, healthy, and true. I was, above all, calm in the face of disease and death. Again…it was the fury thing. See, I was sick today, not because of any natural act of God, or because of simple bad luck like a brick falling on my head causing a subdural hematoma. No, I was ill...*dying*...because an act of war had been declared...an act of premeditated murder.

I wanted to kill the son of a bitch responsible for this.

I believe I would have, given half a chance.

That is, of course, if he wasn't already dead—dead from what would soon kill me.

I tried to calm down—perhaps that would alleviate the two baby dragons currently playing kickball in my head. Strange images filled my mind, coupled with the pain...memories of my wife. I couldn't remember her name for a second...Leana. My beautiful Leana whose life was changed, or rather ended, a year ago by a drunk driver only one block from our house. She died quickly. That gave me some kind of instant, perverse gratification. I missed her terribly right now, and it was the kind of agonizing, pit-of-the-stomach feeling of loss that was almost more unbearable than the headaches that pounded steadily on. Yes, her death had been merciful; for this relief much thanks.

I would not be so lucky; nor would the rest of the country, if this thing wasn't stopped soon.

With an instant act of superhuman will, I forced back the orgy of dark, twisted thoughts that accompanied this horrible truth. I pleaded to whatever gods may be for different images...kinder pictures from my life...a life that five days ago had been what few men could define as happy.

Billy and Andrea.

The pain shifted suddenly into low gear. Did thoughts of my children have some kind of preternatural power over...over *this*? Not possible. Or was it? I would never see them again—couldn't see them again—not even in these final hours.

The pain returned, a resurgent tidal wave of agony.

"Christ!" I heard myself cry out from someplace alien and far away—as if, perhaps, it was spoken by someone other than myself altogether.

How did all this happen? How did we let this happen? We should have seen it coming. God damn us for our blindness.

I realized that I was slipping into a kind of delirium. And so, again, I forced myself to hold on to a very tenuous sanity.

I thought back...

...*back, back, behind the haystack.*

I took measured breaths and, when I opened my eyes, I returned (for the moment) to the real world, this very, very real world.

My medical mind kicked into gear. I thought back to my early symptomatology—general malaise, fever, nausea, vomiting. The good shit that I could have easily dismissed, euphemistically, as "coming down with something." And yet as time went on…as my own sickening fear and premonition escalated…I knew better.

I looked at myself in the mirror of the staff john where I had just finished throwing up. I then raised my shirt, up to my neck, and looked at my chest, then my shoulders. I then dropped my pants, studying all areas of my body, looking for a rash, classic or otherwise. And of course, I saw what I expected.

For one blurry moment, I lost my rein on reality. Denial kicked in, a close and loving cousin to panicked optimism, which had no basis in reality whatsoever. I rode with the flow.

Heck, maybe this was the influenza virus. Maybe I had been wrong. Maybe…

Sure, and maybe death is an illusion, space aliens live among us, and pigs have wings.

I bent over the toilet and vomited once more (*emesis* was the medical term). This subtextual byplay my mind was enjoying of late caused me to laugh irrationally. Mistake. I choked, gasped for air, and wiped snot…

…mucous, doctor, please…

…from my nose, wincing, teary-eyed, at the taste of bile and acid. The barf-fest brought me back to reality once more. And I thought to myself:

Bravo, Dr. Kroose. You had correctly made the diagnosis. Give the man a cigar. You had been the first…all because of…

…a hunch.

I chuckled again…though without a trace of humor.

And for the first time in the past God knows how many minutes, I actually prayed to the universe in complete, abject humility.

I prayed that we were not too late…

Too late…

DAY ONE—7 AM

Always follow your gut. Always.

It was my own personal adage—a rule for life and for living—and it had rarely let me down in the past.

So when I awakened this morning with a kind of vague uneasiness, a nebulous disquiet of things to come, I should have done the smart thing and called in sick. That would have been following my gut.

Today I ignored The Gut—the Voice, as I called it. I began my routine at shortly after 7:01 AM. Esmerelda, my combination housekeeper/nanny knocked, then poked her head into my door.

"*Buenas dias*, Doctor Kroose," she smiled warmly, and I could smell the enticing aroma of brewing coffee and frying bacon from the kitchen.

"Hi, Es," I said, putting my wristwatch on. "Kids up yet?"

"*Sí*, for half an hour now. You did not forget about the play tonight, yes?"

My kids, Billy and Andrea, ages nine and ten, respectively, had been reminding me about the school's production of The Pied Piper for several weeks. Tonight was the grand opening and, of course, I was the guest of honor. I was actually kind of looking forward to it; my work allows me so little time to spend with the children, and since Leana…

"No, I didn't forget. I'll be there at seven, sharp. You, too, right?"

"*Claro*, doctor. I would not miss it," she smiled, then closed the door.

Esmerelda was my own personal angel—my rock. She ran the house with the efficiency of a crew manning a nuclear submarine. The kids loved her, and I'd be lost without her. She had been hopelessly devoted to my wife and, after her death, that devotion, by proxy, was transferred over to me. I didn't mind a bit.

As I showered, I went over a few details of yesterday's events in my mind—a kind of morning mental callisthenic which, more than caffeine, tended to stimulate the system satisfactorily. I had been doing this for ten years—recapped highlights of the previous shift. Don't ask me why this had become habit…it just had. Perhaps I did this because, now, after being on a twenty-four-hour shift, (and after a bit of sleep) there was time to reflect and ruminate, perhaps something to be gleaned or otherwise stored away for future reference. Emergency room doctoring was not unlike combat—once you were in the fight, there was little time to do anything else but to fully commit to the task at hand, relying on training by rote. It was only after the battle that reflection was allowed…where learning was possible, where utility of experience could be more fully appreciated.

I began with yesterday morning—memorable, because it started off with a proverbial bang.

The baby was nine months old, a SIDS patient. SIDS stood for sudden infant death syndrome. The poor kid had been brought in by the parents, both understandably hysterical given that the child appeared lifeless. It was a full-court press. The little one was immediately intubated and IVs were started. We started with atropine to jump-start the heart. Other pressers, such as adrenalin, were given. Usually, these infants arrived dead with little hope to revive them. Everyone, staff and parents, were invariably traumatized when this happened. Thank God this didn't occur that often—and yesterday had been fortunate, as we were able to save the child.

About an hour later, another patient with Pickwickian Syndrome arrived (so named for Mr. Pickwick as described by Charles Dickens in his classic "The Pickwick Papers"). Paramedics had brought in the man—a certifiable Code 3 with sirens and flashing red lights. Apparently, the man had become apneic while sleeping, and the wife called 911. The paramedics were unable to intubate him, and he was brought in this state into the emergency room shortly before noon. The guy's name was Wally Tinsdale, and he easily weighed 500 pounds on the hoof. It required ten paramedics to load him and unload him from the rig. We had to bind two gurneys side-by-side to be able to accommodate his size. He was being kept alive by the use of an Ambu bag, which is a bag a liter in size continuously filled with oxygen from an oxygen tank attached to a face mask that is applied to the patient's nose and mouth. Forcefully collapsing the bag delivers a breath of oxygen to the patient. His size made it impossible for one individual to assist in ventilating him, which is usually the case. It required two pairs of hands to apply the mask to his face and one pair of hands to compress the bag. But the real challenge came when trying to intubate him. Placing the tube in the trachea through the mouth was next to impossible.

I attempted to intubate him several times, however, there was too much redundant tissue, and the tongue was massive. It was impossible to move all those structures out of your line of vision to visualize the vocal cords, which is essential in successfully intubating the patient. I had to give up this futile task and perform a cricothyroitomy, which is placing a tube through the neck into the airway just above the trachea. This, in and of itself, was a great feat. I had to dissect through five inches of fatty tissue before I could identify the structures (the larynx and the trachea) and penetrate the airway. But it was successful; although there was a time we thought we had lost him. Fortunately, most sleep apnea patients weren't this difficult to manage.

"Dad."

A knock accompanied my name on the shower door, and my itemization of yesterday's events momentarily evaporated. I opened the door and glanced down at my son.

"Hey, sport. What's up?"

"You gonna be ready soon?" he asked, impatience lining his face.

"Why don't you give Pop five minutes to finish his shower, okay?"

"Okay, but hurry, 'cause I gotta get your opinion on my moustache."

I was momentarily in the dark. Bill was eleven. Moustaches, beards, and shaving shouldn't be in his lexicon of Things Needing To Be Attended To.

"What moustache?"

He rolled his eyes, giving me a look that seemed to question how I had ever achieved adult status of Dad.

"I'm the Piper," he said matter-of-factly. "I gotta have a believable moustache. It can't look dumb. And Es is making it look all pretty and stuff with her eye pencil."

Water continued to cascade behind me, and soap was beginning to seep into my eyes. Yet I understood the immediate and monumental gravity of my son's dilemma.

"I'll be out in a few minutes, and I'll give you the best darned moustache you ever saw."

Bill grinned, appeased by the promise of great things to come. He turned and trundled out of the room. I shook my head and laughed. I should have remained cheerful after this little encounter with my boy, but again something was lurking in the back of my mind...that inexplicable itch of mine that wouldn't go away. I chided myself.

What was it? The day is just beginning, doc. Don't get antsy.

In fact, I suppose I knew what was bugging me—what had been bugging me now for a year since my wife's death. Shrinks would call it some kind of associative paranoia or fear—post traumatic shock of some sort—usually experienced by those of us who have suffered a great loss, like a family member or a spouse. Some folks when faced with that kind of tragedy would develop bizarre phobias—a fear of leaving the house, terror at crossing a street, abject misery at the thought of eating a strawberry. My continuous and daily sense of impending horror that something dreadful was in the air and about to descend on me like a ton of bricks could be part and parcel with *my* loss. I would have bought this, hook, line, and sinker, had the Voice not been with me all my life...yet today I should have accepted my general feeling of despair and distress as related to that of Leana's passing. It would be a logical deduction.

Still...

I turned the water off in the shower...and realized that I was crying. I shook my head, trying to regain some composure, but none came. I turned the water back on and gave myself a private moment of grief. I would not let it go on for long. I had moustaches to attend to and approve. The call of duty finally stymied the tears...enough so that I could turn the shower off once more and take several long breaths to keep the scaries at bay.

I reached for a towel and buried my face in it, grateful for the darkness.

Today is just another day, Max, so I told myself.

Except, as I would discover soon enough, this day would be like no other.

$$* \qquad * \qquad * \qquad *$$

Leana had been the love of my life.

We were the kind of people who would have been content to grow old with one another. She was the spitfire of the family, smart as a whip, and possessed of boundless energy, not only for her work but also for home and hearth. She had quit her law practice once the children arrived, and that suited me just fine. We were comfortable financially, though by no means rich. I suppose we occupied that statistical strata defined as All-American Nuclear Family.

Though I was an emergency room physician, adjusted to the vagaries, unfairness, and tragedy of life in general (i.e., bad things happening all the time to good people), I never for a moment thought something as monstrous as losing my wife would ever interject itself into my scheme of things. It simply wasn't part of the mix, couldn't be.

Yet that is exactly what happened.

The drunk driver was a kid, barely out of high school. Leana was crossing the street from our neighbors' Ben and Mindy's house on her way back to our place. The kid, ripped out of his mind on several six-packs of Bud, tried to swerve his pickup truck, but even the partial impact threw Leana ten feet into the air. She landed headfirst into our car's windshield and died immediately.

The kid smashed into a telephone pole. Aside from being three sheets to the wind, he wasn't even scratched.

That was a year ago, but it felt like yesterday.

I suppose I could have dismissed the Voice today as being, again, part and parcel with my monumental and unfinished grieving process for Leana...but somewhere deep down, I knew that wasn't it. I remembered a quote from somewhere, I think it was Ray Bradbury, and as I muttered it aloud, I shuddered.

"*Something wicked this way comes...*"

I shaved and got dressed, still anxious. As was always the case with my despairing thoughts for Leana, the recovery process was relatively quick due to the regimented schedule I kept on a daily basis.

When I entered the kitchen, a heated debate on the issue of whether a moustache twirls up or slides straight across the lip was in full force and effect between my son and Esmerelda. Bill was a vociferous proponent for the latter style.

"Es, no!" he admonished my nanny. "I look like Snidely Whiplash if you do it that way."

"No, you look like a fierce bandito!"

"Do not."

"I am personally very afraid when I see you like that," Es said, as serious as a heart attack.

Bill turned to me, an expression of "save me" written all over his face.

I took a sip of coffee and studied my son grimly. I then glanced at Es and shook my head.

"No, Es, he's right. Makes him look far too cute."

Esmerelda, a perennial perfectionist in all things she did, considered her handiwork and frowned. "He *is* cute, doctor."

"I'm supposed to be playing music to lure kids out into the forest. I'm a bad guy," Bill said, as if stating the obvious facts of differential calculus to an audience of nitwits.

I took Es's eyeliner.

"Let me try."

As I began drawing my son's moustache over his lips, I thanked God for the reprieve from recent grief. This was real, this was my life now...Leana was gone, but my children were here and now...and they needed me, and I them.

"There," I said.

Bill twitched his lips, then looked at the small hand mirror Esmerelda had dug out of her purse. He tilted his head to the right and then to the left, an eleven-year-old da Vinci perusing details of moustache art. He then glanced at me and nodded seriously.

"Yeah, that's more like it," he said, then gave Esmerelda a withering look. She tried not to smile, an admirable effort, which she further camouflaged with a cough.

I looked to my daughter, Andrea, who had remained silent and fascinated while watching the moustache scenario unfold. I kissed her on the forehead.

"Hi, Princess."

"Hi, Daddy," she said quietly, then reached out to touch my still wet hair. "Don't catch cold."

She smiled at me—Leana's smile. I leaned in and kissed her, again aware of the tears welling up in my eyes. I just nodded, not daring to speak.

Esmerelda saved the day, clapping her hands.

"Okay, everyone, jackets and lunch pails. We go now!"

This was Bill and Andrea's signal to prepare for the ride to school. Off they ran into the other room, giving me a moment of emotional reprieve. I sat down and took a deep breath, staring at the bacon and eggs that Esmerelda had placed before me.

I then felt Es's hand on my shoulder.

"*Está bien*, Doctor, *está bien*," she said softly.

I did not look up at her. I sniffed and turned away, reaching for some coffee. Esmerelda took the hint and left the room. The kids bolted in, both kissing me on the cheek, and then turning on their heels heading back into the living room. A moment later, the front door opened and closed.

I was alone.

"Okay," I said to myself. "Pull it together."

And as always, I did just that.

$$*\qquad*\qquad*\qquad*$$

Half an hour later, I was on the road, heading for the hospital, again thinking back on yesterday's events in the emergency room.

After Mr. Pickwick had come and gone, Squad Three brought me a traumatic full arrest. Mind you, we're not a trauma center—just a small, community hospital. However, the patient en route coded, and lost his pulses and spontaneous breathing. And it had been the bloody rush hour. The trauma center was 15 miles away. There was no hope for the paramedics to get the patient to the trauma center in a reasonable amount of time. Instead, they were diverted to our facility.

We were initially irritated (okay, try *pissed*) by the arrival of this patient to the emergency room but realized that this was his only chance. He was around thirty years old and had been shot through the chest by his girlfriend during a lover's quarrel. Lost the argument on that one, I guess. *Hell hath no fury*, I thought…though the young lady had clearly taken the altercation too far. The man was lifeless and had lost a lot of blood, but luckily he had only one injury—the kind of injury that commonly is fatal, however, one that we could effectively treat if the treatment is rendered without hesitation.

We were forewarned of his coming so we had everything but the kitchen sink ready for him. He had already been intubated by the paramedics and had several IVs with saline infusing at a rapid rate. All we had to do was crack his chest—that is to say, surgically opening his chest. As we did this, we saw there was a hole in the heart. The great vessels (the aorta and the large veins) were fortunately spared. We sutured the damage and transfused O-negative blood then shocked the heart with a small electrical current, which brought it back to life. With this, we got a good pulse and blood pressure, and he began to breathe spontaneously albeit on the respirator. The dilemma, however, was that there were no cardiothoracic surgeons in the hospital. So now we had to find a way to transfer the patient to a tertiary facility or a facility with a cardiothoracic surgeon. This took longer than we would have liked, but fortunately the patient survived.

That was yesterday; active, but not atypical by any stretch of the imagination (save for the tiff by the young lovers which ended in gunplay). I tried to remember if I was as equally twitchy yesterday as today, as inexplicably…preoccupied.

I knew that this apprehensive mental masturbation about what disaster may befall me on the next shift wasn't going to serve me well. It only gave rise to more anxiety about what the day was going to be like.

I looked up at the clear, bright Southern California sky.

I thought about my kids, about their play tonight. I wiped the events of yesterday from my mind. Today would hold something entirely different, so just go with the flow. I tried to force myself to be cheerful.

It didn't work.

That damned voice of mine…

*   *   *   *

In the days after Leana's death, and even now on occasion, I would look back at my life and try to reconstruct a series of events and choices which had led me to where I was today. It was not an unpleasant exercise, and I had few regrets—something I would imagine few people could declare at the end of the day.

After four years of undergraduate school at Stanford and four years of medical school at Johns Hopkins, I had taken my residency in emergency medicine. To be sure, it was grueling work—yet rarely dull. I was persuaded to accept a three-year fellowship in infectious diseases thereafter. If there was any sense of wonderment in terms of other destinies I could have pursued, I often wondered why I didn't pursue this line of research. It was more of a controlled environment, little or no night call, and none of this adrenaline-pumping, ride-by-the-seat-of-your-pants practice of emergency room medicine.

Glen Hamilton, who had been my mentor in the infectious diseases arena, had encouraged me to stay with this particular field of medicine, but it was the excitement of the emergency room that drove me, which is where I'm practicing now some ten years later. If there is a place where you can make a difference in a life and death situation, it's in ER. And I love that challenge. The more I triumph over death, the more gratification I feel. To me, it was undoing death in an instant in time.

Still, those three years with Glen were life-changing, and it was during this time I believe that the Voice matured into something almost precognitive in nature—and has stayed with me right up to the present.

Glen and I had met at Johns Hopkins. He was an instructor on staff, but his time was mainly allocated to his position at the U.S. Army Medical Research Institute of Infectious Diseases (USAMRIID) at Fort Dietrick, Maryland. He was a key field inspector for studying highly hazardous viruses at Biosafety Level 4 (the highest designation of virulence within a controlled environment). The USAMRIID conducts research to develop strategies, products, and training programs for medical defense against biological warfare threats and infectious diseases. It is the leading medical research laboratory for the U.S. Biological Defense Research Program.

A contract program with universities and other research institutions complements USAMRIID's in-house research program. Johns Hopkins was one of the universities on the list—and I was one of the young doctors Glen Hamilton tapped to join the program and finish out my fellowship under his tutelage.

It was fascinating stuff. The USAMRIID's military and civilian staff at the time (and it has no doubt grown today) numbered 450—physicians, veterinarians, microbiologists, pathologists, chemists, molecular biologists, physiologists, and pharmacologists, not to mention the administrative and technical staff necessary to support the research. We worked on improved vaccines for anthrax, Venezuelan equine encephalitis, plague, and botulism and on new vaccines for toxins such as staphylococcal enterotoxins and ricin. Our research included that for medical countermeasures to viral hemorrhagic fevers and arboviral illnesses.

I followed Glen to North Africa, where I studied amebiasis, Boutonneuse fever, brucellosis, Crimean-Congo hemorrhagic fever, and the dreaded Ebola and marburg hemorrhagic fevers. When I returned to the states, I was part of a study to determine the effects on a given community by a bioterrorist attack. We chose a town called Hope in North Carolina. The simulation was an intentional aerosolized release of Rift Valley fever virus (RVFV). The community was selected because its mosquito population could support transmission of RVFV. We videotaped a series of simulated print and television "news reports" over a fictional nine-day crisis period. In short, we watched people.

Predictably, confusion arose in the community over disease management (e.g., the effectiveness of the antiviral drug ribavirin, the need for RVFV vaccine, and who should receive the vaccine) and over the potential for infected persons to serve as reservoirs and carriers of the virus elsewhere during the few days when viral titers are especially high.

I found it gratifying that the community responded with great courage. Participants in the study generally said they would stay on their jobs in the event of such a disaster but did want all information to be delivered within a chain of command at work. Ranking second as the desired source for such information (public health authorities being first) was the private physician (which I would always remember as being significant). Though I did wonder if this was *not* a simulated outbreak (the choice of RVFV as the disseminated agent does not have the high "fear factor" of some other diseases such as smallpox) but a bona fide bioterrorist incident, if the conclusions drawn at the end of that study period would mirror what would ultimately transpire once such an incident materialized for real.

Today, I would not have long to wait to receive that answer.

However, I did not know this yet. Today I was mind-walking into my past.

Remembering…

Glen tried to persuade me to remain on board the USAMRIID research bandwagon, but I had other priorities.

I had met a girl.

A friend introduced Leana and me as a blind date. Six months later we were married. While I loved the research adventures provided by the USAMRIID, I was still enthralled by emergency medicine…and by the prospect of having a family. I made my decision to leave the USAMRIID two months after my wedding. I had no regrets.

That had been ten years ago.

Ten years. How it all goes by in a blink of an eye…

And that was my life; a little bit of this, a little bit of that. At the end of the day, I was an emergency room physician with a varied and eclectic background.

Would that background ever come in handy for some special emergency?

At the time, I could not have guessed.

As I drove, I was still feeling some of that early (and constant) apprehension, but I thought to myself: It's like a fighter who has butterflies in his belly as he enters the ring. Nerves, plain and simple. Then, as the first punch is thrown, all the anxiety dissipates. Today, as yesterday, all I would have to do is walk through that emergency room door and poof! I'd be Dr. Kildare once again.

There would be nothing to worry about—just the task at hand.

So I thought.

And how wrong I would be.

THE STAFF—7:05 AM

I parked in my reserved spot, damn near hitting a few pigeons that just wouldn't move from what remained of half a muffin. I raised pigeons as a kid and had a soft spot for birds in general, but I had to admit they were among the dumbest creatures on the planet. After honking my horn repeatedly, they decided to forego further dining, favoring not being run over by my 1999 Suburban.

Traffic was a bit heavy this morning, and I was a few minutes late. No biggie; I had good people working for me. They could cover if the need arose.

The emergency room is a structure within the hospital. In essence, this is the most important portal of entry to the place. ER is where patients present when they're acutely ill (*present*, in medical jargon, means simply to arrive). This is a lifeline for the hospital activity. But, more importantly, the staff is what makes the emergency room really tick, and your ER is only as good as your staff.

I happen to have one of the best ER staffs on the planet. Of course, I'm somewhat biased. You know the true grit of your staff when the proverbial shit hits the fan, and this staff had been tested many times over. They were dependable, reliable, had a genuine interest in what they were doing, and they always went the extra mile to accomplish what needed to be done.

Our emergency room is relatively small, perhaps 2,500 to 3,000 square feet. We saw approximately 1,300 to 1,400 patients a month; many of them not acutely ill—but problem cases nevertheless. This month, we'd probably exceed those statistics given the flu season hit pretty hard this year. We were usually staffed with one physician for most of the day and, during the busy season such as now, we would have a student or a second physician during the peak hours. There's usually one physician working either twelve- or twenty-four-hour shifts covering the emergency room.

The rest of the staff consisted of six RNs and one clerk. They also worked twelve-hour shifts. Of course, we had all the ancillary services available at our disposal if and when we needed them, such as during codes or for respiratory therapy. The respiratory therapist, Sergio, was more or less a constant in the emergency room, given we saw many acute pulmonary problems.

As I walked into ER, I realized my apprehension had dissipated. Good. Perhaps this would be a relatively quiet day. I might even get out early, grab a bite, and get to my kids' play on time. Why not? Miracles happen every day. Norma, the head nurse, was at her station. She was the one who assigned patients to the nurses and directed traffic. She would ask for additional resources when they were needed. She knew pretty much what went on in the emergency room and had a finger on the pulse and cadence of the joint at all times. She happened to be the lead nurse on most of my shifts, which I appreciated greatly. She was good at what she did, a no-bullshit personality who was always two steps ahead of the game.

Norma was around forty years old but looked fifty; she had worked hard all her life, professionally and personally, and while she wasn't long on humor, she was kick-ass in detail and department procedure in running the ER. She had been in nursing for about nineteen years and had worked in many emergency rooms before coming here, including some tertiary centers. She had a lot of experience to bring to the table. I tapped her resources whenever I needed to…and, oh brother, she had a wealth of resources. She could cut through a lot of red tape if I needed anything—getting extra supplies, staffing, or settling any political inter-departmental problems.

That latter resource I would greatly appreciate later today.

I grinned at her. "Good morning, Norma, what's new for today?"

"Good morning, Dr. Kroose," she said in her customary quiet tone of voice. "Nothing new. Same old, same old. Got a lot of influenza coming in. The shift has just begun, and you have five patients already with coughs, colds, and fevers. They probably just need notes not to work today."

I can't remember Norma ever having taken a sick day; I could only imagine that she generally took a dim view of anyone who wasn't bedridden with disease _not_ to go to work. If you could walk, inhale, and exhale, by the Norma Mantra for Living, you could bloody well make it to your job. I made a private wager with myself that Norma's children never took sick days, either. Call it a hunch. I couldn't resist, though, so I fenced with her a bit.

"It's not like you to be cynical," I said.

She looked at me and sighed.

"Dr. Kroose, it's not cynicism—it's reality."

End of story, I thought. Norma had all the flexibility for philosophical reasoning as a tiger shark practicing territoriality.

"Who's on staff today?" I asked, feeling the need for coffee.

"The usual," Norma replied.

As she said that, she pointed out to me that they were all listed on the triage board that we had to identify the patients in the emergency room and their diagnosis and disposition. In one corner of this board was the list of the personnel working on that shift. The board was a chalkboard that was hung on the wall to the back of the nursing station—in easy view for all to see what the activities were in the ER. In one corner hung a special for Koo Koo Roo Chicken (which I knew

I would take advantage of in time); the other little items were two discount tickets to the Clippers game this coming Thursday. I would have to pass on that. Football was my game; that and sparring with the Grim Reaper here in ER. It was always fun to keep the bastard at bay. Think it's easy? Try. Just try.

Speaking of the Caped Creep with the Sickle, the place was like a morgue today, though it didn't bother me. It held the promise of reasonable peace.

"Where is everyone?" I asked Norma.

Norma sounded vaguely annoyed with me. "They're placing patients in rooms for you. You better hurry and dress up. I got a feeling that this is going to be a wham-bam-thank-you-ma'am shift."

"Jesus, Norma, give me a sec," I said through a chuckle. "Let me get a cup of coffee before I get started. I might really even party for a few more seconds and make it to the bathroom."

Norma's tone shifted, though she could tell I wasn't really irritated. She knew my off-the-cuff manner well and never took offense. "Sorry, Doctor. I didn't mean to sound pushy. It's just that Dr. Green needs to sign off on his cases…and you were a bit tardy this morning."

Yeah, yeah, bad doctor.

"Traffic," I mumbled. "Aside from those slackers with flu, colds, and fevers, are there any cases for me yet?"

Norma nodded.

"Actually, there's only one. The others are being transported right now, and the one that Dr. Green signs off to you will probably leave in about five minutes. The patient has congestive heart failure. He came in last night. We boarded him overnight until the change of shift."

"Why don't you tell Dr. Green he can go," I said. "He doesn't have to sign off, and tell him not to forget he's covering my last twelve hours tonight. I'm going to check and see what the nurses are doing. Oh, by the way, who's our clerk?"

"It's Jamie."

"Terrific."

I moved off from the nursing station and walked around the corner where Jamie was sitting behind a bulletproof glass window. Sign of our times, unfortunately. She was only too happy to help me whenever I requested extra things from her, such as ordering a meal from one of the local restaurants. Some of the clerks would give me a little flack. In fact, they thought it was beyond the job description. Not so with Jamie.

"Good morning, Jamie. Looks like it's getting a little busy out there."

"Dr. Kroose, good morning! Nice to see you."

Her smile was always engaging, and while Norma wore her age with weary dignity, Jamie was just the opposite. She couldn't have been more than forty-five, but every movement, every gesture—even her smile—fibbed to one and all that she was just a kid in her thirties. She had children and a divorce under her belt, but there was a complete lack of life's woes in her manner.

"Norma just gave me a small riot act," I whispered to her conspiratorially. "We're gonna be busy and, by the way, no time for coffee."

Jamie shook her head and grinned.

"In this place, there's *always* time for coffee," she said.

I gave her a thumbs up and a wink. *Damned straight,* I thought. Coffee was my best friend, especially when the shifts were particularly tough.

And this shift was about to be the toughest of my life.

*   *   *   *

I cruised through the ER quickly to see what kinds of patients they were placing in the rooms to make sure I had ample time to put my scrubs on. My jeans, Doc Martins, and Tommy Bahamas shirt were not considered appropriate attire to see these patients. The administration could be such sticklers on this—no fashion sense whatsoever.

Betty, Cynthia, and Matt—the other nurses—were busy putting a patient in one of the examining rooms. She was an elderly woman, wheelchair-bound and unable to get onto the examining table by herself. I paused for just a moment as the poor thing tried to assist my team—tried to find some strength that would allow her to stand. But the effort was quickly exhausted. She merely looked at Betty and the others helplessly as they took either arm and eased her out of the chair and onto the table. I thought back to my father, who was also eventually confined to a wheelchair due to multiple strokes and just plain old age. The indignity of aging and dying, I thought. How little grace we are given after a certain point—how helpless we can all become.

Old men sitting in the sun, oh dear Lord, one day will I be one?

I decided that further ponderings along this line would just bring on the heebie-jeebies once again, and what good would that do anyone?

Betty caught my eye as she moved the wheelchair against the wall. She gave a slight wave, and I returned it. She was twenty-nine, Filipino, cute as a bug. She was also one of our many clutch performers. Betty shared that kind of preternatural talent with Norma for anticipating my every need at all times. Paraphernalia, procedures, whatever I required or thought of doing, she was there before I was in those do-or-let-die situations. She was now guiding the other two nurses, making sure the patient's Foley catheter and clothing were not tangling on the wheelchair.

Matt was about forty-five and had his initial training as a medic during the Vietnam War. He stood six foot four and was easily two hundred and twenty pounds. He was a huge slab of human being with a bushy beard and moustache and nearly all bald. Matt was not the kind of guy you'd want to piss off in a dark alley somewhere. Not only was he proficient at what he did as an RN, but also with his height and size, he was good at helping with the occasional hostile or combative patient. Once, about a year ago, a drunk trucker was brought in by a few of his buddies, following what I was told had to be the "hands down, no bullshit, biggest fire-up-your-ass mule fight" ever at Don's Watering Hole a few blocks from the hospital. Big Al (as he was constantly being referred to by his pals) had apparently been in the center of whatever altercation had taken place with several other patrons of Don's, and his nose had literally been mashed into a mucilaginous jelly. However, he was in little pain when he was presented, because of course he was still pretty pissed-to-the-wind drunk—and belligerent. When I began my examination of Big Al, he pushed me away, and no gentle shove at that. I was knocked so hard against the wall that my teeth actually rattled. Matt didn't waste a second. He twisted Big Al's arm behind his back and brought the guy to the floor fast, face down, and screaming in pain.

"You ever push the doc around again," Matt spoke in a low, soft voice, "and I'm gonna rip your thumb off and shove it up your ass. Are you reading me, buddy?"

Big Al, drunk as he was, sensed the futility of lashing back, either physically or verbally, against Matt, the human mountain. He just nodded and begged for his arm back.

Matt was a gentle guy at heart, but he had lightning reflexes and immediately sensed a bad situation about to start. I was lucky to have him on my watch.

Cynthia was helping Matt settle the old woman on the examining table, each grabbing an arm and a leg. Not only was she a good nurse, but she also had a great sense of humor, and it sometimes took this to make the long ER shifts more pleasant. She was around thirty years old and, as she put it, a "ghetto girl" from the word go. Damn proud of it, too. "Mind you, I ain't no porch monkey, doc, but I like my roots," so she told me once over a cold beer about a month ago after a particularly tough day in ER.

I poked my head into the room and caught Cynthia's eye.

"Yo, Cynthia! Don't bust a stitch."

She looked at me and smiled. "Good morning, Dr. Kroose. Don't hurt yourself going hood on me. You'll send the black community back a hundred years."

I chuckled, realizing that my attempt at infusing basic Ebonics into my conversation with Cynthia had just been quashed something fierce.

"How's your back? Maybe you'd like to lend a hand," she prodded good-naturedly.

I smiled and then continued to cruise through the ER. I noticed that two other rooms were occupied. Martha had a patient in one who had a red eye, probably conjunctivitis—pinkeye, as it is also known. Martha was a thirty-five-year-old Latina RN, with fifteen years of experience in various departments and, most recently in the past five years, she had worked with us in ER. She had a family of five—two girls and a boy—both in grammar school. She loved her family life and couldn't stop talking about her husband who she was madly in love with. She was part of the A-team and very friendly.

Linda was leading a teenage boy into the last room. She spotted me walking just a few feet behind them.

"Hi, Dr. Kroose," she said.

"Hey, Linda," I found my tongue after a second or two. "You look very nice today."

You look very nice today. Oh, that was smooth.

"Why, thank you," she replied through a perfect smile. She then turned.

"What's this young man in for?" I asked, referring to the boy.

The kid spoke before Linda could reply. "Tetanus shot."

"Ah," I said in a tone of voice that sounded like it held all the secrets of existence within.

"He stepped on a nail this morning. Went kind of deep," Linda said.

Linda held my gaze for just a moment longer then continued toward the last room. She was an attractive blonde—let me take that back—an *extremely* attractive blonde around twenty-seven years old. Not that I'd ever noticed before, of course, but she also had the figure of your basic supermodel; that and aspirations of being a nursing administrator. She was studying to get her masters of business for this purpose. I liked Linda immensely but found myself staring too long at her occasionally.

Reason being, she looked somewhat like my late wife.

And that thought (due out of guilt, I suspect) again allowed my apprehension to return about this day...

*   *   *   *

Okay, don't go there this morning. Just get the bloody coffee and concentrate on the patient roster.

I sighed, probably an audible expulsion of air, as I grabbed a cup of coffee despite Norma's protestations that there was no time for such trivialities. I glanced back to Linda once more, wrestling my anxiety out of my mind. I forced myself to relax. *I'm probably just horny. Yeah, even guys in their 40s get that urge now and then, despite the weight of grief held over their head like the sword of Damocles.*

The thought simultaneously amused and annoyed me. Amused, because I know my wife would accuse me of being terribly hard on myself.

Nothing wrong with looking at a pretty woman, Max, she would say when she caught me doing exactly that if we were out at a restaurant or something equally innocuous.

As long as I don't act on it, right? I jibed back on occasion.

This would make her laugh…and her eyes would twinkle without even a trace of jealousy…only an exceptional grasp of human nature (and the weakness inherent to the male animal at large).

Oh, Leana…I do miss you…

Well, I was doing it again. Stop thinking, I chided myself. Work, I thought. Work to be done. I sipped my coffee and then headed for the doctor's room to dress, determined to do battle against sickness and death with a clear mind and relaxed conscience.

But I did allow myself a final smile to Linda.

And I could practically hear Leana laughing from some place far, far away…

*   *   *   *

The doctor's room was an eight-by-ten-foot place with a bathroom housing a shower, vanity, and toilet. There were hospital beds, which we were able to use sporadically throughout the twelve- or twenty-four-hour shifts. There was a desk made of oak wood with two small drawers on the right side, and a telephone sitting to the left of the desk. There was a swivel chair placed next to the desk. The desk was situated in the room opposite to the bed. At the foot of bed, there was a matching oak nightstand near the entrance to the bathroom. There was an old TV set old enough to have dials, and no remote control sitting on the nightstand.

Old, but it served a purpose during the slow periods of the day. I watch CNN and other news programs, though during the Iraq War I was so demoralized, that I found myself flipping to soap operas or the cartoon channel just to seek some kind of relief from the insanity.

My mind wandered. The Iraq War. Probably a very necessary event, but the doctor in me always chided: The loss of life. Sometimes sacrifice was necessary, but so many of our boys gone. Mind you, I thought Saddam Hussein was living, breathing evil itself…and I had a great fear of weapons of mass destruction—particularly, given my background, those biologically related. And with substantive proof of their existence in any hostile nation, I was all for sending in the Marines and seizing the offending weaponry. I could only imagine the horrors of weaponized ebola, anthrax, or, God forbid, smallpox being utilized successfully against the civilized world by terrorists or rogue psychotics. I believe Iraq (or more specifically, its leadership) would have had no problems dispensing such nightmares to anyone even remotely unfriendly to U.S. interests. Still, I thought, the sooner we could make that particular region stable, the better.

Oh, boy.

I was mentally rambling again. I brought myself back to earth and set my shoulder bag down on the bed which I use to carry all that I may need during a shift: Two or three pairs of scrubs, an extra pair of shorts, socks, a pair of shoes, a medical journal or two, a calculator and a recorder, and a bottle of Motrin for the aches and pains. You never know when you'll need it.

I finished taking my clothes off and hung them up in the small cabinet provided for us along one side of the bathroom and slipped on my scrubs. Now I was ready for the day.

∗   ∗   ∗   ∗

I walked out of the doctor's room to the nursing station where I found Norma. By this time, Norma had assessed all the patients who had walked in and prioritized who I should see first. I started to ask her for the first chart when I heard a voice.

"Excuse me, Dr. Maxwell Kroose?"

I looked to my right and saw a young man no more than twenty-five years old. He was walking toward me with an expression on his face that could only be described as deadly serious.

"Yes?" I said.

I looked over at Norma puzzled.

"I'm sorry, Dr. Kroose. I meant to mention this earlier. You're getting an extern, a student, from UCLA. He'll be with us for a few weeks." She indicated the young man. "This is Andy Goodman."

I shook Andy's hand.

"Welcome aboard," I said. "And you're excused."

"Thank you, sir."

"Get ready for a long day," I said, meaning it.

I wanted to give him the sense that this rotation was not going to be a cake-walk. They were there to work and learn at the same time. Just because these young guns weren't on their own campus did not mean they were not going to satisfy the rigors of their own curriculum. We had an agreement with the local medical school in accepting fourth-year students as externs in the various departments of the hospital for four- or eight-week rotations. In return, those of us who participated became an honorary clinical faculty of the medical school, sort of a quid pro quo relationship.

"Are you from around these parts, Andy?" I asked, as I glanced through some charts.

"New York, originally, sir, but…"

"Max or doctor, Andy. I'm feeling about a hundred-and-thirty years old with the sir thing."

Andy actually flushed crimson at that.

"Sorry…doctor. I'm a little nervous, is all."

I knew the feeling. "So was I when I first did ER. Perfectly natural." I smiled, trying to put him at ease. "New York. Haven't been back East in ten years myself. Too cold for me. I'm a California boy from start to finish."

"I hated the cold, too," Andy chuckled. "That's why I came out here."

At first glance, Andy struck me as a studious, diligent medical student. This I surmised by the thickness of his glasses and the lack of tan on his skin probably from the long hours in the library. He was more than just religiously committed—he was obsessed—not a bad thing, really, for this was the quality that usually made for the finest of doctors. He stood about six foot and was thin but well toned, which suggested an obvious compulsion for natural foods. He looked like he probably hit the local fitness center on a regular basis, which meant that didn't leave much time for a social life. There was no wedding ring on his finger, so he was single. And the fact that he was here on time suggested to me that this young fellow was going to be quite an asset to my ER.

"Okay, Andy, here we go. Dive in, the water is fine," I encouraged. "Norma, let's start him out with Mrs. Franklin." Mrs. Franklin was the elderly lady with the wheelchair and Foley catheter. I thought that would be a good case for him to review and perhaps bestow a few pearls of medical knowledge in the process.

Andy took Mrs. Franklin's chart, and adjusted his glasses.

"Call if you need anything," I said. "I'm only a few feet away at any given time."

Andy looked up and nodded smartly. I half expected him to give me a salute.

And so the day began. Pretty normal, pretty quiet so far. I believed the emotional boogieman I had been fighting with since I awakened this morning was chained up and gone for the duration.

What a fool I was...

THE HOSPITAL—9 AM

The first batch of patients were relatively simple cases. A few colds, flu-like syndromes, fevers with rashes, all the dispositions relatively quick. Andy had seen Mrs. Franklin and finished with her in short order. There weren't many pearls to bestow about this case other than that Foley catheters can predispose patients to urinary tract infections. He made it a point to visit the hospital library to review literature on this issue.

The pace in the morning was brisk but not grossly memorable. By nine, we had seen twenty patients. If this pace continued, we would probably see sixty to seventy people by the end of the day, most if not all with relatively innocuous issues and that was the redeeming aspect of the cases. That is, even though there were that many patients presenting to the emergency room, they could be taken care of fairly rapidly, allowing us downtime and a little R&R. It's hard to work constantly throughout the day. You become fatigued. Sometimes these volumes of patients come in and are complicated cases. When this happens, you get tired, and you know you can't do the thorough job you should do. When they are this complicated, in most cases they get admitted and a second set of hands evaluate the patient, catching those things you may have missed. That's consoling.

Since I had a few minutes, I wanted to touch base with Norma to find out what had happened in the days I was *not* in the ER. Being the emergency room director, I had to keep abreast of all the problems that occurred in the place, and she was my conduit for information.

Norma was at the nursing station directing traffic again, assigning patients to nurses, taking phone calls, and trying to get patients expeditiously admitted. Like an air traffic controller, she stood at the desk with the phone on her left side and a computer screen in front of her. This screen was very important to us. It was hooked up to the blood laboratory computer, cardiology lab computer, and respiratory lab computer where all the EKGs, blood studies, and blood gas results were stored. When we needed to, we could pull out all this information on any given patient. Just punch in the patient's hospital number, up comes the menu, and you select the data you need. This, in many cases, circumvents the need to track down charts. Old hospital charts are sometimes almost impossible to find. The terminal allowed us to know as much as was humanly possible about our ER guests. And after the patients were admitted, it was possible to follow their progress. Norma was on the phone trying to negotiate an ICU bed for the congestive heart failure patient whom she told me Dr. Green had handled earlier.

"Where are we with this?" I asked Norma, irritated. "This patient should have been admitted an hour-and-a-half ago."

She covered the phone receiver and turned to me. "You know, Dr. Kroose, this is a chronic problem. There's never enough ICU CCU beds. They have two patients they're in the process of discharging or transferring to the floors, but they have to get physician orders to do that. The patients are not to leave the unit without orders. Everything's done by protocol, otherwise we're not compliant and somebody gets dinged."

She was right. Everything was based on policy and procedures, and we in the emergency room were always under a watchful eye to make sure we were in compliance with all the rules and regulations. We had to be accommodating to satisfy the needs of those admitting physicians.

She hung up and explained to me that the ICU had just received orders from the ICU patient's physician, and the bed was now available for our patient.

"So he's on his way up?" I asked.

"Yes. I'm going to get Matt to take him to the ICU. I'll send Cynthia along."

"By the way, who admitted him?" I asked.

"It was one of the panel physicians."

The panel physicians. They were our immediate backups. These are doctors who were on-call for us in case a patient required admission to the hospital. The policies and procedures mandated these people be responsive to the needs of the emergency room so that if a patient required hospitalization, the panel physicians are instructed to accommodate us. Policies and procedures also mandated that a patient be seen in a timely fashion so that there is no obstruction to patient flow in the emergency room. Otherwise, our ER could easily become inundated with patients requiring hospitalization. This worked well for us. However, the only mandated services were internal medicine, surgery, and pediatrics. And we were lucky to have pediatrics. For being a small community hospital, we didn't have the services to provide like the larger hospitals or the tertiary centers had (such as infectious diseases, pediatric ICUs, labor and delivery, and others). We had no pulmonary department nor infectious diseases department and other specialties that the tertiary centers had. We had a cardiology lab, but it was used primarily for elective procedures. Unless the cardiologist on-call was inclined to accept a case from the emergency room, we had no cardiology backup. It was really their option. So, our backup was thin. I often had a private bitch-gripe with myself on this, but it was an exercise in futility. These were our facts of life.

Panel physicians were on-call 24 hours. Some take more than 24-hour periods. The advantage to them was that patients admitted to the emergency room that had no primary care physicians were assigned to these folks and, thus, this was used to bolster their practices. The conflicts came when the patient requiring hospitalization were cash accounts, that is, they had no third-party payers. These were considered less desirable cases since there was a good chance the physicians were not going to get paid for their services nor was the hospital. However, both the state and federal governments mandated the hospitals provide the service regardless of payer status. This is why many patients who present in the emergency room for care because they cannot be denied.

"There was one case admitted yesterday by Dr. Green, a patient with chest pain who they're ruling out."

"Yeah? Don't tell me somebody died," I said, obviously trying to be light.

"No, the patient was admitted to a panel physician."

"So?"

Norma took a breath, and then raised her eyebrows. She cleared her throat and looked at me.

"The patient belonged to Dr. Schwartz."

My stomach rolled just a bit. "Oh, shit."

I knew Schwartz and had a few run-ins with the guy in the past. He was a stickler for procedure and was always complaining to someone about something. His was what one would call a *difficult* personality, and there was simply no way to sugar coat it otherwise. Good doctor, but a pain in the ass. And that just wasn't my opinion, either. He had the capacity to annoy not only staff but his patients as well. Linda had mentioned to me that he was astrologically handicapped.

"He's a Pisces," she said. "That explains it."

How could I argue?

Norma let my irritation pass and, after a second, said, "Yeah, and it gets better than that. Last evening, while Dr. Schwartz was rounding on his patients, he ran into *the* patient who was admitted to someone *other* than his service. So, he has this idea that the emergency room is after his cases, and he's making a big issue of it. He's threatening to take this to the Board of Directors if need be."

I hoped this wasn't going to blow up into a stink; I wasn't in the mood for it today. And I was *never* in the mood for Schwartz anyway.

"Boy, and I thought I was paranoid," I mumbled ungraciously.

Norma looked up at me puzzled. I smiled neutrally.

"An inside joke amusing only to me, Norma."

"Well, it's no joke to Dr. Schwartz," Norma said in a vaguely chiding tone of voice. "He's serious about this."

"Make sure I get the chart. Find out why the patient was not admitted to him."

Norma was ready for this. "From what I've heard from the nurses is that the patient did not want to be admitted to Dr. Schwartz. The patient seems to be somewhat timid. He doesn't want to tell Dr. Schwartz that, so we're left holding the bag. It wouldn't be such a bad thing if the patient wasn't well-insured. If it was a cash account, it probably wouldn't have been an issue, but he has an indemnity plan that pays one hundred percent of the services. So, the administrator and Dr. Schwartz are up in arms. The administrator obviously doesn't want to lose Dr. Schwartz as an admitting physician here. So, you get the picture?"

As I listened, I shook my head and felt a little distracted from the patient care I was supposed to be delivering.

"And so what's the second problem, Norma?"

"Well, flu season hit us pretty hard, and we were filled to capacity yesterday. We had a lot of sick patients, and we had to close to saturation. The administrator didn't like that, either."

No administrator likes his emergency room closed to saturation. It's the hospital's lifeline. Patients come to the emergency room; they generate revenues. They get admitted to the hospital; they generate more revenues. Time is money. The longer the emergency room is closed to saturation, the more likely those sick patients who are being ambulanced to hospitals are diverted away from this hospital. So, to him, it's a loss of revenues. If there is one thing that irritates administrators, it is this.

"Norma, make sure I have the statistics for that day. Find out how many patients were here during that period of time that we were close to saturation and the kinds of cases we had before I talk to him about this."

"Already got all the stats ready for you, Dr. Kroose, and I have talked to the nursing administrator, Sharon Blake. She's a good friend of mine. She's in our corner. I don't think it'll be a problem, but I'm sure he's going to want to talk to you about it."

He being our infamous administrator, Jack Kilgorn.

"I think that's a pretty safe bet." I thanked her and was about to leave the nursing station when her phone rang. Norma picked it up, paused, and then hung up.

"It's Mr. Kilgorn," she told me. "And he'd like to see you as soon as you're done with patients. The sooner the better."

"Speak of the devil. Doesn't waste any time, does he?" I said.

She said nothing as she handed me the five charts. I browsed through them and quickly adduced that they were all flu-like syndromes but complaining of high fevers and rashes. Why rashes, I wondered. Maybe it's the measles, although I know many viruses do cause a rash with their presentation.

These patients were not acutely ill. They're the kind of cases that primary care physicians see in their offices, but since they're in the emergency room, I was inclined to see them anyway.

That gut hunch of mine had come back in the meantime.

I just had the feeling that my encounter with the hospital administrator was going to be a royal pain in the ass.

$*$ $*$ $*$ $*$

I finished with my remaining patients and then made my way up the stairs to the second floor where Jack Kilgorn's office was. It didn't take long to see the five cases. All they needed was a little bed rest, fluids, and some Tylenol for the various fevers. I would have taken the elevator, but it tends to be slow and it may take forever to get up to the second floor. It's easier just to walk up.

The hospital had eight floors: Two medical wards and two surgical wards; an ICU, which is located on the fifth floor; and the CCU, which is located on the fourth. There are two other intensive care units, but they had to be closed. There weren't enough RNs to staff the units, thus the reason there was a shortage of ICU beds. Most facilities had more space than they had staff to staff the hospital. Many of the nursing staff works per diem, *lo cum tenets* from other countries, such as the Philippines. Our schools weren't graduating enough nurses to fill the positions needed.

This was also a question of money. Health care was costly, and third-party payers weren't paying the going rates primarily because of the HMO market's stranglehold on the industry altogether. So many hospitals downsized, closing units, to become profitable and that, in turn, affected patient care indirectly. That is, each ward nurse was assigned more patients to care for during their shifts, and that sometimes affected the quality of care.

What a disaster, I thought. If, in fact, there *was* ever a catastrophe, say, a bioterrorist attack—how easily the system would become inundated given the limited resources we have. I was probably the only doctor on staff to be thinking such morbid thoughts, and I know it was because of my background with the USAMRIID. Once an infectious disease counterbioterrorist physician and always—still, it weighed on my mind.

Although eight floors, the hospital's capacity was only ninety beds, of which only seventy to eighty of those were filled at any one time. Before HMO medicine, the capacity was one hundred forty. Times have changed, but private hospitals were not the only ones in these straits, so were the public hospitals. The general hospitals were also having budgetary problems. Most of them were downsizing or closing. So, more and more patients were being disenfranchised from the system that was supposed to be the safety net—a health care safety net. I again thought to myself: There's no way we can be prepared for a bioterrorist attack. We were lucky that the natural disasters we experienced in Los Angeles were tolerable, and that was because there weren't overwhelming casualties. I was on-call during the last major earthquake in 1994. If the flow of trauma patients continued, we would have been inundated in a few hours. But it didn't. There was a quick surge of patients and, just as quickly, the volumes trickled to less than what we would normally see. If there were a bioterrorist attack, my thoughts were that the volumes would be greater and sustained for a much longer period of time.

I opened the door to the stairwell and walked into the hall. The administrator's office was directly opposite. His office was quite in contrast to our emergency room of fourteen beds, high-technology equipment, gurneys, and paraphernalia needed for the various procedures we routinely do in the emergency room. His office was downright plush. Hell, you half expected to see a miniature putting green in front of the desk.

Jack Kilgorn's secretary, Katy, was seated behind her desk at his door entrance, guarding it, if you will, like Cerberus at the Gates of Hell. She was handpicked for her ability to diplomatically accept, divert, or deny entrance to those individuals that he wished or did not to speak to on any given occasion. She seemed to favor me. I smiled back.

"Hello, Kate. Jack just called down in ER."

"Yes, Dr. Kroose. Mr. Kilgorn always looks forward to talking with you."

Sure, like a cobra enjoys swing dancing with a mongoose.

I didn't share this thought with Katy, so I decided that silence was at the moment golden.

"He's waiting for you now," Katy said amicably.

Now *that* sounded ominous to me.

She announced my presence over the intercom and directed me to go on in.

Jack Kilgorn's room was large, measuring about twenty-by-twenty feet in width and length. He had a large window with a view of the ocean. He was sitting behind a cherry wood desk on a plush, black leather swivel chair. On his desk were the various Cross and Mont Blanc pens. There were a couple of Lalique crystal paperweights, one of a lion and one of the world. His laptop was sitting on the right side of the desk, opened. All I could see were charts of costs and revenues.

To his back, he had a floor-to-ceiling cherry wood bookcase enclosed with lead-laden glass doors. The shelves were full of various journals, reference books of business, and several books on tort law.

Not one on medicine, I thought with momentary contempt; though I should forgive Kilgorn on that. He was a businessman, not a doctor, plain and simple.

To his front, there was a wall of plaques: Diplomas from UCLA undergraduate school, USC business school, and Pepperdine law school among other civic awards for community contributions.

He was an accomplished man at forty and he wore it, wearing a three-piece brown Armani suit and a diamond-studded Rolex watch. He wasn't a man who subscribed to a local fitness center nor did he like natural foods; quite the contrast to my newest young Dr. Andy. Kilgorn was a bit overweight, by which I meant to say, he was downright chubby, and I cringed imagining what his cholesterol and triglyceride levels were. His wet bar, which was on the right side of his office, held the best of cognacs, scotch, and brandies. He'd never offered me any of that before (Kilgorn and I could not exactly be called old drinking buddies. I believe, at best, we tolerated each other on many levels).

However, I liked the coffee he always made available. He invariably had a fresh Columbian brew waiting for me.

We shook hands.

"Jack, how're you doing?"

"Good, Max, good. Would be doing better though if we could cut the cost of those cash accounts you see in the emergency room."

Fuck you, I thought. First volley fired, and not five seconds in the door. It rankled me to hear *any* complaints about money issues vis-à-vis my ER (where every penny was uncompromisingly needed). And how many poor souls out there simply couldn't afford insurance? Still, again, I decided to play the silent game. I shrugged, as if to tacitly convey *c'est la vie, c'est la guerre.*

When he saw that I wasn't going to buy into his initial byplay, he moved on.

"How're things down there today?"

"Busy enough," I said neutrally. "We're seeing a lot of influenza, and we're just getting to the peak of it."

"Do you have enough nurses to handle the load?"

"Yeah, we seem to be doing fine right now."

Shooting the shit. *When the hell was he going to get to the point of this meeting?*

Jack took a moment and poured a cup of coffee for me. I waved off cream and sugar and took the offering. He gestured for me to take a seat, which I did. He folded his hands in a steeple and leaned forward in his chair, putting on his most sincere veneer.

"You have a great staff down there," Jack said. "They seldom call in sick. Wish I could say that about the rest of the hospital."

I sipped the Columbian and nodded. "Yeah, we have a tight group. We hate to let each other down, and when we're short, the rest of us suffer."

"I see your point. Anyway it's well-appreciated up here."

That took me by surprise. I didn't anticipate his gratitude, but it was welcomed. He folded a few papers in front of him, a casual gesture.

"Schwartz seems to be up in arms again. Pointing fingers, making accusations."

Here it comes, I thought.

I spoke slowly, cautiously. "His patient—a Mr. Miller—was one admitted to a panel physician."

"Yeah, I heard about that," Jack said, shrugging. "But I'm not going to get into a twist about it."

This comment sideswiped me. *I'm here because of something else, not Schwartz and his tantrums? What the hell?*

"He seemed to be pretty upset," I said.

Jack took a moment with this but eventually waved it off. He seemed preoccupied, as if, quite frankly, he couldn't give a shit about the Schwartz dilemma.

"Don't worry about it," Jack said at last. "Besides, I got a letter from the patient telling me he did not want Dr. Schwartz on the case. I don't know why he just doesn't tell the guy. If you could just smooth it out for us, have a talk with the good doctor—make it seem like it's in his best interest not to take this particular patient."

Jack knew Schwartz and I just plain didn't get along (not that I was in the minority). *Why was he passing this on to me?*

"Schwartz is paranoid," I said, and I know it sounded like a snipe but couldn't help myself. "We have nothing against him, and we do all we can to please him."

"Yeah, yeah, I know. He's a difficult doc, but he's one of the major admitters to the hospitals so we need him."

Administration rote. Money, money, money. Fine, I'd play ball.

"Okay," I said easily. "I'll talk to him tomorrow. Maybe I'll even try to make peace and take him to lunch." I was bending over backwards on this, but I was gearing up for what might be the *real* reason for me being called up here. That reason being a complete mystery to me at the moment.

"Hey, good idea," Jack grinned enthusiastically. "Bill it to the hospital. We'll take care of it. Any other problems I should know about?"

I was beginning to feel annoyed. He was taking his time—maneuvering in for some kind of kill I couldn't even begin to contemplate. Again, I waded through this murky conversation as best I could.

"Well, we were close to saturation yesterday for a couple of hours."

"Yeah, I know. Sharon told me it was unavoidable."

Okay, no problem obviously on this front, either. Norma had talked to the nursing administrator about this to preempt this conflict.

"Sometimes these things happen," Jack said philosophically. "If we were only so lucky to be this busy all the time."

Silence again. Jack leaned back in his chair and smiled at me. A tiger sizing up a gazelle in the Serengeti before the fast spring forward and pounce.

"Max, I've got a bit of a sticky issue I'd like to discuss with you."

I smiled back. "I'm all ears."

Jack took a breath. "It's about the vaccinations."

"What vaccinations?" I asked, clueless.

He met my gaze head-on.

"Smallpox vaccinations."

I felt a pang of dread and uncertainty deep down in my gut.

"What about the smallpox vaccinations?" I said carefully.

Jack stood up, walked over to his window, and then turned back to me. With a casual gesture of his hand, he shrugged.

"Well, I'm thinking about opting out of it."

I let that sit for a moment yet realized every hair on the back of neck was probably standing vertical right about now.

"What do you mean opting out of it?" I said, barely containing a feral growl growing in my throat.

"Well, I just don't think it's necessary to vaccinate our staff."

I no longer felt like being polite.

"*What?*" I declared through a hiss.

Jack studied me for a moment. I don't think he was exactly prepared for my response.

I was caught off-balance. I know there had been nebulous discussions about possible inoculations for this hospital's staff, mainly during the period just after September 11, and while I had been a vociferous proponent for such a measure, the topic had died fairly quickly. Apparently, in some administrative circles, however, it had not expired at all, and if Jack Kilgorn was broaching this subject with me, it means that this subject had been rehashed and discussed exhaustively at the highest levels.

Were we actually this close to receiving approval for vaccinations? It was too much to hope for. And with good reason. Jack Kilgorn, our illustrious hospital administrator, was already making noises about quashing the idea altogether.

I thought to myself, *horseshit,* but I decided to tread carefully.

"You mean, *not* vaccinate our first responders?" I said, as Jack just continued to stare obtusely at me.

Jack's tone was dismissive.

"Yeah, the first responders; I think it's just too risky."

I thought to myself, *how wrong could he be?* I was prepared to do battle about two issues of no relevance now or tomorrow, but this issue was more important and relevant than any other I could think of. And though I hadn't anticipated this conversation, I was ready and willing to engage him on the topic at hand.

"*What* risk?" I snapped.

Jack didn't waste time formulating a careful reply. "Max, people can die from the vaccine."

Oh, boy, I thought. Jack had been listening to too much CNN again. Or more likely, he had other issues factoring into what was apparently already a foregone decision on his part to nix vaccinations for our people. I spoke in my most patient, bedside manner voice—the voice meant to assure and comfort, though images of my hands around Jack's neck wavered fleetingly in the back alley of my mind.

"Jack, it's very rare for someone to die from the actual vaccine. It happens in less than one in a million vaccinations."

"I heard it could happen as many as four out of a million," Jack shot back.

"Depends on the studies you read," I said, pressing. "The most extensive study was reported in the *New England Journal of Medicine* in 1969. They reviewed fourteen million vaccinations. That is the statistics I'm referring to. The others are conclusions drawn from much smaller studies. I think the 1969 report is more valid."

Jack made a motion with both hands—a kind of resignation that only great men blessed with the common touch should ever feel the need to use. Jack Kilgorn clearly saw himself as this kind of individual.

"Max, this is a changing world, and perhaps there are other factors to consider."

"What other factors?" I asked, truly curious.

"Well, vaccines *can* make you sick, if not kill you."

So can lying politicians, flipping through pornography with a faulty pacemaker, and killer bees, I thought. Kilgorn was grasping for straws, and I could see this in his eyes.

"Jack, the vaccine is given on a voluntary basis," I patiently replied. "No one is forced to take the vaccine, and you and I know that complications occur primarily in individuals who have never received the vaccine before. Those who have been vaccinated before run a much smaller risk, and half our staff has had the vaccine before. So, unless they're immuno-compromised, they stand to have an advantage from the vaccine without any side effects. We can screen everyone for AIDS, any other immunodeficiency disorder, eczema, or anyone who's pregnant who wants to be vaccinated. That should reduce the risk."

Kilgorn gave me a vaguely annoyed look. He tapped his fingers against the tabletop. It was my guess that he wasn't expecting this much resistance from me.

"You make a persuasive argument, but I don't know. I just don't feel comfortable with it. Besides, your staff may not want to be vaccinated."

"I *know* my staff, and they've asked about this," I said emphatically. "They *want* to be vaccinated."

Jack again made his waving motion. *Tut, tut*, the wave practically screamed at me.

"Max, the bigger point is that there may not be a *real* danger."

My patience was dwindling.

"I'm not following you," I said. Jack was starting to wander all over the place, and it irritated me.

"I mean, a bioterrorist attack with smallpox. It's just not that conceivable."

"You believe that?" I said incredulously. "After what we saw on 9/11, you actually *believe* that?" It probably wasn't the most politic tone I could have taken, but what Kilgorn was saying was just plain idiotic and dangerously shortsighted.

"A lot of people don't think there is."

My God, I thought. *A lot of people didn't think Hitler was a threat, either.* For a moment, I took a step back. Was I so adamant about this because of my own background, my own exposure to some of the worst pathogens in existence? Was I pounding the drum a bit too hard?

No. I had studied smallpox, knew its history, the weapons programs of both the United States and the Soviet Union—and the terrible possibility that this bug could again be unleashed on mankind by terrorists willing and able to do so. I refused to back down.

"Jack, why do you think the president took the vaccine? Why were all those soldiers being vaccinated in Iraq just before the war?"

Kilgorn sounded patronizing, which further heated my collar.

"It's just hard to justify any illness or death from a vaccine to an illness that has not been around for a long time. I mean, the risks outweigh any benefits."

Dead wrong, and I was going to let him know it. "Not so. Did you know that the last case of smallpox in this country was in 1947? Yet, we continued to vaccinate the people of this country until 1972—some twenty-five years after—even though there was never a case of smallpox in that period of time in this country. There were cases in *other* parts of the world. So, what's the difference now? We know variola exists in this world, and we don't know whether it will be brought to our country intentionally. So, what is different about today?"

I paused, allowing this to digest. Jack Kilgorn continued staring at me, as if perhaps I was speaking a little known dialect of Botswanese.

"If there is a risk," I continued slowly, "*knowing* how devastating smallpox can be, and especially in a community that we have now with no immunity, we should be vaccinated. How else are people going to be immune to this disease? People have not been vaccinated in thirty years, and there hasn't been an outbreak in fifty. These are the only ways to acquire immunity. If it comes back, it's coming back with a vengeance. And the first individuals to get it won't have a chance. Is this what you call collateral damage?"

Jack said nothing, but his smile was gone. So much for parlor courtesy.

"Who do you think the first ones are going to be to get it?" I continued in what must now sound like a minor tirade. "It'll be *us*. Emergency room staff and hospital staff and community docs. Yeah, community docs. You think patients with flu-like syndromes are going to come to the emergency room? Not if they have a primary care physician. They're going to go to their offices first."

"Max…"

"No," I cut him off. "I think vaccinating the first responders is a minimum. We should probably vaccinate all physicians, as well as the public in general. I think there's a false sense of security, in which we think we're going to be able to contain an epidemic if it occurs. And if it occurs, it's going to be unnatural. It's not going to be an epidemic that spreads from person to person. It's going to be spread intentionally. It's going to be spread by individuals obsessed with the thought that killing as many Americans will get them to paradise. And who knows if it will be a natural-occurring virus? Who knows how virulent it's going to be? No, I'll take my chances with the vaccine." I paused. "I *want* the vaccine," I said quietly in follow-up.

Jack stood up, walked around his table, and sat on the edge, facing me no more than a few feet away.

"Max, I know you're passionate about this, but I've got unions asking what happens if the nurses who get vaccinated get sick and can't work because of the fevers, the body aches? Who's going to pay them? And then what if someone develops a serious complication? You hear talk about who's going to sue who? If I give the okay to give the vaccine, my head's on the block."

And so the truth comes out. Jack was covering his ass, plain and simple. *Jesus Christ.* And at the expense of human life. Ignorance and fear and self-interest were coming sharply into focus for me. At that moment, I hated Jack Kilgorn for this manipulative piece of administrative fuckery.

"So, this is what this is all about," I said softly. "Self-serving lawyers and misguided people."

Jack frowned. "Are you suggesting I'm misguided?"

I took the gloves off. "You *are*, Jack. You don't know what you're talking about, and I do. For Christ's sake, this was my field of expertise at one time. Do the right thing and ram this measure down the executive committee's throat. Get us those vaccinations."

Jack glared at me but said nothing. The intercom suddenly blared out with Katy's voice. "Mr. Kilgorn, Dr. Kroose is wanted in the emergency room. Apparently there are a lot of patients who need his assistance right now."

Not turning away from me, Jack snapped back, "Thanks, Katy. He's on his way."

I stood up. So did Jack. "Max, I want your support on this issue. Call it a favor. We can all use favors at one time or another. Friends are good to have around here."

This was not going to turn out well.

"You'll never have my support on this matter, Jack. Get used to it, you'll sleep better."

Jack took another one of his massive sighs and nodded. He stuck out his hand, and I took it.

"Maybe we'll talk later. In the meantime, you better get down there and take care of business."

"Who knows, Jack? Maybe I have a smallpox case right now." It was a flippant thing to say, and I regretted it almost immediately but *not* the look of agitation I received from Jack after I said it.

"If you're trying to butter me up, Max, it's just not working," he said through a smile I'm sure he thought was friendly and politic in the extreme.

"I had to give it my best shot," I said in an equally magnanimous tone of voice. I thought we were finished, but then as he walked me to the door, he said, "Anyway, do let me know how this Miller thing with Schwartz goes. Schwartz can certainly do some damage if he's not appeased. He's got a lot of ears and some powerful friends."

I didn't say a word. We had already covered Schwartz, and this afterthought on Jack's part seemed superfluous.

"I'll see you at the exec committee meeting tonight," he said. "Think about our talk, won't you?"

I walked out the door, and it closed very quickly behind me. And there was no doubt in my mind whatsoever of one thing: Jack Kilgorn, the most powerful man in the hospital, was now my enemy.

10:30 AM

I made my way back to the emergency room, feeling angrier than I had in a long time…since Leana's death, as a matter of fact. Jack Kilgorn may have been a decent administrator (i.e., saving the hospital a buck or two), but he was a damned fool when it came to medicine and anticipating the unimaginable in terms of epidemics. Sure, maybe smallpox would *never* be weaponized and used against this country in our lifetime, but what if it was?

Was it too much to ask for a little foresight, a little ounce of prevention, at least for first responders like myself and my team? I think not.

That bastard. Bad enough he didn't know what he was talking about, but to jeopardize my people with an arbitrary piece of policymaking…

I realized with a sense of futility that Jack would win at the end. I may be the director of ER, but the executive committee was a highly bureaucratic unit—the members would all follow Jack's lead. I could raise hell from here to Tuesday, and the outcome would be the same. No vaccinations. Smallpox is a dead worry and a dead disease. *Leave it to an ER doctor with an infectious disease background to spread doom and gloom and make expensive and potentially litigious problems for everyone.* I could hear the tacit rumble from the committee already.

Still, I would be at that meeting tonight. And I would state my piece. Hell and be damned, I would not let Jack Kilgorn push this thing through without a fight. And if it cost me my job at the end of the day, so be it.

"Be sure to let me know how that thing with Miller and Schwartz goes," Kilgorn had said. *Wasn't like Kilgorn to be repetitious like that…unless…*

Was Kilgorn threatening me? That if I didn't support the quashing of the smallpox vaccine measure, he would let Schwartz run roughshod over me and my department, making all kinds of damaging allegations—all without his, Kilgorn's, defense?

Could be. The son of a bitch. Could very well be.

Or…or was I just being paranoid again. The Voice wagging its subliminal tongue at me. *Watch your back, Max…the sharks are circling…and you're the main course for tonight's festivities.*

"Oh, come on," I muttered to myself and thought through a sigh that I was just imagining things. Jack Kilgorn was a pushy, politically pugilistic apostate for the administration, but he was hardly vindictive. He couldn't afford to be. Could he…

I forced my recent encounter with Jack under the mental doormat. I'd just been called back to ER because things were going haywire. I thought perhaps many more influenza patients had come in, but then again there may have been impending true medical emergencies, and I was about to find out.

I thought of my good friend, Glen Hamilton. If anyone knew the risk of smallpox reappearing, it would be Glen. He had been privy to so many top-secret meetings with the CIA and the FBI while conducting research at Fort Dietrick in Maryland. If I could get hold of him, perhaps I could obtain the newest information and threat levels by which to demonstrate to the exec committee that we needed a proper defense against smallpox. Something current and compelling. Something that would be so inexorable, so indisputable, that Jack Kilgorn and his administrative lackeys would have no choice but acquiesce to securing smallpox vaccines for my people.

And if that failed, perhaps Glen could still help me obtain the vaccine for my staff, outside of this administration's bullheaded jurisdiction. I had to give him a call, but I didn't have his number. I wondered who could help me.

I punched in the code to open up the back door of the department, and I entered the emergency room. I found Norma at the nursing station. She was busy directing traffic. I could see that all the rooms were full.

Suddenly, there was an ambulance arriving in the docking area. I could see the flashing lights.

I was beginning to feel a little apprehensive. The cadence of the day suddenly took that turn for the worse.

Right then and there, worse was a walk in the park.

Eight hours from now worse would be a living, breathing hell.

*   *   *   *

"Norma, what's going on?" I asked, and I could hear the edge in my voice.

"Dr. Kroose, as you can see, all the beds are full. We're getting two runs. This one just pulled up. Squad Five is bringing us an elderly man, about seventy years of age. Apparently, he's pretty sick. Has a fever of 104 and the usual diseases—diabetes, heart failure, and hypertension. He also has a rash over his lower extremities. He may be septic." I knew this suggested a moribund, shocking patient from his infection.

"What are his vital signs?"

"MAC gave us a blood pressure of 170 over 80, and a pulse about 140. Respirations are about 28."

MAC is an abbreviation for Medical Alert Center, which is a communications center for the County of Los Angeles that directs county ambulances to the various emergency rooms in L.A. County. It receives calls from base station, which are emergency rooms designated to assist the paramedics out in the field in delivering emergency care. This is usually done by telephone. Once the patient is stabilized out in the field, the bay station then directs the county ambulance to its destination, which is usually the closest appropriate emergency room.

The elderly fellow, as Norma put it, had a name: Mr. Fuentes—and he seemed acutely ill given his pulse at rest should be about 70 and his respiration 16. But the bottom line was that he was a potential disaster.

"Norma, place Mr. Fuentes in bed one and reassess his vital signs. Why don't we have Andy see this guy?"

"Yeah, Dr. Kroose, it'll probably be a good case for him. It's going to be a long history. It may take him the better part of an hour to do the physical on him."

She smiled as she said this, and I understood what she meant. Medical students tend to be quite thorough, obsessive, and compulsive about taking every bit of the history and physical exam. Although unnecessary in emergency room medicine, he was just learning.

She assigned Martha to take the vital signs and assess Mr. Fuentes.

"What's the other ambulance run?" I asked, by now Jack and his inane conversation with me passing into barely an afterthought.

"Squad Fifty is bringing us an individual; a gentlemen who appears—and smells, they say—like he's been drinking cheap red wine for about a month and lots of it. He was picked up a few blocks away from here. They think he may be going into DTs. He seemed to be a little confused."

"I would be, too, with that much hooch in my system," I said. "How long will it be before they arrive?"

"ETA's about five minutes."

"What else is on the menu?"

"Six influenza patients—four in rooms, two are checking in. And we also have an upper back pain, and another patient who feels he has the flu but says he has a bad cough and can't breathe well."

"Okay," I said, then peeked around the doorway to the clerk's desk and saw Jamie.

"Hey, Jamie, how are you holding up?" I said.

"Oh, Dr. Kroose, okay. I got a feeling it's going to be this way all day."

"Don't jinx us, kiddo," I said, crossing my fingers.

She looked up and smiled. "I think it's too late."

She seemed a little overburdened registering all the patients, but I wanted to talk to Glen Hamilton, and I thought there was no harm in asking.

I asked her to find his number. "He's in Washington, D.C.," I told her. "Johns Hopkins, a faculty member. If he's traveling, they'll patch him through to wherever he may be."

"Okay, Dr. Kroose," Jamie said affably. "I'll see what I can do when I have a few minutes. It's going to take me a while to catch up with all these patients."

"No problem. Just let me know when you have something," I replied.

I continued through the ER. Matt was placing one of the influenza patients in a room and getting vital signs. Likewise, Cynthia, Linda, and Betty were doing the same. Martha was taking vital signs and assessing Fuentes. He had not stopped coughing since I walked into ER. Martha had him undressed and ready for me to see. Andy was coming down from the library, where he had spent a couple of hours reviewing the literature on urinary tract infections. I wanted to make sure Fuentes was stable enough to be seen by Andy. I needed to review his condition with Martha.

"His blood pressure's okay," Martha said. "His pulse is about 140, and his respiration rate is about 28, but his pulse oximetry is ninety-eight percent—normal. His temperature is 104."

His pulse oximetry was the oxygen content of his blood, which was normal, indicating that his respiratory system was functioning just fine despite the respiratory rate (I suspected this was due to other discomfort). A cursory examination of the patient revealed that he was oriented with a good sense of humor.

"Young feller, are you the orderly or the doctor?"

"No, Mr. Fuentes, I'm Dr. Kroose."

"Okay, Dr. Kroose, let me ask you this: Am I ready to go? I'm not sure why they brought me here by ambulance. I don't think I'm that sick."

Although oriented, his judgment was obviously impaired.

"No, sir, you're a little too sick to go home right now. As a matter of fact, there's probably a good chance you're going to stay in the hospital for a few days."

"Oh, there's no need for that," the old man protested.

"Mr. Fuentes, how about you just let me do a little bit of an examination. Dr. Goodman will be with you a little later. He'll want to look you over as well, if you don't mind."

"I get two doctors?" The idea seemed momentarily fascinating to him.

"It's your lucky day." Mr. Fuentes chuckled at that.

A cursory history and a physical revealed a man weathered by his illnesses. He had had several hospitalizations for diabetes, hypertension, and heart failure. His obvious problem, presently, was his high fever. The examination indicated that the source was most likely the skin rash, but what was the cause of the rash? I was going to let Andy figure that out. This would be a good teaching case for him, and I just wanted to give preliminary orders while Andy initiated the workup and whatever therapies he required.

"Martha, get me a CBC, a set of electrolytes, a BUN, a creatinine, and a glucose. Also get a urinalysis, a chest X ray, and an EKG."

These were all basic studies performed to evaluate basic body function. The EKG records cardiac electrical impulses, which helps us evaluate heart function. In this particular case, the heart rhythm was important to know (i.e., whether the heart rhythm was normal or not). The urine study and chest X ray were done primarily to determine whether these two organ systems were sources for the fever. That is, whether there was a urinary tract infection or pneumonia.

"Martha, while you're waiting for Dr. Goodman to see the patient, why don't you give him 10 grains of Tylenol and 600 milligrams of Motrin so we can get the fever down? Also start an IV and infuse normal saline. Challenge him with 200 ccs (boluses) of saline to a total of 600 ccs. Let's see if his pulse comes down as his fever comes down and you bolus him."

Not uncommonly, these patients present dehydrated, so infusion with this common solution using boluses achieves rehydration quickly, lowering the pulse and improving their condition.

I took a breath and recollected my thoughts. "Any other orders?"

"You need more coffee?" Martha asked.

I smiled, grateful. "No, I had one in the administrator's office. Thanks anyway. By the way, how's the family?"

"Oh, everybody's fine, Dr. Kroose. Thanks for asking. Can't wait to get off work though."

"Why is that?"

"My husband's taking me out to dinner for our anniversary."

"What anniversary?"

"Our twentieth anniversary."

"Well, congratulations."

"He's got me a little present."

You could feel the exuberant joy in her expectation.

"I hope it's another diamond ring," I said.

"Me, too. Or tickets to Hawaii," she said and laughed.

I had four other patients to see quickly and, in five minutes, I was getting another run. I went from room to room, examining each patient. All of them had the same complaint—fevers, body aches, headaches, backaches, having a sense of malaise, and severe weakness. Much of their symptomatology, however, could be attributed to their fevers. So, in essence, controlling their fevers made them feel better.

It was a little unusual, however, because two of them had a faint, generalized spotty rash. I had seen this with other viral syndromes but not this often. I prescribed Tylenol, Motrin, lots of bed rest and fluids, and they were discharged in short order.

Mr. Lyle Caruso—who smelled like a small brewery, as promised by the ambulance drivers—had been brought in while I was seeing the influenza patients. He seemed to be stable, however, quite confused. I could hear the struggling in the other room where he was being placed. Linda was assigned to him. She was assisting the paramedics and placing soft restraints on the patient since he was attempting to get off the gurney. He required a lot of encouragement to stay in bed. The paramedics signed off the case to her, and she began her assessment. She got whatever medical history she could, but it was limited. He seemed to be stuttering and repeating himself, making it difficult to obtain much of a history. She gave up on this and began assessing the vital signs, placing the cardiac monitor leads on his chest and the oxygen monitor probe on his finger. She masterfully undressed him. Mind you, he was bound, making this a very difficult task, but she was able to do it with ease.

Norma was busy directing the flow of patients from the waiting room. She brought in the influenza patient with the cough and shortness of breath and assigned it to Betty to assess; and brought in the patient with the upper back pain and assigned it to Cynthia to handle. They were both placed in non-monitored examining rooms, sparing the monitored beds for patients who were more acutely ill and required cardiac monitoring. She returned to the nursing station, where she began to key into the computer terminal the laboratory studies requested on the patient being evaluated in the emergency room.

As I walked toward Mr. Caruso's bed, the red phone rang out. The red phone is the phone MAC calls us to give us the heads up when they're transporting a case to us. To me, it meant another potential disaster.

I diverted my route to where Norma was. As Norma picked up the phone to answer the call, she began to jot down important information on the case they were transporting to us. I couldn't see what she was writing, but she was shaking her head.

"Norma, what are they transporting?"

"A peds case."

"A peds case? We're not a pediatric receiving facility."

"You know that. I know that. They know that. Apparently, the patient can't wait to get to the pediatrics receiving facility right now. They think she's an extremist."

"What's her problem?"

"She has asthma and had an acute exacerbation. They began to give her treatment, however, they can't seem to break it."

"How old is she?"

"Six. They tell me she's breathing about forty times a minute and her pulse oximetry is about 85."

"So what's the ETA on her?"

"About ten minutes. They're still at the site."

"Do we have a bed?"

"Number four," she pointed at the room just opposite her station.

I nodded. "Make sure you get the crash cart there and ready just in case I have to intubate her. I'm going to go see Mr. Caruso and get things started on him. Call respiratory and have Sergio come down."

"Done it already, Dr. Kroose."

Mr. Caruso was confused and, at times, combative. I introduced myself several times, but he continued to repeat the same question over and over again. "Who are you?"

There was no old chart to retrieve information about him since it was his first visit. The best we could do was to review what he had in his pockets—his billfold, what we call in the emergency room a "wallet biopsy"—to obtain whatever little information he was not able to give us. He was fifty years old and came from Michigan. He had no pictures in his wallet or home phone numbers. He had several credit cards and a business card with a business phone number. This we could use to obtain further personal information about him or contact a family member or significant other. He worked for a pharmaceutical company. He was here for a conference. This we gathered from a registration card he had in his wallet. There were keys in his pocket, which indicated that he was staying in a local hotel. The registration card indicated that it was a three-day conference, and the room was going to cost him a fortune. Either he had quite a bit of money or the company was going to cover it.

I asked Linda to follow up on the various leads to see if she could locate a family member who could give us a little bit more history. His vital signs were abnormal, however stable. His pulse was about 130, his temperature 105. His respiratory rate was fast, but I gathered this was from the fever and his drinking given that I could easily have caught a buzz just from his breath. His lung examination was normal. His pulse oximiter reading was ninety-eight percent, meaning that he was oxygenating well. He also had a faint, spotty rash that could be consistent with alcohol liver disease. The rest of his examination was consistent with an individual suffering from chronic alcoholism—rubor facies, pale skin, thinning of the extremities, protuberant abdomen, and a deep, red-colored tongue; all this, not to mention his state of mind, which was all over the map and fairly incoherent.

Linda was making her way back to his bedside. She had left to obtain paraphernalia needed to draw the appropriate blood studies so she could start an IV. I remember thinking how sexy she looked. She had a provocative sway as she walked. I'm sure she didn't do this intentionally. It was just part of her. But I had more important things to do at the moment, so I abbreviated my thought.

"Linda, what studies are you going to draw?"

"The usual."

"Make sure you get the liver function studies, alcohol blood level, and toxicology screens. Oh, and get a core temperature."

"Max…ah, I mean Dr. Kroose, I know. I got a core temperature. His rectal temp was 105, but I haven't had a chance to record it. And I've already told Norma what studies we're going to order, but I will add the toxicology screens."

She turned around and looked at me as she stretched to hang up the saline IV bottle on the IV pole and smiled, as if she knew I was watching her do this. *Subtle, Max, real subtle.*

"We wouldn't want to miss anything," I said to Linda. "His confusion could be due to an overdose."

"I know, Dr. Kroose. It just doesn't explain the fever, does it?"

She was right. It didn't explain the fever, but I had to cover all bases. Liver function studies would help confirm the diagnosis of alcoholic liver disease, which could explain his confusion. The alcohol level should be low or zero if he was truly in DTs, that is, withdrawing from the alcohol. The toxicology screens were just a safe measure in case we were following a red herring. Sometimes we're prejudiced by the presentation of a patient and come to the wrong conclusion as a result of this. I wanted to make sure that I wasn't going to make this mistake. She was right. The fever. It may have been something else causing this.

I walked over to Norma's workstation.

"Norma, is everything ready for the little girl?"

"Yes, we have the crash cart at the bedside, Ambu bag, and Sergio will be here in a minute. Dr. Kroose, what size intratrachial tube would you like to use?"

"Get me a six and six-and-a-half with a cuff."

Intratracheal tubes were the tubes we used to place in the trachea on those patients who could no longer breathe for themselves. I was hoping not to have to use this. It was usually located in the crash cart, which is a large, red toolbox where we keep all the paraphernalia we need in resuscitation of patients who succumb to their illnesses and all the possible chemicals we may need, such as adrenalin, atropine, and sedatives such as Valium and Versed.

I walked over to the bedside to check on all the paraphernalia I would need. The red phone rang again. Norma quickly walked to the phone and answered it. I saw the same expression on her face again. I walked over to her. She put the phone down and jotted down a few notes.

"Norma, what're we getting now?" I asked

"There's a two year old who had a seizure with a fever of 104. They were able to start an IV and give some Valium to suppress the seizure. She seems to be waking up. They're trying to cool her down."

"She sounds stable enough to be transferred to the pediatric receiving facility."

"No, Dr. Kroose, they feel she can't wait, so she's coming here."

As I turned away from Norma, I saw the paramedics wheeling in the six year old. She seemed to be struggling to catch her breath, and I began to feel a sense of impending doom. And now the outside phone rang. Norma answered.

"Yes, this is Ames Community." She waited a moment and then nodded. "Yes, Dr. Kroose is right here. May I help you?"

Again, she listened...and I watched, wondering what *new* disaster was heading our way.

"I see," Norma said. She looked to me and held out the phone.

"Dr. Kroose, it's for you," she said. "It's the school where your children go. Your little boy has been hurt."

11:30 AM

I could feel the blood drain from my face.

I took the phone from Norma (snatched it was more like it).

"Hello, who is this?" I said.

The voice on the other end was female, soft-spoken.

"Dr. Kroose?"

"Yes, that's me. What happened to my boy?"

"He's all right, doctor," the voice assured. "I'm Louise Mahler, the assistant principal. Billy is in the nurse's office now."

"What the hell happened?" I asked, short and not in the mood for pleasantries.

"Billy was playing in the schoolyard, and he had a fall. He has a nasty cut on his head. We've bandaged him, but we wanted to know if you'd be coming by to pick him up and take him home."

I glanced at my watch and looked out over the ER. Not a chance in hell I could get away. Not now.

"I won't be able to do that, Ms. Mahler," I said, relaxing a bit. "And I didn't mean to bite your head off. We're just a bit busy here in ER today. Thank you for calling me."

"Our pleasure, doctor," Ms. Mahler said. "Is there anyone who can pick Billy up?"

"I'll call my housekeeper," I said. "Big question, though. He's in the play tonight. He's not going to be able…"

Ms. Mahler interrupted me, laughing. "I'm afraid Billy's way ahead of you, doctor. He doesn't mind missing the rest of the day at school, but he insists on coming back to do the play tonight."

I smiled at this. Billy, the little scrapper; he's got it all planned out. A whole day of cartoons and playing games (not to mention the inevitable spoiling by Esmerelda) and then come back to the school and be a star.

"Okay," I said and chuckled. "I'll call my housekeeper. Thanks again for the update."

"No problem," Ms. Mahler said and hung up.

I let out a breath of relief and looked to Norma.

"Everything all right?" she asked.

"Yeah, he had a bit of a fall while playing, but he's fine," I said.

Norma told me she was taking lunch, and Linda took over the multitasking of the hour. Meanwhile, the paramedics with the asthmatic little girl were right behind me. I directed them to bed four.

Linda practically ran ahead of me, positioning herself at the head of the bed and ready to set the patient on a monitor. Sergio had just arrived to the emergency room and was making his way toward me as I began to get the history from the paramedics.

Apparently, Amy Sterling was doing fine until two days ago when she developed a cold, which was common for asthmatics. She deteriorated with the onset of a viral syndrome, and this was what she was suffering from. Her parents were on their way, but she was too short of breath to give me much more of a history. She pretty much took a turn for the worst this morning. She used her nebulizer several times without any improvement, at which point the parents called the paramedics. When they found her, she was in acute distress. She was unable to breathe well and tripoding (this is where a child uses her upper extremities to straighten her torso to allow her to take deeper breaths.) She was cyanotic with bluing around her lips and fatiguing. They gave her oxygen and nebulized albuterol, a mist of medication given through a facemask with the intent of dilating the bronchi in spasm in asthmatics. In spite of three back-to-back treatments and an injection of adrenalin, she continued to breathe at forty times a minute and began to fatigue. Her pulse oximitry was eighty-five percent. That is, her oxygen content was much below normal. And in a patient who was struggling, breathing forty times a minute, this suggested that she would begin to succumb to her illness.

I dismissed the paramedics who had other runs to do and began my examination and treatment of Amy. I introduced myself.

"Amy, I'm Dr. Kroose. I'm going to help you. I know you're having a difficult time breathing right now and you probably can't speak very much, but just answer me as best you can. I'm going to begin to give you some medications that will make you feel better."

She responded in broken sentences not being able to answer because of her labored breathing. "Okay…that's fine…thanks…Dr. Kroose."

My heart went out to the child; I could almost physically feel her discomfort, and I fought the lump rising in my throat.

"Amy," I said quietly. "I may have to intubate you, which will help you breathe better. I won't do this unless the medications don't work."

She looked back at me with huge brown, discomfited eyes and nodded.

"I understand, Dr. Kroose," she whispered. "I've had this done before."

I thought of my little one, Andrea. Thank God she was in perfect health, but I could imagine how insane with worry I would be on a 24/7 basis if she was as afflicted with what Amy suffered from.

"I'll bet you have," I said and put what I hoped to be a comforting hand on her cheek.

She was a stoic, strong little girl, mature beyond her years, who probably experienced several episodes of her illness. I applied my stethoscope on her chest. As I listened, I could hear the monstrousness of what tormented her: Nasal flaring, the retraction of the space between her ribs with each deep inspiration, and slight wheezing—the faint breath sounds, all underscoring the severity of her disease. Technical assessment aside, Amy probably felt like she was slowly suffocating, which indeed she was.

I looked to Linda. "Draw up 125 milligrams of Solumedrol and give it through the IV." She had already drawn it. I turned to Matt. "Matt, place her on the cardiac monitor and the pulse oximeter. I need her heart rate and oxygen level continuously monitored. Give her an additional treatment of albuterol and add atrovent to her therapy. All these medications in a synergistic way could help open up her airways."

Sergio interrupted me while I was giving out the orders.

"Doc, I'll take care of inhalation therapy. Let Matt set up the monitors."

"Good," I said. "Watch the pulse. I don't want her above 160. Let's get the pulse oximetry above 90."

If we were successful, we would see the pulse oximetry climb above 90 and the pulse below 140.

Sergio was an ex-SEAL who had come to work at the hospital about three years ago. He was fearless and seemed to bring a sense of confidence to patients that he treated. I could see him interact with Amy, which brought on a smile from me despite the desperate circumstances at hand.

"Also," I said, "do the routine lab. Get me an arterial blood gas and order a portable chest X ray."

"Got it, Doc," Sergio snapped back with military precision.

In spite of the inhalation therapy and Solumedrol, which is a steroid, Amy continued to struggle. Perspiration was running off her forehead. Ten minutes had passed. Intubation seemed to be inevitable, but I was willing to try a controversial therapy. I looked to Linda.

"Get me aminophylline."

"Yes, Dr. Kroose. How much?"

Amy weighed about forty kilos, so I did a quick piece of calculation.

"Get me 240 mg of aminophylline. Run it over fifteen, twenty minutes, and then we'll start a 30 mg per hour drip."

As I gave this order, the ambulance with the two-year-old seizure patient, Jordan Gallaway, pulled up to the docking area." Big day for ambulance drivers, I thought. Busy, busy, busy.

Linda went about obtaining the aminophylline to infuse while Matt closely followed all the vital signs and the oxygen level. Sergio was busy giving back-to-back treatments with the inhalation therapy. I went to assess the newly arrived Jordan along with the mother, Anne. I met them at the ambulance entrance, and I obtained the pertinent information about the transfer from the paramedics.

Jordan had developed a flu-like syndrome earlier this morning. He had subsequently developed high fevers. The mother tried to control the fever with the usual measures of Tylenol and lukewarm baths, however the fever would not break. Then suddenly Jordan developed a grand mal seizure. The mother subsequently called 911 and when the paramedics arrived, they found the toddler seizing (to the tune of about two or three minutes). It was, however, uncertain if the child had back-to-back seizures or one sustained seizure. They started an intravenous line and gave him Valium. With this, the seizures stopped. His fever was just above 104 and, apparently, he was unconscious during transport. However, he was conscious when entering ER. The child had no other illnesses, and a quick cursory exam revealed him to be otherwise healthy, awake, and active. So I directed the paramedics to one of our pediatric rooms. Then I asked Martha to assess the patient and begin the workup. I asked her to obtain the routine blood, urine studies, as well as a chest X ray, and gave her orders for routine fever measures.

It was at this moment that I turned and saw Dr. Maynard Schwartz, staring at me from the ER/main hospital entrance.

"We need to talk, doctor," he said and the tone in his voice portended of gloom, doom, and further irritation for me.

*   *   *   *

I stared at him and weighed my various options. Either talk to Schwartz now or tell him in the highly technical medical jargon I've been famous for to simply fuck off, I'm very busy right now. However, I knew this latter option would only cause monumental repercussions on every level and do nothing to ameliorate an otherwise dismal political conundrum.

"Hi, Maynard," I said and looked around to the various cases I was presented with. I glanced at my watch.

"Can this wait?" I asked him politely.

"Two minutes is all I need. I know you're busy," he said. He would not be put off.

As it were, this was a good time to talk, because my people were handling everything else, and Jordan, my latest case, would have to be directed to a pediatric bed and preliminarily situated.

"Okay," I said. "Step into my office," I indicated, pointing to the doctor's room.

Meanwhile, Martha picked up Jordan off the paramedics portable gurney and took him and his mother to the pediatric room. Although the seizure was a bit longer than one would expect for a febrile seizure, it was my impression that it was only a febrile seizure precipitated by fever, which was probably caused by the influenza, the virus that was in the community at the time. During the day, he looked well. I thought the child would probably do fine.

I closed the door to the doctor's room and turned to Schwartz.

"What the hell are you doing to me, Max?" he hissed immediately.

"I'm doing nothing to you, Maynard," I said. "I know you've gone to Jack about this. You obviously feel like I'm stealing your patients or, if not me, then my ER."

"Feel?" he almost squealed. "It's happened too many times to be coincidence."

"It's happened a few times and not deliberately, Maynard. These were critical cases, they had to be handled quickly, and you were unavailable," I said. "We moved fast to save lives."

"You're supposed to call or page me," he said angrily.

"We did. And it's not our fault if we have to send you the cash-basis clients on occasion. We're not trying to stick it to you…"

"Like hell," he fumed. "If it happens again, I'm going to see that this goes to higher heads than you and me."

I paused at that. "You've already done that, Maynard, by bitching to Jack."

He didn't immediately reply. "Listen," I said, recalling my conversation with Kilgorn. "I want to bury the hatchet. Sure, we've had to shove some pretty shitty cases your way and siphon off the insurance patients, but it was completely unintentional. Why don't we have lunch, talk about things, and see how this becomes less dramatic and traumatizing in the future."

I could hear Maynard taking deep, ragged breaths. He stared at me for a moment.

"You're patronizing me, Max."

"I'm not," I said, meaning it. Hell, if I could get Schwartz off my back, Kilgorn's back, *anyone's* back—this hospital would be better for it. "What do you say?"

He studied me for a moment. "Max, let's cut the bullshit. I know you don't like me."

"That's not true," I said, though half-heartedly.

Poor Maynard. He just wasn't my cup of tea nor most of Western Civilization's either, for that matter. A bit of a prig, as they say...

"No," he insisted. "I know you don't. I know a lot of folks don't. I lack your gift with people—and that may be my major drawback as a physician, since a good bedside manner personally and professionally is critical in this business. But I'm a good doctor. Damn good, and I expect respect. If I feel maltreated, I voice it. I'm pretty blunt."

"I hadn't noticed," I said quietly, trying a touch of humor to pacify my esteemed colleague.

He smiled at this, but it was not a friendly smile. "I'm serious, doctor. I will take these various past incidents to the medical exec committee, and while I may be dismissed as being just temperamental or a bit of an asshole, I'll still cause a stink for you. And you don't need another stink right now from higher up."

"What's that supposed to mean?" I asked, all feelings of a need to ease the tension evaporating by Maynard's veiled threat.

He nodded, and his mouth twisted to the side. "You've been warned, Max."

"Don't push this," I said. "And don't insinuate you can get me thrown out of my department. It won't happen in a thousand years."

He reached for the door and opened it. He then turned to me and raised his eyebrows.

"Really," he said. And then he was gone.

*   *   *   *

My hoped-for peaceful day was obviously now swirling down the proverbial shitter. This latest altercation with Schwartz left me not so much angry as bemused. He had tossed out innuendoes at me as if they were confetti. My paranoia about Jack Kilgorn trying to shaft me if I didn't support his insidious small-pox moratorium rose to the fore once more. I asked myself: Were Schwartz and Jack actually in cahoots with some kind of retaliation if I didn't side with Jack at the exec committee tonight? Had Schwartz made a deal with Jack, if he, as a primary care physician (and a rainmaker, of sorts, for the hospital), supported the obliteration of the smallpox measure, giving Jack's case a kind of detestable medical merit for eliminating vaccines completely?

I ruminated the scenarios. Anything was possible, and I had to admit that between the conversations with Kilgorn and Schwartz, this was turning into the most politically uncomfortable day of my career here at the hospital.

All that aside, I had more pressing duties: My patients—people with true medical emergencies.

I returned to Amy's bedside and found the aminophylline was infusing. I looked up at the monitors and, to my delight, saw the pulse had decreased to 130 and the personal oximetry was at 90. I looked at Amy. Perspiration on her forehead had ceased. She was still struggling, but I saw a bit of improvement.

"Amy, how are you feeling now?"

"I think I can breathe a little better." She looked up at me and smiled. Sergio smiled back and looked at me.

"Doc, you haven't lost your touch."

"No, Sergio. You guys are just good."

He turned around and patted Amy on the shoulder as if to say, "No, she's just a good patient."

I felt more comfortable about Amy. I felt that she had turned a corner, but by no means was she out of the woods. However, her improvement was significant, and it was less likely we'd have to intubate her, and that I felt good about.

I looked up and saw Linda finishing up her notes. I could appreciate the sense of pride as she reviewed all that was being done for Amy, a sense of pride for the team. I thought I had a few minutes while the aminophylline infused. I went back to see Mr. Caruso, with Linda following behind. She'd finished obtaining the EKG a while ago, and I wondered how she was able to do that, knowing how uncooperative Mr. Caruso had been initially.

As I approached the bed, I wondered what was wrong with this picture. Linda had raised the point about the fever. Was this from the DTs or was there something else wrong such as an infection?

"How are you feeling, Mr. Caruso?" I asked.

This time, Mr. Caruso didn't answer. He stared at me through bloodshot eyes, weaving, and trembling.

Okay," I said. "I'll be back in a few moments. You rest easy, while I check out your lab results."

Linda and I exited the room, closing the door behind us. I asked her if she believed the fever was from anything other than the DTs.

"Well, Dr. Kroose," she said. "If I were a betting woman, and you know I'm not or I'd have gone out with you a long time ago, I would say this is most likely from his alcoholism. So, no. No other options."

Hmm. That came out of nowhere, I thought. *Was that an open invitation or what?* She smiled at me, and I was surprised at her boldness…yet I found myself smiling back. That was a much-needed momentary distraction from the various political imbroglios currently proliferating in my life.

What harm could it hurt if you did ask her out for a drink one day? I could almost hear Leana's voice: Do it, Max. Get out of your doldrums, start living again. I won't mind.

Leana wouldn't, either. She had been an infinitely practical woman, and she wouldn't have approved of me cloistering myself off from happiness. Well, I thought, one day, if I have the time, when I don't have a play to attend—one day.

I cleared my throat, regaining my composure. "Uh, we'll have to talk about that some time," I said to Linda. "By the way, did you know that patients who overdose on aspirin present not uncommonly with high fevers? And how do you know that Mr. Caruso hasn't overdosed on something that causes a high fever?"

"Dr Kroose, you're stretching it. This guy has DTs. You and I both know that."

She was right. Chances were that is what Mr. Caruso had. However, there was something wrong about his presentation. I couldn't put my finger on it at the time.

"Something wicked this way comes."…

I was spooking myself again, and I had the feeling that the Voice was being nudged by my unpleasant dealings with Kilgorn about the smallpox issue.

"What does the EKG show?" I asked Linda.

"Normal," she replied, handing me the heart stats.

"I think I'll reexamine him again and make sure I didn't miss anything on the physical. Maybe something else will explain the fever," I told her.

Linda looked up at me and shook her head.

"You're a doubting Thomas, Dr. Kroose. You're just a doubting Thomas."

"No, I just want to be thorough," I defended myself.

As I was about to reenter Mr. Caruso's room, I heard Betty call me from one of the other examining rooms. I went over to see what she wanted.

"Dr. Kroose, I think you should see Mr. Villalobos next."

Fernando Villalobos had been brought in about five minutes ago.

"Why is that?" I asked.

"I don't think he's doing that well. And there's something else."

"What?" I asked, feeling impatient.

Betty hesitated for just a moment. She looked me directly in the eye, and she was dead serious.

"He scares the hell out of me."

✻   ✻   ✻   ✻

I just stared at Betty. I was expecting her to elaborate, but she stood there resolutely letting this last statement speak for itself.

"He scares you?" I repeated her words, a bit incredulously. Satan, the prince of darkness, couldn't scare Betty; she was fearless on every level.

"Yes, doctor," she replied evenly. "Please, come with me."

I nodded, curious to see what kind of human being instilled so much trepidation in one of my top nurses. I followed her into Room Two—the room of Mr. Fernando Villalobos.

"What's going on with him?" I asked.

"He came in with a fever. He's had a cough, and his pulse oximetry is low. It's at 89. He's also tachycardic."

Fernando Villalobos, to me, anyway, didn't look remotely Latin, but his chart said he was born in Milan, Spain. Fine, I thought. Michael Jackson didn't look white, either, but most of the world was now willing to accept he was, thanks to mega-millions of dollars' worth of cosmetic surgery.

Villalobos was coughing as he stared at me—and, I have to admit, his gaze was somewhat unsettling. Betty wasn't exaggerating; he looked menacing, though the poor guy was probably just sick as a dog and wasn't feeling too terribly friendly, thus the ill-tempered glare. He was twenty-something and was just a little shorter than myself, roughly six feet. Not thin, not fat, his physical build was average.

"Hello," I said, offering a smile.

I was greeted with silence.

"How are you feeling?" I asked him.

"Bad...No good." he said, though his words were barely audible.

"Okay, let's see if we can find out what the trouble is," I said. I took his wrist, and he snatched it back.

"What are you doing?" he asked, sounding downright petulant.

"I was going to feel your pulse," I said. "Don't worry, it won't hurt."

Villalobos stared at me as if I were an alien strain of bacillus. Then, tentatively, he extended his hand.

"Thank you," I said.

His pulse was racing at 130 beats per minute. I glanced at Betty.

"Betty, what's his temperature?"

She was staring at Villalobos, distracted.

"Betty," I said, nudging her. She looked to me and nodded quickly.

"It's 103, doctor. Sorry."

My initial impression was that Fernando didn't look that sick; incongruous with the high temperature reading, to be sure. I took the chart that Betty was holding in her hand and looked into the patient's eyes.

"When did you start to feel ill?" I said.

Villalobos coughed again. "A day ago."

"Any vomiting?"

He paused at this word.

"Any throwing up?" I said.

He shook his head no.

"Chest pain?"

Again, no.

"Are you bringing anything up? Sputum?"

He coughed again and shrugged. Mr. Villalobos, I was learning, had a wonderful thrift of language and communication.

I pulled at my stethoscope and listened to his chest. There was definitely congestion, and I was beginning to formulate a pretty good idea of what was afflicting this guy.

"Okay, hang on a moment, I'll be right back," I said to him, nodding to Betty. She followed me out of the room.

"I think he has more than just the flu. Probably pneumonia. He's going to require hospitalization. Let's go ahead and do some routine blood studies. Get me a chest X ray, and let's move him to the monitor bed. I'll ask Linda to help out. We'll put him on 5 liters of oxygen by nasal cannula, and let's start an IV."

Betty looked at me and smiled. "Dr. Kroose, somehow I thought you would say that. I've already ordered the chest X ray and the blood studies, but I think he also needs blood cultures."

I loved my staff. Sharp as tacks. Sometimes I wondered why I even came in some days; they could have saved me the trouble, so efficient were they.

"You're right, Betty. Get blood cultures and, after you do that, let's give him some IV antibiotics."

"Dr. Kroose, don't you want to wait to confirm the diagnosis of chest X ray?" she asked.

"Do you have any doubts?" I asked her good-naturedly.

She smiled and nodded.

"No, I guess not."

I reentered Villalobos' room and explained to him what we were going to do.

"Fernando, you're pretty sick. You're going to need to stay in the hospital for at least a day. You probably have pneumonia, and you're not breathing well for that reason."

He started nodding his head back and forth. "No, no, I no can do that. I must leave."

"Why is that?" I asked.

"I have business. It no can wait. I go," he said.

With the kind of fever he had, he wasn't going to go very far for very long. He was already getting off the examination table when I put my hand on his shoulder.

"Mr. Villalobos..." I began and was cut off by his next statement.

"Touch me again without permission, and I kill you."

Betty actually gasped.

For my part, I was not immediately alarmed—with his high fever and some probable disorientation (not to mention what kind of life this man has had to provoke such a response), I merely sighed.

"Forgive me, sir," I said. "I didn't mean to offend you. It's just that you're very ill. And I mean *very* ill, sir."

Villalobos considered this under half-open eyes. He coughed again.

"Look," I pressed, "if we can just keep you in the emergency room for a little bit while we evaluate you, then you can make a decision. Would you do that for us?"

That seemed to appease him. My hopes were that he would come to grips with the severity of his illness and allow us to admit him, so I left it at that.

"Very sorry about what I say," he relented. "Feel very...bad."

I nodded and decided not to prolong this moment.

"Betty, when you get the work done, go ahead and set up the admission. Call the admitting physician."

She was staring at Villalobos again. When we both left the room, she turned to me.

"God, he gives me the creeps," she said. "And I don't think he likes women."

"I'm not entirely sure he likes *anyone*," I said.

"No, I'm serious," she said. "When he looks at me—it's just a sense, Dr. Kroose, trust me. If you were a woman, you'd understand."

I tried not to smile. Betty was particularly twitchy with this patient, and I was amused.

"Did he come out and say as much, Betty?"

She glanced at me, annoyed. "Yes, with those eyes of his." I nodded, very willing to get past this part of the conversation. She glanced down at her chart.

"Dr. Kroose, you know he's a cash account, so whoever gets him is not going to be very happy, and they'll probably try to get us to transfer him out."

"But he's too sick," I protested. "Besides, there's no county facility that will accept this transfer as sick as he is."

County hospitals, the general hospitals, is where cash accounts—that is, patients with no insurance—are transferred if they require hospitalization. However, these transfers are acceptable only if the patient is deemed stable for transport, that is, the patient's condition should not deteriorate during the move. And since the patient with this illness has the potential of deteriorating during transport, the county would not allow this type of transport. This is mandated by the federal government through the COBRA law—the Combined Omnibus Budgetary Reconciliation Act—that was passed in the 1980s, otherwise known as the antidumping laws. It was intended to prevent an inappropriate transport of sick patients requiring emergency care simply because they did not have the funds to pay for that said care.

"Fine," I said, "Who's on the on-call list today? Who are we going to admit this patient to?"

Betty hesitated and bit her lower lip.

"I think it's Dr. Schwartz."

Well, of course. That made sense. From bad to worse.

"Dr. Schwartz."

"Yep," Betty said and bit her lip.

"Jesus Christ," I muttered.

Did it have to be him?

"Great!" I said in a voice that conveyed clear unhappiness.

Betty was not aware of the conflict that had occurred moments earlier, but she knew that Dr. Schwartz was our resident problem child of sorts. I looked at her and just shook my head. I walked in the other room looking for Norma to see if she was back from lunch. She usually only took fifteen or twenty minutes in the nursing lounge; she didn't like to leave ER for too long…a kind of proprietary mother hen syndrome that she could not escape.

I wanted to know where we were—how many more patients were there to be seen. Sure enough, Norma was back at the nursing station inputting lab results into the computer and retrieving reports on the patients we were evaluating.

"Norma, where are we?" I asked, still chewing on the Schwartz debacle, past, present, and future.

She looked at me and nodded for me to come closer.

"Dr. Kroose, I've just had a very quick meeting with Sharon."

"Ah, our friendly nursing administrator," I said. "What's up?"

Norma glanced around the ER. "Dr. Schwartz just came back from meeting with some of the medical exec committee members. He's not a happy man."

I smiled wearily at her. "You have no idea. He does appear to be our star of the day."

"In any event," Norma continued, "the committee has been informed, formally, that your handling of patients—patients that are supposed to be directed to Dr. Schwartz—is under scrutiny."

I thought about this with renewed trepidation. I'm not surprised that Maynard Schwartz would have gone kicking and screaming to someone (again!) about alleged wrongdoing. And he and Jack Kilgorn might be in bed together on some political issue involving myself vis-à-vis this whole smallpox matter, but this was all I should be worried about—a little political infighting that would stay among we happy three.

"The medical committee," I said to Norma, "won't even glance at this until next month."

Norma shook her head. "No, doctor. The administrator has put it on this month's present agenda."

This stopped me cold. "Really," I said after a few seconds.

In reply, Norma nodded. "It sounds like Dr. Schwartz is basically waging war against you and this department."

Well, yes, that's sure what it did look like. My God, how foolish and entirely unnecessary for Maynard to take potshots like this—especially at a committee that generally approved of most any way I ran my ER.

There were several ways to handle this: Accept the slap of the glove and come out shooting, damn the torpedoes, full speed ahead (as Maynard has clearly just done)—or—exercise a lit bit of political leverage of my own.

"Thank you, Norma," I said, grateful for her loyalty. "I'll see what I can do to diffuse Dr. Schwartz' histrionics about patient theft."

It was the first time I heard Norma laugh in a while.

"So let's leave this matter alone," I said, "and you can tell me where I'm at right now."

"Dr. Kroose, the same place you were five minutes ago."

I sighed and gave her a look of wearied irritation.

"No, I mean how many patients do we have left to go with right now, and what about the patients that we've just seen? How about not busting my chops right about now and just work with me." I said this in a way that was not adversarial but almost teasing, yet with a touch of edge.

"My, my, getting a little snappy, aren't we?" Norma gave me a rare smile. "Here's the list of what's next, Dr. Grumpy."

This Schwartz matter had put a damper on my whole day. And Billy was weighing on my mind—which reminded me, I had to call Esmerelda. I asked Norma to do this for me.

Things just weren't going the way I wanted them to go, and I fought to rid myself of this general churlishness coursing through my system. I could feel the adrenalin in my body rise. It was as if I knew something was going to break loose, and all I do could was wait to see what it would be.

"Did I overhear you say that you're going to admit Mr. Villalobos?" Norma asked.

"Yep," I said.

"What about Mr. Caruso?" she asked.

"Yes, he's going to need to be hospitalized also. But I need to get a little more information on him before I can transfer him out. Mr. Villalobos, though, we can go ahead and start admitting him."

"And Mr. Fuentes?"

"Chances are we're going to admit him also, but they need a little bit more information on him, too. Do you have any labs back on him?"

"Not yet, but we got his chest X ray, and it's normal."

"Can I take a look at it?"

"Yeah, here it is."

I took a look at the chest X ray of Mr. Fuentes and found there was nothing there. His congestive heart failure was compensated and well controlled.

"Is Andy done with his history and physical?"

"Almost done," Norma replied.

"Good, I'd like to chat with him as soon as I can about Mr. Fuentes. What about the two-year-old?"

"Martha is working on him," Norma said, nodding. "Jordan seems to be doing well, although he still has a fever. Blood has been drawn, but they're also pending. We haven't got the chest X ray on him yet. The IV is in place, and we're infusing saline."

"What is the boy's weight?"

"About 19 kilos."

"Good. Give a fluid challenge of 400 ccs, and then we'll reassess him. I think he probably just has the flu and a kind of febrile seizure. Plus, he's also a little dehydrated. How's Amy?"

"Making a comeback. I think she's out of the woods now," Norma said.

"Great. I'll go see her right now. Who else do we have in the waiting room?"

"A couple of flu-like syndromes, lacerations, minor burn."

"Do you have anyone else I can see right now?"

"Not just yet. Cynthia's putting a couple of patients in rooms now. We're getting full. We'll have to disposition these folks, otherwise we'll get inundated."

"As soon as you get those two patients in, I'll see them, and we'll see who we can transfer out of here. Oh, by the way, the back pain, what happened to that one?"

"Cynthia was on that one. He seems to be stable, though still with the backache. We're wondering if you want to get a chest X ray or other X rays before you see him."

Good idea, I thought. "What part of his back is hurting?"

"The upper."

"Why don't we get a T spine, a thoracic spine, and a chest X ray? Are his vital signs okay?"

"They apparently are. He's a little sweaty. It's probably from the pain."

I went back to Amy's bedside to see how she was doing. Norma was right. She had made a comeback. Her pulse was down to 80, and her pulse oximitry was 98. She was more comfortable and no longer tripoding. Her nose was no longer flaring. She was speaking in full sentences. The aminophylline had apparently done the trick.

"Amy, how are you feeling now?" I asked her.

"You were right," she brightened. "The medicine worked. I'm glad you didn't have to use that tube. They had to do that once before, about a year ago. I remember being awake with a tube in my mouth. It was so painful, but it saved my life. Anyway, thank you."

God, she was smart, I thought. *When I was her age, I could barely put two coherent sentences together...*

"You're welcome, Amy," I said. "I'm just happy to see that you're doing better. Your mom should be here within the next fifteen minutes."

I thought to myself how lucky we were. We had dodged the bullet. Kid intubations are not easy, and sometimes they go wrong and sometimes, regardless of what you do, even after you intubate a patient with asthma, they just don't do well and die from their disease. Matt had overheard my conversation with Amy and walked away from her bedside with me. He gave me an update and ended with a question.

"Do you think we're going to have to admit her?" he asked.

"Nah, I think if she continues to do as well as she is now, we'll probably let her go home in the next couple of hours."

Matt broke out into a grin. "Good job, Dr. Kroose."

"Thanks, Matt, but it took teamwork to get her through. And sometimes, in spite of our efforts, it just doesn't work out, so it also took a little luck."

Norma suddenly started running toward us.

"Doctor, Matt," she said, a bit breathlessly.

"What's wrong, Norma?" I asked.

"Mr. Villalobos," she said. "He just walked out the door."

12:30 PM

I sprinted toward the sliding entrance doors to ER, with Matt hot on my heels.

Villalobos was walking (more like weaving) down the sidewalk. He coughed continuously and stopped for a moment, holding onto a pillar. He looked around, as if he were disoriented, confused.

I caught up to him, and Matt placed himself strategically in front of the man, leaving no room for doubt that he was not going to allow him to pass. I was particularly careful not to touch him—in his currently agitated state, he might do something dumb and start swinging at Matt, who would have the inclination to put him down for the count.

"Mr. Villalobos," I said, "I thought we agreed you would stick around for a while."

He stared at me—those eyes again. I remembered Betty's nervousness around this guy. "No, gotta go."

"I really think you should stay. In fact, I insist," I said.

He looked like he wanted to protest, but then he broke out into another coughing paroxysm. I took him by the arm, and Matt did the same; this time, Villalobos put up zero resistance. We led him back through the ER doors. I offered to take his jacket, which he clutched onto and held close to his chest.

"No, don't touch it," he snapped, again falling into his strange, frenetic kind of combativeness.

I glanced at Matt; he shrugged, and I nodded to Villalobos.

"I would just hang it up in your room," I assured him.

He glared at me. "If I want to hang it up, I will."

Villalobos was not about to win any popularity contests in the near future. I didn't push him further as we walked through ER.

"How long do I have to stay?" he asked, as I led him back to his room. With every word he spoke, I was more and more convinced that this guy was about as Spanish as I was Swahili. I didn't know at the time why this was such a glaring point for me. Not until later—and then it was too late.

"Give me an hour," I said. "Let me run a few tests. I know you're in a hurry."

Then he said something to me that seemed terribly strange.

"You don't know *anything*."

He coughed again as I released his arm and let Matt lead him back to the examining table.

You don't know anything.

It wasn't the statement itself that was strange, but the way Villalobos said it. Threatening was the word that leaped to mind. Once he was back on the examination table, I whispered to Matt.

"Keep him in sight for a while," I said. "Bit of a loose cannon."

"No shit, doc," Matt shot back, and I smiled. "Guy's crazy as a shithouse rat, if you ask me."

"Very picturesque comparison," I said, nudging him in the ribs good naturedly.

It was lunchtime, and my first order of business was going to get Jack Kilgorn on the line and do some political reconnaissance. First, I saw the two viral syndromes, probably the flu, who also presented with the same symptoms as fevers, body aches, and a generalized scanty faint rash. They were quickly disposed, as well as the minor burn, simple laceration, and a fracture that was referred to orthopedics. I then paid Mr. Caruso a visit for some unresolved questions I had about his presentation. As I began to reexamine him, I scanned the petechial faint rash over his face and upper extremities—that kind of rash one sees with chronic alcoholism. In these patients, after many years of alcohol abuse, their livers become irreversibly injured. As a result of this, their spleens swell, trapping many important components of blood, including platelets, the little cell that circulates in blood that is essential in the clotting process. When the numbers of these small cells decrease, patients tend to bleed more readily, and the consequence of a low platelet count is a petechial rash, which Caruso seemed to have. It was, however, a bit faint. There were other causes for this manifestation but, given his history of alcoholism, it was my presumption that this was the cause of the rash.

But why the fever? I asked myself. It is well known that patients who develop DTs can develop high fevers with no other concurrent illnesses to explain it. However, I could detect the odor of alcohol on his breath. This was the conflict in my mind. Why should he have alcohol on his breath if he is withdrawing from the booze? His alcohol level should be low to zero, yet the stench suggested otherwise. If the alcohol level were high, then Mr. Caruso would be suffering from other than withdrawal syndrome. That was the puzzle. One would have to invoke another infectious disease. I continued my examination, attempting to remove the sheets off the man.

"How are you doing, Mr. Caruso?" I asked.

He looked at me through bleary eyes. "Could use a drink," he muttered.

"Looks like you had a few too many already," I said.

"There a bar nearby?" Caruso asked.

I put my hand on his shoulder. "Mr. Caruso, you're pretty sick right now, and I don't think another shot of tequila, or whatever you were sucking down, is going to help."

"Might not help you, but I'd feel pretty darned good about it," he said, chuckling.

I gave him a tight smile as an answer. My brother had died of alcoholism ten years ago. He was only 31. Smart guy, too. Thank God he was unmarried and no kids, but I remembered trying to wean him off the booze. His disease frustrated me because I was torn between the two philosophies that alcoholism was simply a chemical dependency versus an emotionally debilitating disease, the genesis of which originated deep within an individual's damaged psyche. Dillon drank from morning until dusk, easily putting away the equivalent of two or three bottles of vodka *daily*. It was startling given that this much alcohol could generally kill someone much faster than over the course of years; it could destroy within a day. Yet, some individuals could assimilate and weather this much and more, with only a bad hangover the following morning. Ultimately, of course, the body protests, resists, and then succumbs to the onslaught of abuse.

My brother Dillon died not from cirrhosis, but from kidney failure. The ancillary organs to the liver simply shut down. He went into congestive heart failure and, within a day, it was *adios, hermano.*

My mother never recovered from Dillon's death and, in fact, I am convinced this is why she succumbed to cancer a few years later. Dad, already hit with strokes and Alzheimer's, stuck around for six months thereafter. I was the only survivor to the Kroose clan…the thought momentarily depressed me, though I accepted my familial demises as more or less normal in the great scheme of things (save for Dillon, who steadfastly had refused to curtail the drinking thing and almost seemed to want to get off the planet posthaste).

I looked at Mr. Caruso and wondered even now, if he would cease the abuse of liquor, that his chances for survival would improve. I surmised that physiologically he would heal…but could that be sustained? Would he eventually go back to the bottle in earnest? Probably so. Caruso was fifty years old; unless he pursued some aggressive rehabilitation therapy, his alcoholism would continue to spiral.

"I'll be back, Mr. Caruso," I said. "Try to rest easy, okay?"

He held up his hand, assuring me he would behave. "If you feel inclined, bring a six-pack of cold Coors back with you."

"I'll see what I can do," I said, realizing that he must be feeling like warm crap right about now. I bit my tongue, wanting to suggest Alcoholics Anonymous, but this was not the appropriate time for that kind of recommendation.

I noticed Andy at the nursing station, and Norma directing him to the bedside of Mr. Caruso. I had put Andy off long enough and decided that it was as good a time as ever to talk to the young doctor.

"Dr Kroose," Andy called out to me. "Do you have a minute? May I present Mr. Fuentes to you?"

"Sure," I said. "Let's go to the nursing station. We can discuss the case there."

As we were walking toward the nursing station, I found myself glancing back at Villalobos' room. He was on the examination table and coughing up a storm. Matt was leaning against the entrance door, doing what I would call a fair job of looking engrossed with a chart but, in fact, watching Villalobos like a hawk.

"Okay, Andy, what do you have?" I said absently.

"Mr. Fuentes is a 72-year-old man who presented to the emergency room with a history of diabetes, high blood pressure, and congestive heart failure. But, most recently, approximately seven days ago, he developed a rash."

I listened, thinking back to my own days of being a medical student. My first presentation must have been ten pages long. I probably bored my attending physician to bloody tears, but I learned later that the important stuff is the salient, not detailed, history. That you leave for your dictation or your written documentation. The highlights are what the attending consultants are expecting to hear. This was a good lesson to learn.

"Andy," I said, "let's presume you have ten cases to see and take care of. And let's say you have to sign these cases off to the oncoming residents. Save the long presentations for your documentations. What I want to know is the nitty-gritty. Give me the pertinent positives, pertinent negatives."

"Yes, sir, Dr. Kroose. A paramedic run from a convalescent facility brought him in, and he has diabetes, hypertension, and congestive heart failure. He has a fever, fast pulse, and a pustular rash over his lower extremities. His chest examination is normal, as well as his heart and abdominal exam."

Not bad, I thought. Dry, to the point, no razzle-dazzle.

"Dr. Goodman, that was excellent. Now what do you think he has?"

"Well, sir, he has a rash which most likely has given rise to his fever."

"Andy, just call me Dr. Kroose. Forget the sir," I begged.

"Yes, sir."

That provoked a smile from both of us.

"Do you think there could be another source for the fever, such as pneumonia?"

"As long as the lungs are clear, he doesn't have a cough, so no, I don't think he has that," Andy said.

"What about a urinary tract infection?"

"He has no symptomotology consistent with this nor does his physical examination suggest that kind of problem, but we have a urinalysis pending which will confirm our impressions."

"What about an intra-abdominal process giving rise to his fever?"

"Mr. Fuentes seems to be clear of mind and is not complaining of any gastrointestinal symptoms, and his abdominal examination is also normal. So no, I don't think there's a source for fever there."

"You make a good point," I agreed. "If this gentleman were confused and unable to give you the clear history, then you would have to suspect all these other ideologies. So what is the cause of the rash?"

"Well, Dr. Kroose, it's a long differential."

What he meant was that there was a long list of possible causes for the rash. But, in medicine, from a long list there are usually only one or two strong candidates.

"Tell me about that," I said.

Andy took a moment to mentally stockpile possibilities.

"It could be a bacterial infection, such as *staphylococcus aureus*. It could be smallpox or anthrax or an allergic reaction."

I didn't immediately reply. The smallpox or anthrax options were remote at best, but I found myself considering the possibilities and feeling the hair on the back of my neck rise a bit—especially given my contentious encounter with Kilgorn this morning.

"Do you seriously think this could be anthrax or smallpox?" I said carefully.

"Smallpox does give rise to a pustular rash."

"Yes, but so can anthrax," I countered.

Andy seemed to be unsure about this point, so I took it as an opportunity to teach. I realized that the nurses were gathering around the nursing station to listen to our discussions, so I directed my comments to all of them.

Oh, no, the old man is pontificating again, I could almost hear my staff think to themselves. However, they all appeared generally interested, so I got on the proverbial soapbox. And it was fun to remember knowledge from a time long ago—when my life had been so different—so very different indeed!

"Anthrax is caused by an organism called *bacillus anthracis*. It's a gram positive rod and is found in nature in soil. It releases spores that are hardy and can withstand weather for long periods of time, thus it's very difficult to destroy it. Naturally occurring anthrax organism is acquired by coming into contact with animals infected by the organism or carrying it. It usually causes a painless sore at the site of the infection, which is more commonly on the extremities, and gives rise to the classic black, crusty scab which ulcerates. It is a relatively slow-advancing infection. However, if untreated, it can be fatal. What we're hearing about in the media is not about naturally occurring anthrax. This anthrax has been engineered to be airborne, thus the most common presentation of an infection with this anthrax will be a person with a flu-like syndrome and pneumonia. This form of anthrax is most often fatal unless treated early with a vaccine and an antibiotic. Pulmonary anthrax can also be found in nature, but this is more rare. This would occur if the individual inhaled a spore on a windy day in an endemic area where the spore is found in the soil, and the wind blows it up making it airborne."

Betty seemed anxious to make a comment.

"Dr. Kroose, doesn't anthrax mean black?"

"Yes, it connotes black, so we can eliminate this from the differential. So this is a pustule not an ulcer."

Linda also wanted to make a point. "Is a smallpox rash a pustule?"

"Yes, it is," I said.

"Could this be smallpox?"

I should have answered immediately but found myself reminiscing about this morning's talk with Jack Kilgorn and again feeling a surge of anger.

"Smallpox," I said slowly, if not decisively, "was eradicated in 1980. There hasn't been a known case of smallpox in the world since 1977. Besides, Mr. Fuentes' presentation is not typical for smallpox. These patients usually appear with a flu-like syndrome called the prodrome, which begins after approximately a twelve-day incubation period."

"How long does the prodrome last, Dr. Kroose?" Betty asked.

"About four to five days, and then the rash appears. When the rash appears, these patients are usually afebrile. That is, they no longer have a fever when the rash appears. Mr. Fuentes' rash is also atypical and inconsistent with smallpox. These folks usually develop initially a rash over the upper extremities and face. It begins as a little red spotty blush, which subsequently develops into a blister-like rash, and these blisters subsequently fill with pus. That's the pustular rash. The rash then generalizes over the lower extremities and torso. These patients are usually prostrated. They don't appear as well as Mr. Fuentes, although Mr. Fuentes is very sick and probably has a generalized bacterial infection which, if untreated, could be very serious.

"As in, he could die?" Linda asked.

I nodded. "Yes."

"If smallpox was eradicated in 1980," Betty asked, "why is everybody worried about it now, Dr. Kroose?"

I wished some people were more worried about it than others. Yes, Jack Kilgorn, I'm thinking of you.

"That's a good point. The problem is, even though they've not seen smallpox in some 25 years, we know the virus that causes it exists in certain repositories, one in this country and one in Russia. However, what is more worrisome is that it may have fallen into terrorist hands. We don't know if this is supposed to be a fact, but we also don't know that it's not, and that's the dilemma."

"But Dr. Kroose," Linda said, "isn't it just like the influenza virus? So we get sick, we get better, and that's the end of that."

"No. This virus kills thirty to forty percent of the individuals it infects. In the past century, it was probably responsible for as many as half a billion deaths worldwide. There's a real reason to fear this virus."

"So when are we going to get vaccinated for it?" Linda asked.

My nursing staff had asked this question in the past. I looked at all of them and sighed.

"I don't know, but I'm working on it." I looked to Andy. "Which brings us to you, Dr. Goodman. Have you contemplated what the rash is in our patient? I have to make a quick phone call."

"It's probably *staph*," Andy said without hesitation.

"Excellent choice, although drug reactions can also present this way. I don't think he has this. Perhaps you could review the literature on that. We can sit down and talk about it during lunch."

I excused myself, stepped into the doctor's room, and punched in the extension to Kilgorn.

Katy would probably say he's out to lunch but what the hell, I thought.

A final push for political peace was worth this extra effort before I would have to go for personal reinforcements and this thing turns ugly in the extreme.

*   *   *   *

"Max, long time no talk," Kilgorn said.

I had no difficulty getting past Katy, which means, possibly, Jack had been expecting my call.

"Jack, you know I wanted to keep you in the loop about this Schwartz mess."

"Yes, thanks for that. Anything new?"

A smokescreen. He approved the damn present month's agenda just an hour ago…and now this butter-would-melt-in-his-mouth attitude.

I felt myself get angry once more but resisted the urge to tell Kilgorn that he was a lying, manipulative son of a bitch. Bad form that would be.

"I had my talk with him a little while ago," I said.

"How did it go?" Jack asked.

Fishing I was—though I think I already bagged the big one. "Not well. He feels personally hamstrung by myself and ER. I even suggested the lunch thing to mend a fence. He didn't go for it."

"Yeah, yeah."

Silence. I waited. Then Kilgorn sniffed. "Well, let's just see if this dies down a bit before losing our minds. I have a few ways I think I'd like to handle the scenario. I'll give them a mental whirl and see where they land."

"Thanks, Jack," I said amicably. "You're right. It's probably the best way to go on this."

"Have you thought about our little problem?"

"Ah, the vaccine thing," I said. "No, it's been hectic down here. And I'm pretty married to the idea of acquiring this vaccine for my people. Sorry, Jack."

"Pity to hear that," Jack said.

"Pity we can't make it work," I said.

"Okay, then, thanks for the Schwartz flag. I'll talk to you later."

Then he hung up.

I looked at the phone for a moment and then placed it back in the cradle. Kilgorn had just made another ploy, albeit much subtler in the morning than now, for my support at the executive committee meeting tonight to shoot down the smallpox vaccinations. I had turned him down.

And, by his final words, I knew he was gunning for me.

*   *   *   *

Now that I had a little time, I wanted to go back and finish my evaluation of Mr. Caruso. Norma was helpful in that area.

"His liver function studies are back, and they're slightly elevated," she said. "But his electrolytes, kidney function studies, toxicology screens, and his glucose are all normal."

"What about his platelet count and the alcohol level?"

"Those are still a no-show."

I thought at least the liver function studies would establish that he had liver disease. And the toxicology screen ruled out the possibility of an overdose of some kind, giving rise to his altered level of consciousness as well as his fever. However, the platelet count and the alcohol level were crucial in establishing the definitive diagnosis.

"When are we going to get the platelet count and the alcohol level back?" I asked Norma.

"The analyzers are down so this may take as long as an hour to get those studies."

I was making my way to Mr. Caruso's bedside to finish my evaluation when I heard Cynthia calling from bed three bedside.

"Dr. Kroose, I need you here STAT."

This was the patient with the upper back pain. Why would she be calling me STAT?

1 PM

Betty, Norma, Matt, and I responded to Cynthia's call. As I approached the bed-side, I could see Mr. Smith diaphoretic clutching his chest in severe distress. I looked at the monitor, which revealed a bradycardia, which is an abnormally slow heart rate. His blood pressure was 90 over 60, which is also abnormally low, how-ever his oxygen level was normal.

"Cynthia, what's going on?"

"He's the gentleman who presented with upper back pain initially. We sent him for a chest X ray and a thoracic spine X ray."

She showed me the films, which I reviewed quickly, and they were normal.

"But now he's complaining of chest pain. And, it turns out, he now tells me that he's had chest pain all along, but the back pain was worse. Then I noticed his pulse slowing and his blood pressure dropping."

I looked to Mr. Smith. "Mr. Smith, are you having chest pain right now?"

"No, my back."

I was somewhat confused by his answer and then realized he was parsing his words.

"Are you having pressure, tightness in your chest?"

"Oh, yeah, it's pressure. I think it feels like an elephant sitting on my chest."

Patients often do this. When asked whether they have chest pain, they deny it. Then they don't subsequently volunteer that they're having some type of discomfort. My feeling is it's a form of denial. However, I've learned not to accept no until I was absolutely sure when they said no, they had no chest pain, that they had no discomfort of any kind.

"How long have you had this pain?"

Mr. Smith fought for breath. "It started about nine o'clock and has been unre-lenting since then. I took a couple of aspirins. That seemed to help out a little bit, but it keeps coming back."

"Do you have diabetes or high blood pressure?"

"No."

"How is your cholesterol?"

"I've never had it checked."

"Does your chest pain go into your neck?"

"Yes, I have a choking sensation around my neck."

"How about in your left shoulder?"

"Yes, my shoulder hurts, too."

"Do you have a family history of heart disease?"

"My dad died at 42 from a heart attack."

Norma was busy obtaining an EKG. But even without the EKG, I knew this gentleman was suffering from a heart attack.

He had all the harbingers for this disease. Cynthia had already placed the patient on oxygen. The patient, by his own account, had already taken aspirin. Cynthia had also already started the intravenous line. As I examined the patient, except for the abnormal vital signs, everything was otherwise normal. He was beginning to deteriorate quickly. His heart rate went from a bradycardia to what we call an AV Block, which is a condition where the electrical impulses do not get into the ventricles. And without electrical impulses to the ventricles, the heart stops pumping, precipitating sudden death. His blood pressure now was 60 over 40, and he was losing consciousness. He no longer was responsive to verbal commands.

"Mr. Smith, can you hear me?"

However, Mr. Smith was down for the count. Matt was bringing the crash cart close to the bedside. Norma had already called Sergio to assist us, but he was applying the defibrillation pads to the chest in case we would need to defibrillate him. Cynthia was assisting the patient with Ambu bag respirations and had already started an intravenous line. Matt and Betty had earlier surmised the patient would require intubation, so they began to assemble the paraphernalia I would need to intubate the patient. They had already set up the suction apparatus, which I would use to suction foreign material and secretions from the oral cavity to make the airway visible, and Matt prepared the proper size intratracheal tube required to perform the intubation.

I looked at the monitor. Suddenly Mr. Smith was in ventricular fibrillation—sudden death. He had no blood pressure. I looked at him. He was lifeless.

*   *   *   *

I had no choice. We had to go for the defibrillators.

"Norma, give me 200 watt seconds. Come on shock him. Clear the bed."

Everyone removed his or her hands from the patient and the bed while Norma pressed the red button on the defibrillator, releasing the electrical impulse. The patient's body jerked as the electrical impulses discharged. I looked up at the monitor. Mr. Smith remained in ventricular fibrillation. I looked at Norma. Norma gave me 400 watt seconds.

"One more time, people. Clear the bed."

Everyone stepped away from the bed and the body while Norma discharged the defibrillator again. The body jerked. I looked up at the monitor. We were still losing him.

We shocked the patient again.

"Clear the bed."

Again, everyone cleared the bedside while Norma released the third electrical shock. I looked up at the monitor. The heart stubbornly stayed in ventricular fibrillation. Time was running out. The increasing watts of electric energy failed to convert the heart. I looked at the pulse oximeter, and it was reading seventy percent. That means the patient wasn't adequately oxygenated. This may have been the reason why the patient did not respond to electrical shocks.

"Matt, give me the ET tube and laryngoscope."

The laryngoscope is an instrument used to remove the tongue from the back of the throat allowing me to visualize the vocal chords, which is necessary to introduce the intratracheal tube. I positioned myself at the head of the bed and placed towels underneath the patient's shoulders in order to hyperextend the neck. This would give me a better view of the vocal chords while introducing the laryngoscope. Sergio had just arrived and assisted Cynthia in ventilating the patient. Norma prepared the paraphernalia and made sure that the suction catheter was ready. I held the laryngoscope in my left hand and the ET tube in my right hand.

"Okay, everybody, on the count of three. One, two, three."

At that point, Sergio stopped ventilating the patient. I introduced the laryngoscope into the oral cavity, lifting the tongue away from the throat. Then with the neck hyperextended, the vocal chords came into view. I easily inserted the ET tube and secured it.

Sergio quickly attached the Ambu bag to the ET tube and began to ventilate the patient. I listened to both sides of the chest to ensure that the tube was perfectly placed. There were good breath sounds; the intubation was successful. I looked up at the monitor. The patient's oxygenation was improving.

"Norma, give a milligram of epinephrine."

She had already drawn the milligram and was ready to give it.

"Okay, Norma. Now let's crank it up to 400 watts seconds, and let's give it the fourth shot."

Everyone cleared the bed again. Norma pressed the red button, discharging the defibrillator. Mr. Smith jerked again. I looked up at the monitor. Bingo! A normal sinus rhythm was displayed. Betty checked the femoral pulse. The femo-

man ?

ral artery is the larger artery, which is much easier to palpate. It's found in the groin and much easier to identify a pulse when it's present.

"Dr. Kroose, there's a strong pulse."

"Matt, give me a blood pressure. Sergio, set up the ventilator with the usual parameters."

"Right, Doc. 800 ccs of tidal volume. A backup rate of twelve, and one hundred percent FIO_2, and an assist control setting."

"You've got it."

"Norma, get me a chest X ray and make sure the tube is in place. And Cynthia, order all the routine blood studies, including the cardiac enzyme."

Cardiac enzymes are enzymes released by the heart muscle when it is injured. This would help establish the diagnosis of an acute myocardial infarction—that is a heart attack. His EKG showed changes consistent with a heart attack. However, this, in and of itself, was not enough to make the diagnosis.

"Betty, give the patient 100 mg of lidocaine so we can prevent another episode of ventricular fibrillation. And put him on a 2 mg per minute drip."

This medication was commonly used to control this type of arrhythmia.

"Norma, let's call the cardiologist on-call. He needs to go to the cardiac cath lab."

"You're in luck," Norma said. "He has a private physician and a private cardiologist. Both of them admit to this hospital. I'll give him a call so you can discuss the case with him."

"Good, Norma."

She winked at me and walked away proudly. I could hear her faintly say, "Great teamwork." I walked over to the other corner of the room, and I saw Andy observing everything. He was intently observing all that was occurring. He seemed to enjoy the excitement. He seemed eager to assist in the care of this acutely ill patient. These are all good qualities that make a good emergency room physician.

"Andy, have you ever intubated a patient?"

"No, Dr. Kroose. I've seen many."

"Around here we have an adage. That is you see one, you do one, you teach one. So the next one you'll do."

"I look forward to it."

He walked over to talk to Sergio about the respirator and the appropriate setting for this kind of patient. I went back to the bedside and could see the patient was becoming livelier. He was triggering the respirator, which is a good sign for an individual who had just suffered sudden death. That meant there was a good chance of a complete recovery. I felt we had snatched another one from the Grim Reaper's anxious hands and that this was the worst the day would get.

That was a wrong assumption.

Way, way wrong.

1:15 PM

I made a quick call to Esmerelda to check up on Billy.

"He is fine, doctor," Es told me in her heavy accent. "And he wants to make sure you're on time tonight for the play."

"I'll be on time," I assured her. "Don't spoil him too much, okay?"

"I no spoil anyone," she said. "I am now on my way to pick up Andrea."

Esmerelda sounded vaguely annoyed at me, and I couldn't help but smile to myself. Of course I knew she would baby Billy something fierce, buying ice cream, potato chips, anything the kid wanted after his encounter with the playground cement. It wasn't that Esmerelda would disobey my instructions—not deliberately, anyway—but she was a mother herself with seven grandchildren. She would do what she damn well thought was best for Billy, and if that meant extra helpings of chocolate pudding sprinkled with Oreo cookies to alleviate the trauma of the day, then that was her call.

"Thanks, Es," I said, feeling that the conversation had kind of dried up at this point.

"Have a good rest of day," she told me and hung up.

I glanced around the ER. There seemed to be a kind of intermission at this point, a welcome lull. I wanted to get back to see Mr. Caruso, but I was also getting very hungry and wanted to get a bite to eat. It would give me a chance to sit down with Andy and discuss the cases further.

But first there was the damage control. I made my first call to Nathan Powell, our chief of staff. We generally talked once a week and brought each other up to speed on our various departments—his one department, of course, overseeing not only ER but everyone else. He, among several other members of the executive committee, would now be my focal point in this subplot of political machination for the next hour. During that time, I would also concentrate on my patients. This whole mess infuriated me. I liked absolutely *no* distractions from my patients.

"Max, how goes it?" Nathan asked. "How are the kids?"

Nathan and his wife, Miriam, had been our guests for dinner parties on numerous occasions. They were good people. Nathan and I, in particular, got along well. A long time before he marshaled the many forces of hospital staff and operations, he was an ER doctor.

Pity, I thought, he wasn't our hospital administrator.

"Kids are fine, Nathan. Thanks for asking. Miriam?"

"She torments me on a daily basis, and for my own good. This damned diet she has me on: Low salt, no sugar. Hell, I'm pissing holy water, I'm so pure."

I laughed. Nathan had just turned 68 when he had his triple bypass, concurrent with diabetes. That was a year ago, and nothing slowed him down. He still worked nine hours a day and jogged every morning. Even took Viagra—and loved it, he confided in me once.

"What can I do for you, Max?" he asked. "I'm up to my chin with staffing reports."

"Fair enough," I said.

Then I laid out the events of this morning's conversation with Kilgorn, my failed plea for consideration of smallpox vaccines—and lastly, my unfortunate encounter with Maynard Schwartz. I told Nathan I was reluctant to bring him in on this, but it had all the makings of an avalanche and, at the end of the day, I just wanted him to be on record—kept in the loop, as it were. If I was going to be buried (which I sincerely doubted—but, at the very least, stomped on by Kilgorn and Schwartz), I wanted Nathan to know.

"Kilgorn's an ass, and Schwartz has the temperament of a spoiled schoolgirl. I say fuck them both," Nathan said.

I had expected an answer like this. The chief of staff and Kilgorn had butted heads on numerous occasions, and poor Schwartz (the perennial object of dislike for everyone) Nathan simply couldn't stand.

"I can live with Schwartz and his bellyaching, Nathan, but it's the smallpox issue that really counts. I can't be the only baby on a highchair pounding my spoon on this. It's too important and, for Christ's sake, we're doctors, and we have to recognize the potential horrors if 9/11 happens again on a bioterror level."

"Agreed, Max. No argument there," Nathan said. "I, for one, will back you up a hundred and ten percent."

I closed my eyes and breathed a sigh of relief. "Thanks."

"Make no mistake, Kilgorn's got his cronies that will support him, staffers and docs alike. I'm afraid, as you've discovered, our little smallpox idea may hit some brick walls. Reason being, of course, some folks just can't visualize it happening. That, and they'd rather see revenue diverted elsewhere."

"Tell me about it," I said dejectedly.

"Listen, I'll make some calls. Folks we can trust. Bob Schuster, in endocrinology, and Whit Hudson, over in hem-onc."

"Both good men," I concurred.

"I'll get back to you. Let me hit the phones."

"Right. Take care. Thanks, Nathan. This can only help everyone in the long run."

"You don't think I know that, son?"

I smiled.

"I'll wait for your call," I said and hung up.

Now if I knew Nathan, he would call Schuster and Hudson first, have them ring me, and not wait for the executive committee meeting tonight to debate his administrative counterpart.

He would deliver a proverbial power-punch to Jack Kilgorn, either by phone, or by marching down two doors to give him a piece of his mind.

✳   ✳   ✳   ✳

Which is exactly what Nathan Powell did.

I was to learn that the scene, which transpired between chief of staff and hospital administrator, was rather epic in nature. Before I got those details, however, I was pleased to receive several calls from Drs. Schuster and Hudson in short order—giving allegiance to support for acquisition of smallpox strains. I thanked them profusely; no, they said, thank you.

Andy was finishing up with Sergio and was making his way out of Mr. Smith's room, so it would be a perfect time to go out to the cafeteria since there was nobody in the waiting room. Jamie poked her head out of her reception area and caught my attention.

"Dr. Kroose, I've got a surprise for you."

"Yeah?"

"I've got your friend on the line."

How fortuitous, I thought—and not just a little coincidental given my political hurly-burly this past morning. It'd be great talking to Glen Hamilton. I hadn't had a conversation with him in two years since the ID conference we were both attending at the time. We had a little catching up to do.

"What line is he on, Jamie?"

"Line two."

I rushed back to the doctor's room to pick up the phone.

"Glen, you old mole. How are you doing?" I said. "How are things up in the Ivy Tower?"

"Max, jeez, it's good to hear your voice." Glen said in a rich, authoritative baritone voice. "How's the ER?"

"Crazy as ever. The influenza this year's been pretty bad," I said. "I'll bet it's nuts on your end, too."

"Yep. The fellows have been asked to consult on several ID cases."

"I have ten consults here, seven of them are from the ER. Four of them have flu-like syndrome. Three have rashes. Everybody wants to know whether it's other than the flu."

"If it smells like the flu, looks like the flu, it's got to be the flu."

That was just like Glen, speaking with unquestioned clarity. "So, Glen, how are metabolic rounds?"

"I haven't had any time for metabolic rounds. Too busy with research and all these public health issues, not to speak of all the responsibilities that I have as the chair of this ID Department."

Glen had graduated high school at age twelve and then took a leave of absence for about a year to travel around the world. His family thought it would be important for him to learn to socialize, more so than what he could during school time. They hired a tutor to finesse his social skills in order to allow him to socially acclimate. When you're too bright to socialize with kids your own age and too young to socialize with individuals who have your intellectual skills, it is necessary to bridge the intellectual/social gaps. At the age of thirteen, he entered Harvard and earned a BS in biology and a PhD in microbiology at the age of nineteen. He did his thesis while in medical school on DNA recombinant technology and taught as a student in his medical school, having the PhD to do it. In addition, he had written a book by that time on the conquest of infectious diseases and man's longevity.

He continued his research at Johns Hopkins, pioneering work on new antibiotics available and recombinant DNA technology. He worked on the sequencing of the variola virus at Fort Dietrick and, since this was top secret, found himself in the midst of privileged meetings with the military intelligentsia, CIA, and the NSA. Throw in the NSA and DIA just for good measure. He continued his top secret research at Fort Dietrick and chaired the Department of Infectious Diseases at Johns Hopkins, as well as co-chaired the microbiology department. He was a busy man. However, for his students, he always took the time to socialize with them and to get to know them more personally. This he did usually during metabolic rounds where we'd sit around, have hors d'oeuvres, a few bottles of beer, and discuss pressing issues in medicine, specifically infectious diseases. In those days, you'd find him wearing a pair of jeans, a T-shirt, and long hair. He had a beard and moustache. He was a nonconformist, and he had the intellectual power to pull it off with grace and charm, without appearing eccentric. We all admired him. He also had a good sense of humor, such as all the time while on rounds, he'd tell us how in the days giants walked the earth, they would have to taste urine to determine whether a patient had diabetes because there was no simple clinical study to determine that. We all grinned and took this story as tongue-in-cheek, but he was serious. So that evening, when we had metabolic rounds, he filled all our glasses with a light, amber-colored ale and, as we toasted to the good times and we were taking our first good gulp down, he pulls out a urine cup filled with urine from behind the bar and sets it on the counter. It was the same color as the beer we were drinking.

Then he said to us, "This is diabetic urine."

The beer tasted a little sweet. We all began to spit the beer out. He broke out into a roar and managed to say, "No gentlemen, you're drinking ale. This—" as he held up the urine cup, "is diabetic urine."

I miss those days. I missed that clarity of purpose. Now, I deal with assholes like Jack Kilgorn and paranoid doctors.

"Glen," I edged into the conversation, "what public policy are you working on?"

"A smallpox vaccination program."

"Curiouser and curiouser," as Lewis Carroll once put it. On the same day I fight this major battle with bureaucrats and administrators for this very kind of program, Glen is well on the road for a major public push.

"Are you talking such a program solely for first responders?"

"No," Glen said. "I'm trying to hammer out the policy whereby everybody gets vaccinated. I think it's probably necessary."

The timing of this conversation was almost scary. I wished that Jack Kilgorn could be listening in on this, not that it would make a whole lot of difference. Kilgorn was still into "saving a buck" versus saving lives. I felt myself getting angry once more.

"What a coincidence" I said. "This is what I wanted to talk to you about."

I then explained to my friend that our illustrious (and let's just throw in ignorantly parsimonious for good measure) administrator wanted to opt out of the vaccination program for the first responders, and that I wanted the vaccine given to my staff. I told Glen that Jack seemed to think that there wasn't a clear and present danger. He was more worried about the lawsuit and the demands made by the labor unions.

"Isn't that like them?" Glen said. "When it comes time to make the right decisions, they're all looking out for political correctness. They don't want to take the heat. Nobody wants to take responsibility even if it's for his or her own life. Lawyers are always so willing to blame somebody else. But, yeah, I've heard there are hospitals opting out of the voluntary vaccination program. They just don't get it."

"No, they don't," I agreed readily.

Glen continued. "They don't seem to recall what they're dealing with. Smallpox is a natural killer. It kills enough only to survive. It's like a lion, a predator. It will only kill and eat what it needs to sustain itself and not a bit more. It allows the herds of gazelle and other animal herds to grow and continue to provide it ample food resources."

"I'm having a difficult time comparing a hungry cat to variola," I said.

Glen chuckled at that. "Think about it. Variola only kills enough to stay alive. Otherwise, if it were to wipe out the human race, there would be no other host, and it would vanish from the face of this earth. There's a theological reason why it only kills thirty or forty percent of the individuals it infects. Imagine if it killed fifty, sixty, or seventy percent? Pretty soon there wouldn't be a human race. Man would cease to exist. Only man does that. When man hunted the herds of buffalo, he did so to its near extinction. Man has also engineered this virus to kill more than it needs to." With that, there was a pause, as if Glen had said more than he wanted to.

"Go on," I said, fascinated. These were facts I was pretty much aware of, but to hear Glen articulate them in his own special style gave me new reason to have goose bumps.

"You know," Glen said, "variola has been around for thousands of years and has developed a symbiosis with the human species. It has killed many of us but, in so doing, it has also immunized us. So there were always a percentage of us that were immune to it before it was eradicated. Then when Edward Jenner developed the smallpox vaccine, cowpox at that time, we found a second means of immunizing man against variola. But, in this country since 1972, there hasn't been a case of smallpox or vaccinations of the general public. So, in essence, there is no immunity in this country to stop or inhibit the smallpox outbreak."

This is what I had tried to tell Jack Kilgorn, all to no avail.

Glen pushed on. "I made that point to those involved in the great debate concerning the destruction of the variola virus after the eradication of smallpox. They didn't accept my argument then, or they had hidden agendas, and they aren't willing to accept the perils now. Those that were involved with the eradication of smallpox then find it difficult to accept the possibility that what they achieved by eliminating smallpox was not an accolade but a disaster in the making. It is as if they can't accept the fact that it exists. No, Maxwell, it exists.

Though it is touted to be contained in repositories, one in Atlanta, and one in Russia, we know better."

"Yes, unfortunately we do," I said, feeling suddenly demoralized.

"Listen, Max. We don't speculate. We know that the Russians were developing it as a weapon of mass destruction. And we know that they probably succeeded."

Glen was speaking as an authority on the issue. He is, in essence, a counterpart to Ken Alibeck, the Russian defector who was a doctor and one of the project directors of Vector doing research on biological agents of mass destruction. Glen knew more than he could say, but he was still telling me quite a bit. I took in every word.

"If the Russians knew half of what we knew, and they probably knew more, they realized there was an easy way and a hard way to weaponize smallpox and other agents. There was nature's way, and then there was our way. Our way was too tedious, requiring the analysis of specific genes for production of activated protein, RNA, manipulating genes to produce catalysts for intracellular replication of the virus and to produce proteins to inhibit the human immune system. These were far too complex, expensive, and time-consuming processes, too daunting to accomplish. But then there was nature's way, a much easier way. Think about it this way, nature had billions of years to make the likes of variola with the specificity to men, with the ability to kill just enough and to adapt. It is not by chance that one of the most virulent viruses to man is also one of the most complex with some 186,000 genes having the ability to turn on and turn off function as it sees appropriate."

"It seems to act almost consciously or intelligently, when you think about it," I said.

"If not consciously or intelligently, certainly with one hundred percent determination and self-interest. Once in the human cell, it is like Hal in the spaceship in the movie *2001: Space Odyssey*. Hal had the ability to control the entire ship to turn on and turn off whatever system it thought appropriate. It had an immense databank with all the programs available to it. So variola is the same. With its complex DNA module, it has an immense memory databank. And once in the human cell, it can pretty much do whatever it wants to. Turn it on, turn it off, destroy it. It was the perfect killer. We knew that, and the Russians knew that."

The renewed sense of horror at what Glen was alluding to, the possibility of *weaponized* variola, swept through me. I pushed him just to see if he would divulge more.

"Glen," I said slowly, "is there a weapon form of variola in existence now?"

He hesitated. Continents could have risen and fallen in the span of time it took my friend to respond.

"Let me put it this way," Glen said neutrally. "Variola is variola, but it can be manipulated. There is a vast variation in virulence. But to answer your more specific question, we know that it exists and is not only in Russia and Atlanta. We're certain it is in North Korea and Iraq. And, if I were a betting man, I would bet that some terrorist group already has it."

"Jesus, it boggles the mind," I whispered. Those pricks in Al Queda wouldn't hesitate to use a weapon like this if they could.

Glen had skirted my question, but he told me what I already suspected. He was convinced that smallpox was a menace, even now, with more than two decades of absence.

"Glen, will the vaccine work?" I asked, point-blank.

"The vaccine has always worked."

"That's not my question. Always in the past doesn't mean always, as in now."

Glen sighed on the other side.

"Max—that's all I can say. I'm sure you understand."

This was in the pretty high-classified stuff category that Glen was speaking in, and I knew he felt his hands tied on most every level. I knew I couldn't push him anymore on this issue, but I continued with my request.

"If my administrator succeeds in preempting the vaccinations from my department, is there somehow I can get it from you?" I asked, not reluctant at all to call in a favor.

"That's a tall order, but I'll see what I can do, Max. I do think you should have it. It's only a matter of time and something may happen, and I'd like you to be prepared for it. By the way, did you know I was in L.A.?" Glen said, shifting gears.

I felt instantaneous delight—and relief, for a reason I did not quite understand, though a plot was hatching in my mind.

"Are you free later this afternoon? I could take a half-hour break and meet you near the hospital," I said.

"I'm pretty busy, Max."

"No, I understand. What are you doing here?"

"Working with the FBI," he said distantly.

"Really. On what?"

There was a moment of silence. Then, "Not really at liberty to say, Max. I'm sure you understand."

"No, of course. Any chance at all?"

"Tell you what. Give me a call when you think you're free, and I'll try to carve out some time. Deal?"

"Deal," I said, and he gave me his message service if I couldn't get him directly.

"Okay, let's talk later," he said.

"Sure. Will do. Great hearing your voice, Glen."

"You, too, Max." Then he added, "You're right to be concerned about the vaccinations. Very right indeed."

Then he was gone.

1:30 PM

My plan with Glen began to crystallize after we spoke. It was my thought to bring him to the executive committee meeting tonight and ram the facts from a top brass government honcho like Glen Hamilton down Kilgorn's throat. Forget Kilgorn, even—the *whole* committee's throat—so much so, that at the end of the day, they would have no choice but to vote unanimously for widespread inoculations for my staff.

This was my hope, anyway. Glen said he was busy with FBI stuff. He was very tight-lipped, and probably for good reason.

Shit.

That was the sticking point. Perhaps he really didn't want to be compromised like this—but I was pulling out all the bunnies from the hat at this stage of the game. I had nothing to lose. All Glen could say was no—courteously, of course.

The conversation with my friend concerned me. I became more worried about the reoccurrence of smallpox, making me a little suspicious about the cases I had seen that morning. It was a reflex, knee-jerk reaction—or overreaction, as Jack Kilgorn would have ventured to point out. Although nothing that presented to the emergency room smacked of smallpox, I wondered whether the weaponized form of the disease would present atypically and in stealth or perhaps with a different rash or no rash at all.

I took a moment to mentally breathe. I had rashes and smallpox on the brain. These two party poopers had obsessed me all day long.

However, the gut was talking to me again and the Voice.

Party poopers themselves, the little devils.

I wanted to get back and examine boozy old Mr. Caruso, but I was hungry and I had to meet with Andy. He was waiting for me at the nursing station, so I grabbed him, and we rushed down to the cafeteria to have a bite to eat. We found a quiet spot where we could talk, and I grabbed a hamburger with fries and a diet Coke. As I thought, Andy grabbed a salad with a little oil and vinegar and a diet Coke.

I looked over at Andy and said, "Healthy devil, aren't you?"

He replied, pointing at my hamburger, "That's not good for your heart. You know that."

"Red wine, my friend, and a life of moderate sin makes a heart healthy, wealthy, and wise. That, and a jog every day. Besides, knowing my luck, I'll be hit by lightning in the prime of my youth."

Andy laughed at that, though he kept his gaze on me, a quizzical look at that.

And I knew why.

I had changed over the course of the year.

I imagine I had become, though I tried to conceal it, bitter. The death of a wife can do that sometimes. It never crept into how I treated my staff—but the edge in my voice (and thoughts)—well, I recognized it. It even screwed with my sense of humor.

And Andy was right. The burger was unhealthy as hell. A year ago, I was a vegetarian. Now, I didn't give a shit. I ate what I wanted. Extra grease, if you please.

Ah, well.

We sat down and began to eat our meal and discuss Mr. Fuentes' case.

"Why didn't we wait for blood cultures or at least the gram stain from the pustules to confirm that it was a bacterial infection?" Andy asked, nibbling a carrot.

"When there's time for recourse then we can wait for such studies to come back," I said. "But your impressions based on the current findings were sufficient to make a presumptive diagnosis and treat on that basis. Mr. Fuentes, who has diabetes, is predisposed to a more severe infection, one that causes sepsis and ultimately shock over a very short period of time. He may appear stable right now, but untreated, within hours he could deteriorate. Thus, there's no time for recourse, and he requires immediate therapy with antibiotics. If we were to wait for his admitting physician to begin IV antibiotics, who knows when that would be?"

Andy nodded, took out a small notebook, and jotted down a few things. After our earlier discussion, he had gone to the library and reviewed the available literature on drug reactions. He found in his literature research that there were case studies describing the same type of rash in patients with drug reactions. Fortunately, Mr. Fuentes was not on new medications and probably was not suffering from this. He, however, had questions about smallpox.

Topic of the day, I thought. *The only thing that could make perfect timing and coincidence is if we actually had a case of smallpox in our ER.* I shuddered at this thought. *Don't go there, doc,* I warned myself. Just don't friggin' go there.

"You know that while I was at Fort Dietrick doing research on the influenza virus, I heard of an atypical presentation for smallpox," Andy said.

I was genuinely surprised. *A coincidence again?*

"Andy, you were at Fort Dietrick? When was this?" I asked, dumbfounded.

He smiled. "I know, you went there, too. That's why I specifically asked to be assigned to this ER."

I laughed. "And just when I thought there was some kind of divine serendipity at work here. You're a bit of a manipulator, Andy."

He shrugged. "I just want to be around people I can learn from. Call it selfish to an extreme."

"Duly noted," I said. "So, Fort Dietrick?"

"Two years ago I did a research externship there," Andy dove in. "I was there for about two months during the summertime. Instead of taking the two months off for the summer vacation, I decided to do a little research there."

"Well, it's interesting. I was just talking to my friend, Glen Hamilton, who's also doing research there. He's a good friend of mine." I didn't mention my talk with Glen today, or my intention to meet him later, if possible.

Andy nodded, clearly impressed.

"I had the pleasure of meeting him the last month I was there. He was our project coordinator. He's a famous man. He seems to have his hands on a lot of things. He's written a lot of books about antibiotics and DNA recombinant technology. He wields quite a bit of authority at Fort Dietrick. When you wanted things done, they were done, and they were done quickly. I recall my research project was on the chopping block. They were about to pull the funding from the project. The department heads thought it was a waste of time, but it was one of Glen Hamilton's pet projects. He resolved the problem with one simple phone call."

"That's Glen," I said. "He was my mentor during medical school, and I was one of his fellows at Johns Hopkins."

I finished wolfing down my burger and looked at Andy. "Did you do any research on variola?"

"No, just on the influenza virus," he said, sounding a bit dejected.

"So, where did you hear about the atypical presentation of smallpox?"

"Through some lectures I attended. It was rumored that they were doing research on the replication of the variola virus, and Dr. Hamilton's team found an ingenious way of manipulating this."

Reflecting back on my earlier conversation with Glen, I realized there was a lot he had not told me.

"Apparently, they had found a way of accelerating the replication of the virus. I don't know what became of the research though," Andy said, finishing his salad.

What Andy was referring to is probably top secret research. And what Andy also didn't know was that they were probably attempting to weaponize smallpox.

We were still messing with The Dragon. We never seem to learn from our mistakes.

"Andy, what atypical presentations did you learn about?"

Andy took a moment to ruminate. "Apparently the virus—I'm not sure if this was in the naturally occurring virus or the one engineered—but apparently there are strains of smallpox that will present either without a rash or a *different* type of rash and not the pustular rash. But I don't recall the specific characteristics of the rash."

"What research were you involved with?"

"We were studying the influence virus. However, we were trying to understand the proteins, the enzymes, or other co-factors that allowed the virus to replicate so quickly. That's why it had an incubation period of about three days, and that's why it was so infectious and spread so quickly."

"And Glen was also overseeing this project?"

"Well, Dr. Kroose, you probably know him better than I do, but he was involved with many projects, including mine."

I thought to myself, *this is one way of making variola more infectious, more virulent*. But it seemed to me a bit like making more powerful nuclear weapons. If your intent was to use them one day, you could pretty much count on eventual self-annihilation. It made absolutely zero sense to me. This is where, I suppose, I would have failed miserably as one of those politicians espousing *mutually assured destruction—the fear of both sides killing one another with a doomsday weapon*.

"We've got to get back to the emergency room," I said wearily. I was sure we were behind, and I wanted to see Mr. Caruso again.

Something about his case disturbed me.

No, that wasn't it. It was something more.

It was terror; irrational in the extreme—but terror nevertheless.

2 PM

We made our way back to the ER. We found the waiting room full along with all the rooms. Mr. Fuentes had received his antibiotics and was ready to be admitted. I talked to the attendant who happened to be one of the private physicians with admitting privileges to the hospital, so it was a simple procedure. With the fluid challenges we had given him and the antibiotics, he seemed to be doing a little better, although I was sure he would require several days of hospitalization.

Norma approached me with a grave and worried expression on her face.

"What is it?" I asked her.

"The administrator's office called. You are to call back immediately when you returned from lunch. Those were his words, his secretary told me."

The gloves are off now, and we're off and running, full tilt boogie for combat.

I thanked Norma, then turned to Andy and excused myself. I entered the doctor's office and called Jack's extension.

"Mr. Kilgorn's office," Katy's voice came on pleasantly.

"Hi, Katy. Max Kroose. I got a message from Jack to give a ring."

There was silence for a moment. Katy then whispered into the phone, "Max, he's a bit upset."

"So am I, Katy" I said. "So am I."

"One moment."

I opened my door and waved Andy over, asking how Amy was doing. The child had improved, so I was informed. On my repeat examination, her wheezing had completely resolved. The aminophylline drip that I had placed her on was now stopped, and her parents had come by to visit with her. Given that everything had improved so remarkably over the time she was in the emergency room, I thought it was reasonable to discharge her. Her parents were happy to hear that she could go home. Having been through this several times before in many cases, weathering several days of hospitalization, those must have been hard times for the two of them.

"I'll take care of it," Andy said.

I then closed the door once more. Then Jack came on the line.

"Kroose, you son of a bitch," he said in a low, feral voice.

"Hello right back at you, Jack," I said easily.

"Do you realize that Powell thinks I have some kind of conspiracy against you? He told me that, flat out in my office. He told me. That's a laugh. He was screaming like a deranged lunatic."

The time for mincing words had finished. "Jack, what kind of horseshit do you really believe I'd buy? That you hadn't placed Schwartz' idiotic complaint on the present month's agenda? That you didn't do that to try to humiliate me in front of that committee? You bet I went to Nathan."

"And," Kilgorn continued, as if I hadn't said a word, "you have people screaming and shouting for smallpox vaccines. I told you, I'll never approve it for the budget, and I have other medical reasons that I've already discussed with you."

"Medical reasons, my ass."

"You trying to get into a tail tangle with me is only going to get you into more trouble, my friend."

"I've lasted through three administrators, including you, Kilgorn."

"There will be no smallpox vaccines. Get used to it."

"I think there will. With or without your consent."

"Pissing match ain't your style, Max," Jack said, changing his tone. "You're a doctor, not a politician. Again, I'll ask you nicely not to butt heads with me. You'll only lose. Maybe not the battle, but, at the end of the day, the war."

This was becoming tedious. Kilgorn's ego was now bruised, and he wanted blood. It didn't really bother me, but it was now a waste of my time, for myself and for my patients.

"I told you this was a passionate issue for me, Jack. We, as first responders and in this new world of ours, *need that vaccine.*"

"Fuck you, Max. As far as I'm concerned, you're finished in this hospital. I don't have a way yet, but your days are numbered here."

"Can I take that as a formal threat, Jack?"

"Watch your back, pal," Jack said with genuine menace. "I'm after you now."

"Careful, Jack, you're sounding a bit like Schwartz now."

Click. The phone disconnected, and dial tone heaven began.

*   *   *   *

I had four other cases to disposition, three admissions, and Jordan, but I had to see these new patients first. I assigned Andy three flu-like syndromes and a simple laceration. There was also a young woman who had felt burning on urination beginning after her honeymoon. It was probably just a case of honeymoon cystitis, or even more simply put, a bladder infection.

I used to tell Leana about these occasional cases. She was amused.

Too much hoochie cooch will do it every time.

Worth it, don't you think? I countered.

You bet.

Then we'd laugh. After our honeymoon, she also had a case of cystitis.

Andy went about taking care of all of these patients, while I took care of the difference. I just finished the last case and was on my way to see Mr. Caruso when I ran into Norma.

"Dr. Kroose, here are the labs on the influenza patient."

"Which one? We've seen several."

"The one we're admitting?"

"Oh, Mr. Villalobos," I said, remembering how restless he had been and how anxious he was to leave our hospital. That, and his threat to kick my ass from here to hell and back if I touched him again.

"Yes," Norma said. "Matt's been keeping an eye on him, making sure he doesn't try to leave again."

"Okay, let me see those labs," I said.

What was notable was the white cell count, which was low, as well as the platelet count. We thought these were both consistent with a viral syndrome, perhaps the influenza virus. Urinalysis was normal, but the blood gases revealed an oxygen level of 50, half of what it should have been.

"How is he feeling?" I asked, still pondering the results in my hand.

"Much better now that we have him on oxygen. And we've brought his temperature down with Tylenol, Motrin, and fluids. But here's his chest X ray. I think it's abnormal."

She handed me the chest X ray, and I reviewed it. She was right. It was not just abnormal—it was *bloody* abnormal. There were infiltrates, spotty shadows over both lung fields, not just the right or the left but both lung fields. Mr. Villalobos had a diffused pneumonia, and that's why his oxygen level was so low. Influenza typically does not give rise to pneumonia, but it can. However, I wanted to be sure I wasn't missing a diagnosis. It was still possible that this is a bacterial infection, one that would require antibiotics.

"Norma, this is probably influenza, but it doesn't commonly cause pneumonia. I'm worried that this may be a little secondary bacterial infection, like staph."

"You're right. We've had similar cases in the past. Do we have time to give him antibiotics right now?"

"Yes, they're both admitted."

"Dr. Schwartz called back, and I told him about the two cases. He wasn't too happy about it since they're both cash accounts."

"Perhaps we'll see a more quiescent Dr. Schwartz in the near future," I mused hopefully. Hopefully, because maybe Nathan had a little talk with him just after his cordial discussion with Kilgorn.

"You know, it's interesting. He didn't put up too much of a struggle, come to think of it. He said not to bother with calling him, just to send all the labs and the X rays with the patient so he could review the charts. If he had any questions, he'd give you a call."

This was unusual. Typically, when we admitted, the admitting physician wants a report from the emergency room doctor. Perhaps he felt a little embarrassed (I'd like to think scared as hell) and decided to give me some space for a bit.

"Martha, why don't we give him two grams of Rocephin IV before we send him up." This was a commonly used antibiotic given for such an infection.

Martha went on her way to order the drug for Mr. Villalobos. I wanted to see him before he left the emergency room department just to make sure nothing had changed. Sometimes these patients begin to deteriorate very quickly, and it's important to identify the problem as soon as possible to adjust your therapeutic regimens. I also wanted to see Mr. Caruso before he was admitted.

As I began to walk toward Caruso's bedside, I saw Betty walking out of the other monitored room and then start waving to me as if to tell me to come to see Mr. Villalobos. I was getting a little annoyed with all my interruptions. It was if they were intentional to keep me from seeing my alcoholic friend in Room Three.

"Betty, what is it?"

"Dr. Kroose, come in. I want to show you something."

"Can it wait? I'm busy." I was wondering what new evil she was seeing in Villalobos, baby duckling killer, possibly. I realized this was unfair to Betty; I was still a bit out of sorts with my political day thus far.

"It will just take a sec."

"I'll look at it later."

She would be annoyed at my dismissiveness of her, but I thought she'd get over it. I walked into Mr. Caruso's room and, as I began to examine his abdomen where I had left off on the previous examination fifty years ago (so it seemed), I noticed that he was still talking nonsense. Blabbering, really.

"I ain't no goddamn gin peddler—good salesman—not a peddler."

"I'm sure you're not," I placated him, continuing the exam.

"And she's a bitch for sayin' it—a plu-pural, slap-on-the-ass bitch...charged too much for a simple blow job, too."

Mr. Caruso was no doubt rambling out one of his late nocturnal excursions, mixing and mashing various disjointed thoughts into barely coherent sentences. Clearly, this last statement was one of fiscal impropriety by a certain young lady.

"Fucking bitch," he said under his breath, then shut up.

His skin was hot, clammy. Oh, sure, he had a fever, in spite of the antipyretics we had given him. And the rash that I noticed before was unchanged; it was over his upper extremities, his face, and, to a lesser extent, over his neck. I'm sure that it was a petechial rash, the kind of a rash that you see with alcoholic liver disease. Over his left upper abdominal quadrant, I could palpate a very large spleen. And over the right upper abdominal quadrant, I could palpate a large liver, as we would expect to find in one with alcoholic liver disease. This could also explain the petechial rash. As I began to undo the sheets to examine his pelvic area, as well as his genitalia and lower extremities, I heard Norma.

"Dr. Kroose, Dr. Crow the cardiologist for Mr. Smith is on line Two."

It seemed I would never finish my examination of Caruso, in this century or the next. However, I'd now grown used to the interruptions.

"Thank you, Norma," I said wearily.

I walked up to the wall phone, which is located in the examining room. I pushed line two.

"This is Dr. Kroose."

"Dr. Kroose, this is Bill Crow. Listen, I hear you have Mr. Smith there. He's a very good patient of mine. I've known him for ten years. What happened?"

"Hi, Bill," I said. "He came to our emergency room a couple of hours ago complaining of upper back pain. As we evaluated him, we realized that, in fact, what he had not told us was that he was having concurrent chest pain. His description was of a chest discomfort, but he had focused on his back pain. He subsequently dropped his blood pressure and pulse. An EKG was done, and we realized he has an anterior wall MI."

Of heart attacks, this is perhaps the worst type of heart attack one can have, because this is the larger part of the left ventricle, which is responsible for pumping blood to the rest of the body. If one loses the entire anterior wall of the left ventricle (i.e., the left main chamber of the heart), one ultimately suffers cardiac shock.

"Got it. Thanks, Max. Don't feel bad about that. It doesn't surprise me he didn't tell you he had chest pains. There's a reason why he's seeing me. His wife brought him in about six months ago because he kept rubbing his chest. Smart lady. Brought him in by his ear, practically."

"That's why married men live longer than single ones," I said.

"True, but they're also more willing to die." We laughed momentarily, until Bill continued on, "Anyway, I got an EKG at the time and that was normal, but the characteristics of his pain were very worrisome. I suggested doing a coronary angiogram. He refused. I left it at that, and he was supposed to get back to me if he had a change of heart. So how is he now?"

I was happy to give good news. "He seems to be comfortable. He's intubated, and I've sedated him. The problem is I don't know if he's having pain and, given his EKG abnormalities, I think he needs to go to the Cath Lab."

"Agreed," Crow said. "I've already called the lab, and we're set up to see him. I'll be there in about ten minutes. If you can get the nurses to transfer him up to the unit now, I'll cath him when I get there, and we'll take care of his problem."

"Sounds like a plan," I said.

"Do me a favor—go up with the nurses. I don't want anything to happen to him. He is on a vent, and we'll probably have to bag him while he's up there while we're doing the dirty deed."

"You're absolutely right. Sure, no problem," I said, feeling just the opposite. *Another distraction*, I thought dismally to myself. Perhaps I'd actually get to evaluate Mr. Caruso, my problem drinker, sometime by 2023 at this rate.

However, I liked Bill Crow, and he'd done me a few favors in the past. Bill Crow was also on the executive committee. I was doing some back scratching. I hope I'd get mine scratched later, with respect to support for vaccinations. In any case, that notwithstanding, during the transport of a patient for procedures like this is when the patient is most vulnerable. Anything can go wrong with the ventilator, or he could develop another complication from his heart attack, and I had to be there to prevent that from happening or to take care of whatever unexpected problems occurred. Mr. Caruso would have to wait.

But that damned rash—it stuck in my mind—and his fever. Were they truly a manifestation of his alcoholism? Was he really going through DTs, or was this an atypical presentation of some other illness?

That was my concern, a manifestation of my own paranoia.

And that paranoia had a name attached to it: Smallpox.

2:30 PM

It had taken the better part of forty-five minutes to wheel Mr. Smith to the cardiac cath lab to perform the angiogram and the angioplasty that would most
likely save his life. Ultimately, I was glad I went in. Smith had several episodes of
sudden death that required resuscitation, all of which were successful. Dr. Crow's
associate came in at the tail end of the procedure, which allowed me to return to
the emergency room.

I wasn't sure how many patients had arrived during that period of time, but I
thought I probably would have a few cases to see before I attended to Mr.
Caruso. I was surprised to see that Andy had taken care of all the cases. He was
suturing a minor laceration when I got back. He had grown quite a bit in the few
hours he was in the emergency room, taking charge of the cases. Norma was quite
impressed with his clinical acumen and his maturity for a fourth-year student. I
went to the bedside of the patient he was working on to observe him.

"Good work, Dr. Goodman."

He looked up. "Ah, you're back, Dr. Kroose."

"Yeah, it took a little longer than I expected. Is there anything I can do to help
you?"

"No, I've got things under control."

"I can see that. When you're done with your suturing, we'll go over all the
other cases you've seen so I can sign off on your charts."

I made my way back to Mr. Caruso's bedside and realized that he was no
longer there. I went over to Norma, who was at the nurse's station finishing up
the paperwork on the admissions.

"Norma, where's Mr. Caruso?"

"I took him up while you were at the cath lab," Norma said.

I nodded and almost laughed. Why was this not a surprise.

"Did we get all the laboratory results back on him?"

She keyed in his hospital number into the computer and punched a button,
and the printer began to print out the laboratory reports. She handed them to
me, and I began reading. The urinalysis was normal. There was no evidence of a
urinary tract infection, thus not a source for a fever. The electrolytes were also
normal, as well as the kidney function studies. I had already appreciated that the
liver function tests were elevated, consistent with alcohol liver disease in support-
ing the diagnosis of alcohol withdrawal symptoms. And the white cell count was
low, which could also be explained by an alcohol-related illness.

So why did I have a hunch that it was other than an alcohol withdrawal syndrome? I wanted to convince myself, without a shadow of a doubt, that DTs was the diagnosis. However, the platelet count, that would help explain the rash. What was it? I reviewed the lab again, and somehow something was omitted.

Some of the results were still pending.

"Norma, I notice that the platelet count is not reported. Why is that? Did you talk to the lab?"

"Yes, I noticed that. I called them. They said they were having problems with the coulter counter, but that it should be out pretty soon."

"Can you check to see if it's been fixed?"

"Of course."

I felt the urge to go up to Mr. Caruso's room on the fourth floor to complete my examination, to look for other clues, or to verify the diagnosis. And I wanted to control the sense of mounting fear. There was no logical reason why I should suspect any other illness, such as smallpox, anthrax, or some other biological agent. I continued to review the labs and realized the alcohol level was also not reported.

"Norma, the ETOH level, it's not in the report. We have the other toxicology results, why not the alcohol level?"

"I called the lab about the alcohol level also. That was a sendout, so it takes a little longer to get those reports. They generally take another forty-five minutes, and that was fifteen minutes ago, so perhaps in the next half hour or so we should get the report back."

Norma was waiting on the phone for the results of the platelet count.

She nodded and then thanked the party on the other line. "Dr. Kroose, the platelet count is 48,000."

There was really nothing to worry about.

I gave the reports back to Norma. Sometimes you just have to look at the facts, and the facts will point you in the right direction. Sometimes they're just irrevocable. Andy had just finished the suture and was making his way toward me.

"Dr. Kroose, let's sit down and talk about these charts so we can sign off on them."

"That's a good idea. We have a few minutes. Let's do them before another deluge of patients comes in."

I caught Martha in the corner of my eye, coming out of the room where Jordan was. Yes, Jordan. I forgot about him. We had begun the evaluation, but I hadn't gotten back to complete the process. As far as I knew, he was doing well.

"Dr. Kroose, we're still waiting for blood studies. This is his X ray."

I took the X rays from Martha and put them on the light box, which was located next to the nurse's station. The one seemed to be clear, no evidence of any infection.

Martha continued, "But I don't think he's doing as well as when he first got here."

"What do you mean?" I asked.

"Well, he seems to be a little more listless, not as attentive, and he's not crying much now. His pulse has gone up a little. But with the fluids we gave to hydrate him, I would have expected his pulse to decrease."

I did not like the gestalt of what Martha was describing. Children sometimes precipitously, without warning, deteriorate, so I urgently needed to reexamine him again. I looked to Andy, who waited patiently nearby.

"Why don't we defer discussion for a little bit? I need to go see Jordan."

"You bet," Andy said.

Martha had already returned to Jordan's bedside and was about to obtain a rectal temperature, a core temperature, when I heard her yell out, "Dr. Kroose!"

It was an expression of alarm and fear. All in the emergency room could hear. They all began to make their way to assist Martha. Norma, Matt, Cynthia, and Betty were all at the bedside when I arrived. Jordan was convulsing. His body was stiff, frothing secretions were spewing from his mouth. His eyes were turned up. His arms and legs were stiff, and he let out a high-pitched shrill sound. Then, within seconds, he began to rhythmically jerk his upper and lower extremities with his back arched and his head hyperextended. He began to turn blue. Respiration ceased. His skin began to mottle. This all happened suddenly as we all descended upon his bedside. Matt turned Jordan to his side to prevent him from aspirating, as many do during a seizure as a result of vomiting during the attack. Betty applied a facemask and began assisting Jordan's ventilation with the Ambu bag. Norma called the respiratory Sergio, STAT, to the emergency room. She then rolled a crash cart next to Jordan's bedside.

The anxiety, apprehension, and fear were palpable in all that were present at the bedside. The room was small, barely accepting all of us and the crash cart. Cynthia ushered the family to the waiting room, while we began our resuscitative measures. Martha placed cardiac monitor electrodes on the toddler's chest. Linda placed the pulse oximeter probe on Jordan's finger to measure the oxygen level. In seconds, the monitor was displaying the vital signs that I needed to assess the boy's condition. Jordan continued to seize. His oxygen level was dropping. It was at 85. His pulse was 200, and his respiratory rate 0. If this continued, hypoxemia could result and not only a pulmonary arrest, but also a cardiac arrest. We had to interrupt the seizure quickly.

"Norma, give me 4 mg of Valium through an IV."

As Norma complied, I noticed Jordan was profusely sweating. And superimposed over the motley tone of the skin, a faint rash began to appear, a few dots all over his torso and a few over his extremities. I began to fear the worst. I thought, *my God, this could be smallpox.* However, I quickly subdued that paranoia that kept hounding me.

This was not smallpox.

This was meningococcemia, and this child was in danger of dying—and dying quickly. I listened to the lungs. They were clear, with the assisted ventilation that Sergio was providing. He had just arrived. The abdomen was soft, and the pupils were beginning to dilate. Jordan became more cyanotic, bluer, every second that ticked away. Then Jordan stopped seizing. The medication had worked, but he still was not breathing. His pulse was over 200, and he couldn't sustain this condition more than a few seconds. He needed an airway so that we could deliver the oxygen he needed. If we didn't, he wouldn't survive this.

"Norma, we're going to intubate him," I snapped. "Get me the ET tube in a 3.5 and a 4. Sergio, continue to bag Jordan. Let's put him in the supine position."

Then I went to the head of the bed. These intubations are the most difficult. All the anatomical structures are much smaller, making it more difficult to visualize the vocal chords in order to successfully intubate the patient. Norma continued to record all the events as they occurred, timing every procedure intervention that we performed. Betty placed another intravenous catheter in case fluids and medications were required, one IV used for fluids, the second for medications. Matt, using the controls of the bed, elevated the bed to a level to make it possible for me to more easily see the vocal chords. Linda placed her index finger on the right groin area to count the strength of the pulse, knowing that if the pulse weakened, Jordan's condition would worsen. I looked at Linda for that input.

"Is it strong?"

"It's pounding right now."

"Cynthia, get me a blood pressure."

The staff had not noticed the rash that I had seen earlier. However, before our eyes, the rash was becoming more apparent, more diffused, and, in some areas, confluent. It was so impressive that it took everyone in the room by surprise. Betty was the first to comment.

"Jesus, Dr. Kroose, do you see the rash? This is like Ebola"

"No, it's not that."

Sergio then chimed in. "Holy shit, it's quickly developing. I've seen this before, but I can't remember what it is."

The others were also equally amazed. I took my paraphernalia—the laryngoscope and the intratracheal tube—and was ready for the intubation. Cynthia reported the blood pressure.

"Blood pressure's 50 over 30."

This was low. This is consistent with all the other vital signs, signs of a moribund patient.

"Betty, increase the IV rate," I said. "Let's bolus the patient with 400 cc of normal saline."

I was hoping to improve Jordan's blood pressure and decrease his pulse somewhat, knowing that he was septic. That is a generalized, overwhelming infection that, in many cases, is fatal. I looked at Linda for an update on the pulse.

"The pulse is weakening," Linda said, in view of the monitor. "It's still fast. Two hundred ten beats per minute, and the oxygen is seventy-nine percent."

I had no time to wait. It was time to intubate the boy.

"Everyone—on the count of three—one, two, three."

Sergio stopped ventilating the patient with the Ambu bag. I cleared the throat using the suction catheter, which was filled with frothy pink mucus. I introduced the laryngoscope, swept the tongue away from my visual field and, with the fiber optic light, I could see the vocal chords. I introduced the ET tube and secured the tube to Jordan's chin. Sergio began to ventilate Jordan with the Ambu bag. The child was still in a coma, not responding, pupils dilated.

"Linda, what's the pulse right now?" I asked.

"Still weak, Dr. Kroose."

I listened to both lung fields as Sergio ventilated the patient. I could hear good breathing sounds, right and left. I looked up at Betty who was in view of the monitor.

"Betty, what are we showing?"

"It's looking better. Pulse oximeter's now 85. Pulse is down to 190, and his blood pressure's 60 over 40."

I walked away from the head of the bed, allowing Sergio to maintain the airway as well as ventilate. I positioned myself next to Jordan. As I did so, Linda stepped away from the bedside, and I placed my hand in the right groin area and could feel Jordan's pulse, and it felt bounding. I looked up at the monitor now that I had a view of it and saw that the pulse oximeter was over ninety percent now. The pulse was down to 170, and the blood pressure was 70 over 35. Matt had recorded the temperature at 105. The rash that had begun just a few minutes before was now generalized; in other words, a diffused small, spotted rash spreading and screaming at all those who observed it.

Sergio looked at me. "Dr. Kroose, I remember. The rash that I saw that was similar to this was when I was training as a SEAL. There was a lecture that we attended about biological agents and their presentations. There were some viruses that gave rise to a similar rash, but the peculiar part about that case was that it was only present over the face and upper extremities."

I interrupted Sergio. "Sergio, this isn't a virus. This is meningococcemia. It's a bacterium, and it gives rise to meningitis. Many of these patients die from it."

Sergio didn't look entirely convinced, but he said nothing.

Although Jordan had improved, he was still in peril. I had to begin antibiotics to try to control the infection.

"Norma, let's give Jordan two million units of penicillin IV and also Rocephin 2 grams IV."

Martha had already begun giving Jordan second doses of Motrin as well as Tylenol. We also increased Jordan's IV infusion rates, knowing that he would require more hydration to help keep the fever down and maintain his normal blood pressure. Sergio, with Matt's assistance, placed Jordan on a ventilator, knowing that it would take a while to transfer Jordan to a pediatric facility where a pediatric ICU was available.

"Norma, let's call MAC and see if the Children's Hospital has an ICU bed. If they do, let's contact the hospital and arrange for the transport. They'll probably want to medevac Jordan out, so we'll need to call the police department so they can clear the intersection so they can land the helicopter."

It was three o'clock and rush hour had just begun, so transferring Jordan by ambulance across town could take too long. I needed to talk to the parents to present them with the good and bad news.

"Cynthia, can you bring the parents and place them in one of the examining rooms so I can talk to them?"

Betty went back to assist Mr. Villalobos who was ready for admission, and Linda assisted Betty in infusing the antibiotics ordered. Andy, who had assisted me with intubating Jordan and provided me with all the paraphernalia I needed, seemed a little disappointed.

"Dr. Kroose, I thought the adage was, 'You see one, you do one, you teach one.'"

I had forgotten in the excitement and apprehension of all we were doing to save Jordan's life that I had said that.

"Yes, Andy, but I think it's only fair to let you try on a case that's an adult. Kids are very difficult, and this is one, you and I both would agree, could not tolerate any delay."

"I understand, Dr. Kroose, but the next adult I'd like to try."

"Absolutely, Andy. You'll get your chance. The day is young. The way this day is going, I'm sure you'll get your chance."

It was a Freudian slip, for as I prepared to talk to the parents, I couldn't help but think, "Is this the snake in the grass? Is this what I've been anticipating all day long or are there others?" I could not help but feel that there was something impending, so much had already happened.

And Sergio's comments about biological agents didn't help, but I was certain that Jordan was suffering from meningococcemia. Was it possible for us to misdiagnose one of these cases and miss an index case of biological agent, such as smallpox?

Max...get off the smallpox thing. You're seeing it in every nook and cranny. Not like you, old boy. Not like you at all.

So my inner voice told me.

Then again, this day had been like no other for me since my first day of employment.

Stick around, kiddo.

It's gonna get worse.

I chided myself. Then I realized that my paranoia was pretty natural given it had only taken up virtually the whole day in one form of another. How could I not see smallpox everywhere?

Hell, next I'd see large white rabbits with hat and cane, looking for a party. Late, I'm late, for a very important date, no time to call, no time to chat, I'm late, I'm late, I'm...

I killed these rambling thoughts as I talked to the parents and Children's Hospital in preparation for the transport by helicopter.

3 PM

Jordan remained stable throughout the rest of the emergency room evaluation and treatment. After the antibiotics were given, he seemed to improve. He began to awaken and trigger the respiration on his own. This does not require as much support as he had had earlier. The rash, ever present, had not changed any since the antibiotics were given. I find it amazing our immune systems are capable of overcoming overwhelming infections. As physicians, all we need to do is sometimes just urge the process on, and I think that's what the antibiotics had done. This organism was apparently very sensitive to the antibiotics I had given. Jordan's blood pressure remained stable. His pulse had come down to 130. His temperature was down to 99. The laboratory studies we had ordered looked consistent with the diagnosis. Betty had suggested ordering the buffy coat, which was not unlike Betty thinking about these things. She was absolutely right. The buffy coat was the perfect study to do. This is a concentrate of white cells from a drawn blood sample that the laboratory subsequently stains, making it possible to identify the organism causing Jordan's illness. We deferred performing a lumbar puncture before a definitive diagnosis, because it would be too time-consuming. The helicopter was on its way. The police department cleared the intersection, which was catty-corner to the hospital, so that the helicopter could land safely. Jordan was subsequently transferred out of our emergency room uneventfully. The parents were obviously traumatized, having seen their child normal only hours ago and learning now that he most likely would not be normal again if he survived his illness. I was glad Cynthia had gone along with me to talk to the family. She had the ability to soothe patients and the families in such traumatic events, and it was unmatched by others in the emergency room. She was able to draw a smile from the mother when she said, "He is a real fighter."

I added my own two bits, "You can tell by the improvement he has made in these past few minutes. Who knows? He may surprise all of us."

My nurses were also somewhat traumatized by this case. Everybody became somewhat quiet and went about taking care of their assigned patients. Andy and I discussed the cases he had seen, and I signed off on his charts. The emergency room had quieted down for the first time that day. The only thing I had left to do before some R & R was to see Mr. Villalobos and Mr. Caruso. So I headed toward the monitored beds, only to realize Mr. Caruso was no longer there. I went back to check with Norma.

"Where's Mr. Caruso?"

"He's admitted to the ICU."

"I'll have to go to the ICU to see him. Where's his labs?"

"Not ready yet Dr. Kroose."

"What about Mr. Villalobos?"

"I want to examine him again. Do we have his labs back?"

"Yes, everything seemed to be normal except for the white cell count, which is about 3,000."

I thought to myself that was probably a little low in a patient with his illness. Then again, the influenza virus tends to suppress your white cell count, so it was not an alarming result. I would let Villalobos rest on his own for a bit, then check in on him shortly. I headed for the nurse's lounge where there was a coffee pot and a TV. I wanted to sit down and relax, have a cup of java, and watch CNN to catch up with the latest news.

It was my last quiet moment of the day.

*   *   *   *

I called Esmerelda at home. Billy was doing great except for the stomachache.

"Stomachache?" I asked.

"He had a little too much pudding," Es replied, without a trace of remorse. I decided I wasn't going to fight this battle today. If my child would have asked for heroin, she might have complied with the request, simply because Billy was a child who had been hurt; who, in fact, needed comforting. I smiled inwardly. Es, you old softie.

"Yes, that would do it. How's Andrea?"

"She take nap right now. You no be late tonight, okay?"

"I won't be late. Tell Billy that's a promise."

"Okay, I do."

"Gotta go, Es."

I hung up then and gave my neck a twirl right and left, fighting the stiffness.

Matt had beat me to the lounge and was already at the coffee station. He looked up at me as I entered the lounge.

"Hey, Dr. Kroose, want a cup of my fine brew? I brought this from home. It's what I use when I'm out backpacking, but I gotta warn you, it packs a helluva punch."

"Sounds like a good idea, Matt."

"What would you like in it?"

"Cream and sugar, two sugars."

Matt prepared the two cups of coffee, one for himself and one for me, and we began to chitchat about anything other than the cases that we had seen.

"So when's your next trip, Matt?"

"I'm going to the High Sierras in the next couple of weeks."

"Isn't it a little cold out there?"

"Yes, we're going to do a little cross-country skiing. I'm going to take my two sons and teach them a little bit about survival out in the cold."

"About how high are you going to be?"

"We plan to hit the 12,000 foot level."

"Watch out for high altitude sickness."

"I know, but it hasn't bothered me in the past. I think we'll be okay."

I noticed on the tube that CNN had a special on weapons of mass destruction. *The perennial topic of the day*, I thought. I was about to turn it up to listen to the discussion when Andy walked into the lounge, poured himself a cup of coffee, and sat down next to me.

"Dr. Kroose, that's too bad about Jordan."

"Yeah, I know. I hate to see these kinds of cases, because you know, invariably, they don't do well."

Andy sipped on his coffee and looked at Matt.

"Matt, you must have been in the military."

Matt smiled at Andy and said, "Why do you say that? I'm sure it's not my beard."

"Well, it's your strong coffee." Andy replied.

Matt laughed at that. "Yeah, I was in Viet Nam. I was a medic in '68. Served my year and left. How about you, Andy?"

"Nope, haven't had the pleasure," as he smiled back at Matt. "Anyway, it's great coffee. I like it."

Matt nodded at Andy as Sergio entered the lounge and began to talk to Matt and Andy about Jordan's precipitous deterioration. I was trying to listen to the CNN program. They were about to talk about smallpox. Matt said to Sergio, "That was an impressive rash. Did you see how quickly it developed?"

Sergio nodded. "Yeah, there was nothing and all of sudden his entire body was covered with this red rash. Dr. Kroose, have you ever seen anything like that?"

"Yes, I have. This rash can appear quite suddenly and is associated with the deterioration of the patient. I've had a few cases that presented this way. That's why I knew it was meningococcemia."

Sergio appeared somewhat pensive at this point. Matt commented, "This is the first case I've seen. Dr. Kroose, since we've been exposed, do we need prophylaxis or some kind of medication?"

"You're right, Matt. We'll take Rifampin. I've asked Norma already to order the Rifampin from the pharmacy so we can all have our appropriate doses."

Sergio suddenly interrupted me.

"Dr. Kroose, now I remember."

"What's that, Sergio?"

"The rash I was telling you about."

"What rash?"

"The one I told you I remembered seeing before that was similar to this rash."

"What rash was it?"

"During training we had lectures of various biological agents. There was a slide show reviewing the various types of rashes associated with these biological agents. One slide was a rash was an atypical presentation of an agent caused by a virus. This virus usually caused a pustular rash, but it was altered. And, as a result, it presented atypically and was very lethal, killing some fifty percent, maybe eighty percent of the people it infected."

Being an ex-SEAL, it was very plausible that Sergio had had some formal instruction and training in biological warfare, and so his story was very credible. All in the room were focused on what he was saying, listening to his every word. So I pressed Sergio on the agent.

"Are you sure it wasn't a bacterium, such as anthrax?"

"No, this was a virus, a virus that typically causes a pustular rash."

"You're not talking about smallpox?"

"No, I don't think it was smallpox. We're vaccinated against smallpox."

"So it wasn't variola?"

Sergio vigorously responded, "Yes, that's what it was. It was variola. It was variola that caused the rash, and it was atypical. It didn't cause a pustular rash. It was a flat, red-dotted rash like the one we saw on Jordan."

Andy then contributed his experience. "That's right. When I was at Fort Dietrick, we had a lecture and a slide show about the *atypical* presentations of smallpox or variola, and one of those presentations was a macular flat, red-spotted rash that appeared over the face and the upper extremities initially. Many of the patients expired before they developed the classic pustular rash, so these patients were never diagnosed."

"Exactly."

"Many of them were diagnosed as the flu or as measles."

Sergio concurred. "Yes, that's right. The distinguishing characteristic of the rash was that it was over the face and upper extremities, and these patients expired relatively quickly."

As I listened to the conversation, I reviewed the characteristics of Jordan's rash in my mind, but I was absolutely sure that Jordan had meningococcemia, otherwise he wouldn't have responded to the antibiotics. My paranoia began to take control of me. I became troubled by the description of the rash Andy and Sergio had both given.

But why was it so troubling? I knew Jordan did not have smallpox. Then I became alarmed. It was Mr. Caruso, his rash. It was over his face and his upper extremities but not over his lower extremities. Then I realized that I had not examined his lower extremities. I didn't get a chance to. There had been too many distractions. The others could detect the concern on my face.

Sergio commented, "Dr. Kroose, I wouldn't worry about it. I'm sure you're correct in your diagnosis. It's probably meningococcemia. I don't think it's smallpox. His rash was all over his body."

"No, no, I don't doubt that he had meningococcemia."

There was still something gnawing at me about Mr. Caruso. I decided in this relative quiet time to allay my fears, which I'd forgotten about for about five minutes. I looked over to Andy and said, "Andy, take care of the ER. I'm going to go see Mr. Caruso and see how he's doing."

Okay, I'll admit it.

I was worried about Caruso and the possibility of smallpox.

I was determined to put those fears in the grave right now.

However, I really should have been thinking about Villalobos.

*   *   *   *

Plain and simple, I didn't want to alarm the others in the emergency room as much as I did not want to embarrass myself, speculating that Mr. Caruso had smallpox. I needed to see for myself whether the rash was over the upper and lower extremities. And what about the alcohol level?

I hadn't received the results yet.

I walked up to the nurse's station, picked up Mr. Caruso's ER record, and keyed in his hospital number into the computer, scrolled up the menu, and requested the laboratory results.

There they were.

All of them were completed, and the alcohol was there.

Now I became more concerned. Then I began to question Mr. Caruso's diagnosis. Was it really DTs or was it something else? His alcohol level was 250, more than three times the legal intoxication level, a level that would render most of us inebriated. Mr. Caruso should not be withdrawing with such a high alcohol level. So what did he have?

This was crazy. There hadn't been a case of smallpox in more than 50 years in this country. Why should Mr. Caruso have it? He's an alcoholic. His liver function studies are piss-poor elevated. His white cell count is low. His platelet count is in the basement.

So what is it, doc? the Voice asked me.

I thought to myself that the labs explained the petechial rash. I did not have to evoke any other etiology for any of his physical findings or symptoms or abnormal laboratory.

Another terrifying thought suddenly invaded my psyche.

In fact, if Mr. Caruso has smallpox, am I exposed then? Is everyone else exposed? He did have a cough but no open sores. The chances are he would not be contagious. Prodrome. Not contagious. All good things...

I moved away from the terminal and high stepped it to the ICU where Mr. Caruso was admitted. I could see him moving his arms as if to pick something out of midair, something that wasn't there. He was obviously confused. He was talking to himself, a lot of continued nonsense about monkeys, expensive whores, Kansas—all in continued disjointed commentary.

I approached his bedside. He didn't acknowledge my presence. *Shitfaced* was the term that nonmedically leaped to mind. I noticed the rash on his face and his arms. A sheet covered his lower body. I could feel the anxiety rising in my body. I felt the chill. If the rash was *not* over his legs or groin, it was no joy in Mudville, kids.

My paranoia kicked in.

Yeah, it's not there. The old drunk has the pox. I knew it just had to be.

I untied the sheets, which were tied to bind Mr. Caruso to prevent him from falling out of the bed. As I did, I exposed his everything below the bellybutton. He had a patient gown on so they were completely visible.

The rash was present.

My stomach did the funky chicken, and I suddenly felt about as smart as Elsie the Cow.

Why would I doubt the diagnosis?

Why should I doubt myself?

I never had experienced this degree of apprehension and paranoia before. What was so different about this day?

The Voice.

The Voice that has never let you down before.

Bullshit! You missed the boat today, Mr. Gut. Hallelujah!

I walked up to the ICU nursing station and pulled Mr. Caruso's chart out. Dr. Schwartz had already seen the patient and placed him on some antibiotics to treat a possible occult infection—that is one that was not apparent on our initial evaluation, but the one which could be identified by our blood study in a couple of days. That was a wise intervention. I asked the head nurse who the nurse was taking care of Mr. Caruso, and she pointed her out to me. Her name was Jackie.

Jackie was perhaps the smallest Japanese woman I had ever seen in my life with perfect porcelain features.

"Jackie, hi, I'm Dr. Kroose. I'm from the emergency room. I took care of Mr. Caruso when he was down there. I noticed he's still confused."

She smiled a little at that.

"Yes, he's been confused since he got here," she said. "But he's doing a little better. His pulse is down to about 100. His temperature's down to 99. We're hydrating him, and Dr. Schwartz has started him on some antibiotics."

"So he concurs with my diagnosis?"

"Oh yeah, this is full-blown DTs. He's presented this way before."

Again, relief flooded through my entire system.

"So he's been admitted here previously?"

"Not here. Dr. Schwartz called one of his hometown hospitals, St. Jude's, and apparently he's been admitted for DTs in the past. His typical presentation is confusion, fevers, the rash, and the tachycardia. Funny thing about it is his alcohol level is always high. One of the ER notes on one of his ER visits when he was inebriated reports an alcohol blood level of 500 mg percent, and he was walking."

I thought to myself, *fucking amazing.*

Anybody with a 500 mg percent alcohol level would be in a deep coma or dead. Yet this man apparently survives, continuously, perhaps even maintains himself at levels much higher than most of us would be able to tolerate. I thought back to my brother, Dillon. He had the same incomprehensible tolerability to the gentle grape. Of course, it ultimately killed him—still, even when presented with these facts, I find it amazing how the individual human body works.

"Ok, Jackie, thanks," I said.

I was about to head back to ER when I heard the intercom above.

"Dr. Kroose to ER, STAT."

3:30 PM

"What the hell is going on here?" I asked Matt under my breath, watching Villalobos, who was weaving back and forth in his bed. He was muttering gibberish, at least I thought at the time.

Or something else.

Arabic?

"Betty and I were trying to get him to let us have his jacket to hang it up for him."

"He wasn't happy about that once before, remember?" I said.

"Yeah."

I looked to Mr. Villalobos and smiled. "Sir, it's Dr. Kroose, you remember me?"

He stared at me through bleary, almost deranged eyes.

The guttural sounds continued, and then I was sure of it. He was speaking Arabic, maybe Hebrew, I couldn't be sure.

"We just want to hang your jacket up, right over there." I pointed at a nearby rack easily accessible from the bed.

"No," he finally managed.

I looked at his mouth; slivers of drool seeped out of either side.

Then he said in a low, hoarse voice words that chilled me to the bone.

"You're all going to die."

*   *   *   *

Matt saw it first—thank God for that background of combat.

Villalobos reached into his jacket and pulled out a small gun—a .22, it looked like. He aimed it directly at me.

Matt caught his arm and snapped it back.

"You Jew pigs!" Villalobos screamed, his first clear sentence of the day.

Betty backed up in horror as I grabbed Villalobos' other arm. Matt snatched the gun with one clean gesture that disarmed our deranged guest within half a second.

"Jesus Christ," Betty screamed.

Villalobos suddenly just crumpled against both Matt and I, appearing somewhat comatose—whatever his sickness was, it allowed for only marginal effectiveness in terms of movement.

I looked to Matt. "Where were you when I was on the wrestling team?"

Matt didn't smile but raised his eyebrows. We lowered Villalobos to a prone position.

Then I saw something that made me freeze.

"I'll call the police," she said.

"No," I said softly. "Don't do that. Not yet."

I didn't answer her. What I saw on Villalobos wouldn't let me immediately find speech.

Matt and Betty looked at what I was staring at.

On Villalobos' face and shoulders was a rash.

"I should call…"

"Don't call anybody, Betty," I looked at her sternly. She immediately shut up.

"Did anyone notice this rash before?" I asked.

Betty sighed, staring at me.

"I was trying to tell you about that earlier, doctor. Remember?" she sounded righteously peeved.

I remembered and nodded. "Yeah, sorry, Betty. Okay. Okay."

I wanted Mr. Villalobos admitted where he could be under constant observation.

"Betty does Mr. Villalobos have a ICU bed?"

"Yes, Dr. Kroose, he has a bed in the ICU, and they are waiting for him."

"Have Matt and Andy take him up to the ICU."

"What do you want me to do with this?" Matt asked, indicating the gun.

I frowned and then held my hand out. "I'll take it for now."

Matt handed it to me and asked me quietly, "Why don't you want to call the police, Dr Kroose? This guy was carrying a dangerous…"

"I have my reasons, Matt. Trust me on this one. I'll take full responsibility."

Matt stared into my eyes for a moment, sighed, and then nodded.

I looked out into the hall; despite Villalobos' outburst, there was practically no one moving about. *Fine*, I thought. Okay, first things first. This is probably just another Caruso Scare Syndrome old Dr. Kroose is having once again. A little extrapolation and investigation was in order.

I walked out of Villalobos' room and found a computer terminal, Mr. Villalobos' chart, and hospital number. I punched in the hospital number and scrolled up the menu, selected the laboratory results button, and up came all the numbers. I clicked the cursor on the platelet count, and the results were 250,000, which was normal.

No reason for the rash.

Fine.

No, not fine, the Voice said. Not fine at all, because if Crazy Boy with the Gun doesn't have the rash below the fun zone, then...

Betty interrupted my cerebration.

"Dr Kroose, Matt's on the line. He wants to talk to you."

The guys had taken Mr. Villalobos to the ICU in a quick clip, understanding the need to keep him in a controlled environment. I took the phone.

"Matt, what is it?"

"Dr. Kroose, this guy's taken a turn for the worse. His breathing is for shit. He may need to be intubated."

I turned to Betty.

"Call Sergio and tell him to meet me in the ICU."

Betty exited the room to make the calls.

Villalobos had a fever, was short of breath, had pneumonia and a rash, and now seemed to be fighting for his life. The influenza virus can do this, but the platelet count was normal. I thought, *why did he have that fuckin' rash?*

It's probably the influenza virus, but...

...it could be smallpox...

...an atypical presentation...

My paranoia began to get the better part of me.

I had to verify that the rash was only over his face and upper extremities, but I was hoping it was generalized.

It was more than a hope.

It was a prayer.

4 PM.

I glanced over at Betty who was at the nurses' station. I pointed at her directly. "Not a word about the gun, Betty. Clear?"

She stared at me, her face registering only a blank look of puzzlement.

"Promise me," I said.

She nodded and then whispered, "Promise."

With that covenant, I went on my way.

*   *   *   *

I made my way to the ICU and through the glass doors, sealing the ICU from the rest of the floor. I entered through the glass doors and approached Mr. Villalobos' bedside. He appeared in severe respiratory distress. He was obviously struggling to breathe. I could detect the cyanosis, the blueness to his skin, in spite of his Mediterranean olive-colored skin tone. I thought to myself, *His accent.* I recalled that his accent, a Spanish accent…

Bullshit, Spanish. That was Arabic.

…sure sounded funny.

However, he wasn't speaking now. He was confused, moaning. Nothing remotely articulate. He was diaphoretic. He was struggling with the ICU nurses. He obviously did not appreciate the fact that they were trying to help him.

As I approached his bedside, I looked down at Mr. Villalobos' legs, but they were covered with a sheet.

There's probably a rash, I thought, that is, I hoped.

Fuck, I can't let this get to me.

However, I didn't panic this time. I had made an error with Caruso, this was probably just another. *Do your homework this time*, I said to myself. I had other immediate concerns about the patient. He was about to code—he would either have a respiratory arrest or a cardiopulmonary arrest, so I focused on the task at hand.

I considered Villalobos' distress. The influenza virus could give rise to his presentation, all his symptomotology, and physical findings. Yes, this was probably the case.

I looked up at the monitor, which was suspended from the wall above the head of his bed. The pulse oximeter read sixty percent. His oxygen level had dropped from the time we'd seen him, and he was on supplemental oxygen so it should have been normal. Now he was more moribund, and we had to interrupt this process.

I took in the immediate stats, along with my team. Villalobos' pulse was up. It was about 160. His blood pressure had started to drop. I looked up at the monitor. It recorded his blood pressure at 80 over 60. His normal should have been 120 over 70. He was breathing roughly thirty-six times a minute, and his oxygen level was more or less sixty percent.

Whatever Mr. Villalobos had, it was very aggressive, and despite the antibiotics given, the fluids, and other measures, he was deteriorating quickly. This was somewhat unusual for the influenza virus. This individual had fallen sick only a day, day and a half ago. That's what he told me in the emergency room, anyway.

Patients with the influenza virus don't precipitously die. If they have a stormy course and succumb to their illness, it usually takes several days. But here, in a day and a half or less, he's on his deathbed. This is not supposed to happen to a patient in his age group, not from the influenza virus, not to someone in his thirties. I looked at Mr. Villalobos, and I could see the red-spotted rash over his face and upper extremities. I looked up at Andy and Matt and began to give orders.

"I need a crash cart. Get the Ambu bag." I looked to one of the nurses in the ICU. "We're going to have to intubate him, and we've got to do it now. Matt, help the nurses restrain him."

I looked at the charge nurse. "Give me 5 mg of Versed." This is an agent we used commonly to sedate the individual and to relax them enough to allow the intubation. I began to clear the bed of all unnecessary paraphernalia. The head of the bed was moved away from the wall to allow me to stand at the head of his bed. Hospital beds are made with removable headboards to allow for such procedures to be done with ease, so the headboard was removed. All the nurses knew their routine. One of the nurses began to bag Mr. Villalobos. Sergio arrived soon after, and we began to prepare for the intubation.

"Dr. Kroose, you have another one."

"Yeah, lucky me," I quipped, feeling about as lucky as Typhoid Mary at the moment.

Sergio looked down at the bed and realized it was Mr. Villalobos.

"Hey, Doc, I thought he was doing okay. I hadn't seen him since he left the emergency room, and they haven't called me about him, so I presumed that he had begun to improve. What does he have?"

Oh, just smallpox, Sergio. Just the most deadly thing to ever afflict mankind. That's all. No, really. Don't be alarmed. See how calm I am?

I shut the Voice up. "He has influenza, and he has a secondary bacterial infection. And pneumonia. That's probably why he's deteriorating."

Mr. Villalobos was fighting everyone, struggling to be released, pulling his IVs, so we had to restrain him and sedate him. Andy prepared all the instruments for the intubation and had them on a mayo stand next to me. Matt was helping restrain Mr. Villalobos. The charge nurse had the Versed in her hand and recorded all events and interventions occurring, while the nurses were adjusting the cardiac electrodes, pulse oximeter, and the blood pressure cuff so we could follow Mr. Villalobos' vital signs accurately. I ordered the charge nurse to give 2.5 mg of the Versed IV. With Sergio assisting Mr. Villalobos' ventilation, his oxygen level did not drop below sixty percent, but he couldn't sustain that level for long.

I looked at my watch. Forty seconds had passed since the Versed was given. Villalobos began to relax.

Sergio commented, "He's much easier to ventilate now, now that he's not resisting."

I couldn't see the monitor from the position I was in at the head of the bed, so I asked Matt for a reading of the oxygen level.

"So, what's the pulse ox now?"

"It's seventy percent."

I looked at Andy to see if all the instruments were prepared, and they were. I looked at Sergio.

"Sergio, stop bagging him for a sec. Let me check to see if he's relaxed enough."

As he did so, I attempted to position Mr. Villalobos' head in the hyperextended position. As I did this, he coughed.

Spray hit me in the face.

Panic set in, but I quelled it.

I won't die from influenza.

True, but what if...

I wiped whatever the hell Villalobos spit on me. I asked Sergio to start ventilating the patient again. I looked at Andy. As I was about to ask for the laryngoscope, I caught a special expression. He seemed to be a little disappointed, then I realized why: The adage.

He was about to give me the laryngoscope when I said, "Andy, do you want to do this one?"

He broke into a smile. "Absolutely."

We switched positions. He took the position at the head of the bed, and I took the instrument and said, "It's your call. You're the lead. Tell us what you need."

He looked at Sergio and to the rest of the staff and assessed the anatomical landmarks. He asked for the intratracheal tube, measuring the length of the tube relative to the airway to determine how far to introduce it to. I could tell that he had rehearsed this many times before, although he had never performed one prior.

He looked up, "On the count of three," he said. "One, two, three…"

Sergio stopped bagging the patient. I handed Andy the laryngoscope. Sergio, understanding what Andy needed, handed him the suction catheter. Andy introduced the laryngoscope, swept the tongue away from his line of vision, and used the suction catheter to remove any unnecessary secretions. As he did this, Mr. Villalobos coughed again. Andy quickly wiped his face, reached out for the intratracheal tube, which lay next to Villalobos' head, took it and smoothly introduced it into Mr. Villalobos' airway.

The intubation was successful. I took my stethoscope to listen to both lungs to make sure that he was adequately ventilated. I stepped away from the bed to look at the monitor. It was pure physiology. He improved the patient's ventilation, gave him supplemental oxygen, and the patient responded by incorporating that oxygen into his blood. And there it is on the monitor, his pulse oximeter now read ninety percent.

I patted Andy on the shoulder. "Good job."

I asked the nurses for a fresh set of vital signs. I wanted the blood pressure and the temperature. Mr. Villalobos' pulse was still 160 in spite of his improved oxygenation. However, he was still sedated from the Versed, so I couldn't tell whether the improved oxygenation had improved his mentation—a fancy way of saying, his confusion. I looked back up at the monitor, which now indicated blood pressure of 70 over 40. The charge nurse had taken the core temperature.

"Dr. Kroose, his temperature's 105."

As she removed the rectal temperature probe, I caught a glimpse of his legs. The rash I had forgotten for a moment was not there. I removed the sheets, lifted his hospital gown, and there was no rash anywhere else. It was only on his upper extremities and his face. I felt a cold chill and weakness beset me. I could hear the charge nurse asking in the distance something, but her voice sounded so far away.

I felt stunned.

This couldn't be. This couldn't happen.

The rash must be there. I began to examine his lower extremities. There was a gooseneck lamp next to his bed. I turned it on and shined it on his legs and his torso. There was no rash. It was only over the upper extremities and his face.

This man had smallpox. Get used to it. Just me talkin'…the Voice, remember?

I didn't want to believe it, but I had to. There was no other explanation for his presentation, his clinical course. I felt someone tugging at my scrubs, my shirt.

"Dr. Kroose, what did you want us to do about the temperature and his blood pressure?"

I was momentarily silent. Oblivion beckoned ahead of me, but I found my voice at last.

"Ten grains of Tylenol, 600 mg of Motrin, and open up the IVs. He's probably dry. And let's call Dr. Schwartz and let him know the status of his patient. He may want to get a pulmonary consultant and maybe an ID consultant."

I wanted to tell the charge nurse what my thoughts were, what the patient likely had—smallpox. I needed to share this *now* with someone, anyone at all.

But I couldn't, not yet.

I realized that we needed containment, a course of action not to let this spread. And I found myself thinking that I had to speak to Jack Kilgorn. I needed him on this, the bastard. But would he believe me after today's events? Would he even listen? I had to convince him that, against all odds, I was probably right, so he could take the necessary precautions, maybe even quarantine the hospital. I had to do something now without alarming the staff, but what?

The charge nurse approached me and asked, "Dr. Kroose, do you think his pneumonia's infectious? Should I be taking any precautions?"

What a break!

Yes, it was perfect. That's what I could tell the nurses. The patient may have an infection with an MRSA organism, that is a Methicillin Resistant *Staphylococcus Aureus* infection. It had been a problem in the hospital before. It's a bacterial organism that is resistant to almost all antibiotics and very difficult to treat. Once present in the hospital, it spreads quickly through sheets, utensils, and to every part of the facility. This would provoke the strictest of isolation protocols. It was the perfect alibi.

"Yes, I think we have to be careful," I responded to the nurse. "As you know this patient has the influenza virus, and they can become secondarily infected with *Staphylococcus Aureus* organisms. This may be a Methicillin Resistant Organism."

"You mean an MRSA infection?"

"Yes, so we're going to have to isolate the patient. Everybody's going to have to wear gloves and gowns and facemasks."

The nurse nodded in understanding. "Absolutely."

"Nobody comes into contact with him without the appropriate precautions. I don't want this getting out all over the hospital."

The nurses went about isolating Villalobos. The sliding glass door to his room in the ICU was closed. No one could get in or out without putting on the appropriate attire, gloves, gowns, head caps, facemasks, and shoe covers. I was relieved that at least this much could be done before we secured the diagnosis. But how was I going to convince Kilgorn?

How could I now convince my worst enemy in the world that we had a case of smallpox?

$$* \qquad * \qquad * \qquad *$$

Man has, for centuries, been tormented by plagues, epidemics, and pestilence, unable to prevent them or successfully combat them, only having prayer, phlebotomy, and witchery to confront these diseases. Not until the seventeenth century, with the inception of public health policy and the public health system, were they able to make inroads in the prevention and the treatment of these diseases. Something as simple as washing one's hands was discovered as preventative in the transmission of diseases, as well as clean water and eliminating stagnant water to eliminate the vectors that carry diseases such as yellow fever, dengue fever, and others. Later they realized that quarantining patients who were ill helped prevent the spread of the illnesses in the communities.

Although initially not done for altruistic reasons, but rather to protect commerce in our growing young nation and others, these new public health policies and systems served the populace well, resulting in the life spans of men and women increasing from approximately thirty years of age to eighty years.

What an irony, I thought, that there were individuals willing to use these contagions to inflict pain, suffering, and death, to reduce the life expectancy of some, and to reverse the efforts of humanity over the past several hundred years for the sole purpose of supplanting an ideology. The irony that the knowledge used to prevent disease and prolong life was now used to shorten it.

With the advent of antibiotics and vaccines in the twentieth century, further inroads were made in conquering almost all infectious diseases to such an extent that now efforts in preventative medicine focused more on preventing cancer and heart disease and less on infectious diseases.

However, one of man's greatest accolades, so we thought, was the eradication of smallpox. The smallpox vaccine was used over two centuries to ultimately corral, corner, and eradicate it in 1980. How were we to know that in man's great capacity to rationalize evil over good that we would come to the conclusion that saving the final strains of smallpox was in humanity's best interest, knowing very well that there are those in this world who would exploit that weakness giving rise to by the elimination of smallpox—that weakness being the lack of immunity of humanity to the variola virus which causes smallpox.

And this is because, since the eradication of smallpox in 1980, there had been no smallpox vaccinations given to the general public, and there had been no epidemics because few of us, if not all of us, had no protection against smallpox if it were to reappear. The irony is in the fact that as a result of the eradication of smallpox, we found ourselves in a more perilous set of circumstances.

4:45 PM

Matt and Andy helped the nurses in caring for Villalobos and setting up the isolation protocols. I communicated with Dr. Schwartz, who was, as usual, even after today's political brawls *not* in his favor, a renewed pain in the ass.

"Why wasn't I called earlier?" he asked.

"This is the earliest any definitive information could be passed on to you, Maynard. Okay?"

"So you say."

However, he did thank me, albeit grudgingly, for taking care of his patient. I also suggested a pulmonary and an infectious diseases consult.

"I don't mind the pulmonary consult, but why an ID man?"

"Just to cover all the bases, Maynard. This fellow is from overseas, who knows where he's been or what he's been up to. Simple precautions from a guy who used to dabble in ID work himself."

"Oh, yeah. Right. You did that. I remember."

He thought about it for a minute. Then, true to his prickish personality, he said curtly, "Nah, we don't need the ID. But you're right about containment. Thanks, Max."

Click. The phone disengaged.

So now Schwartz had his revenge.

I was beyond anger at this point. I was now entering the fuzzy, warm waters of leg-shaking terror. I began to think of what strategy I should follow to confirm the diagnosis that I suspected.

I needed Glen Hamilton, and I needed him now.

I called his office directly, and they told me he was out. I left a message, and then called his message service, my hands trembling as I held the phone. Again, only the service engaged.

Shit.

I left a message nonetheless to call me. Because I realized his was a high-security system, I did not leave details as to the nature of the call. I defined it as an emergency. I knew that would get his attention. It still left me up shit's creek in terms of other matters.

If Kilgorn failed me—and odds were goose eggs to gum drops he would—I needed a backup plan. I could not just order the appropriate studies—the viral cultures on chick embryo yolks or the electron microscopic studies of oral or nasal swabs. There were no quick serologic assays or screens for variola available, although these were recommended by a consensus statement in *The Journal of the American Medical Association* in an issue in 1999.

These studies had to be ordered by an infectious diseases doctor.

And, although I was an infectious diseases physician, my status in the hospital was that of an emergency room doctor. I was not credentialed as an infectious diseases doctor and, therefore, I could not order these myself. Therein lay the dilemma.

So I would circumvent Kilgorn's authority and get an ID man myself—and fuck my career. But I figured, if this was smallpox, we could kiss it all good-bye, and pretty soon at that.

Who was on-call for infectious diseases? I wondered.

The name came to me a split second later. William Jenner. I knew him well. I had a good chance of convincing him. He knew my credentials. But this was Friday, and it is hard getting consultants in on Fridays. However, that was a problem down the road...

Matt, Andy, and I set out to get back to the emergency room. I took the stairs. They noticed that I was in a hurry. As we got to the door to the stairway, while catching his breath, Andy put his hand on my shoulder to slow me down. "Dr. Kroose."

I turned to him—and he looked at me with frank eyes.

"Now, I know you don't think that was MRSA."

The kid was good, and he'd learned a year's worth of experience today. Tragically, I feared his knowledge would continue to grow exponentially.

"If Mr. Villalobos has a staphylococcal infection, which he may well have, he didn't acquire it in the hospital. It would be community-acquired. There is little chance of it being MRSA."

I could not immediately respond, my mind a whirl of options. I did not know whether I should divulge what I was thinking, but I had to at some point. If, in fact, this was smallpox, he was involved, Matt was involved, and all my medical staff was inextricably—and inescapably involved.

Matt jumped into the conversation. "Yeah, Dr. Kroose, in all the years I've worked in the emergency room, I've never seen a patient suffering from influenza virus his age die. Sure, if he had AIDS, but otherwise I think that would be very unusual."

I found my tongue at last. "You're right, and based on the social history I was able to get from him, I don't think he has AIDS. But that's yet to be seen. The AIDS studies won't be back for a day."

"So what gives, Dr. Kroose?" Matt asked.

I remained silent again. It was Andy who let the cat out of the bag.

"You think he has smallpox." It wasn't a question, either. Andy had guessed my worst fear.

I took a breath and looked out a window.

Andy pushed on. "I saw you examine him for the rash he had. I noticed the same thing. He had it only over his face and upper extremities."

They both had read me right. I would remind myself never to play poker with these guys; my ability to bluff was about as effective as a neutered bull. Thus, I had to tell them. I couldn't have them discussing this with other people—with the rest of the staff—before I was sure. Or at least before I could convince the administrator or the infectious diseases doctor to do the appropriate studies so we could make a definitive diagnosis or rule it out.

I threw the door of the stairwell open and pushed the two of them through. I then closed the door and leaned against it, making sure no one would try to pass through. It was more private there. I could have my conversation with them in confidence.

"Okay," I said, "you're both right. I think this patient has smallpox, but I can't prove it. It's an atypical presentation. Who's going to believe me? The dilemma is I can't order the studies that will prove it one way or the other."

Andy paused for a second. He began to appreciate my problem. "But you seem sure of it. Why?"

I bit my tongue momentarily.

Well, Andy, I consulted my alien leaders on NaNoo NaNoo, and they passed on to me the wisdom of the ancients. Sugar, spice, everything nice, including puppy dog tails, all leading me to believe…

"It's a gut feeling," I surrendered at last.

Andy almost smiled at that.

Matt nodded in understanding. "That's why you didn't want us to call the police about the gun. This place would be swarming with cops, there'd be questions and…"

He paused and said through a whisper: "And possible exposure that could not be properly contained."

I nodded. "It was another gut feeling. I was looking at the worst-case scenario that this might be smallpox, and a strain that we know nothing about, where police after their investigation could leave this hospital and further spread…" I did not finish.

Andy pestered me about the gun threat, and I filled him in briefly. He considered me for another moment.

"A gut feeling."

The answer momentarily defied his understanding and practice of modern conventional medicine. For a second, he looked at me as if I was suddenly given to healing people using the Force.

I tried to help him. "Well, it started as a gut feeling, but there were other things, not medically related, which disturbed me."

"Like what?" Matt asked.

"Like the language he was muttering, even half out of his mind. Don't tell me that was fucking Spanish. If he's Spanish, I'm Darth Vader."

Matt looked at me, his face brightening. "You're right. I remember that now."

"Oh," I said, "and what about his carrying a gun and trying to kill us?"

"So?" Andy said, playing devil's advocate. "It proves nothing. He was a wacko who carried a gun."

Matt frowned. "He's an Arab. That's it." Then he looked to me, new horror dawning on his face. "Oh, sweet bleeding Jesus, you think he's a…"

I interrupted his chain of thought. "You've heard the rumors that smallpox is believed to exist in Iraq or Iran. Is it just a coincidence? The other thing, this man is prostrated. Very few illnesses cause prostration in a young man like him. Not only is he prostrated, but, in a day and a half, he's moribund."

I let that settle for a moment. Then: "Yes, I believe this is an *atypical* presentation of smallpox. Something we've not seen before."

Silence.

Andy nodded, though his expression was numb. "At Fort Dietrick, I read a book about smallpox in its various presentations. It was called…"

"*Smallpox* by C. W. Dixon," I said.

"Yeah," Andy said. "It's a pretty extensive review of smallpox in its various presentations."

I continued. "Right. I recall reading a description of a particularly aggressive form or strain of smallpox. He referred to it as "sledgehammer smallpox" or "malignant smallpox." Patients affected with this type of smallpox tend not to develop a typical rash, and it may have been because they succumb to the disease over a short period of time. He describes that many of these patients died within a day and a half. What was also peculiar about these cases is that these patients appeared to be relatively well, presenting with flu-like syndromes, and then suddenly, precipitously deteriorating and dying within hours. Now, Mr. Villalobos has been sick for just over a day, twenty-four hours. Now he is moribund. It's too coincidental for me to ignore. Now, you may argue that this is a relatively rare form of smallpox, and you would be absolutely right. So, if smallpox were to reoccur, why would it be this rare form? And that would be a good point, if it weren't for the fact that if it reoccurs, it would probably not be a naturally occurring epidemic of smallpox."

"Not a naturally occurring epidemic of smallpox," Andy repeated, still not fully understanding the implications.

"No," I said slowly. "It would be perpetrated, and the perpetrators are not going to release the most benign form of smallpox. They're probably going to do quite the contrary…"

"A terrorist," Matt said, more a whisper. "A goddamn terrorist. Son of a bitch."

Andy was stroking his hair back several times. He looked at me. "What are we going to do? I'm beginning to believe in your hunch. And, if you're right, this is a catastrophe in the making. And what about all those influenza patients we've seen earlier? Many of them had a rash. I didn't quite pay attention to the distribution. What if these were similar cases?"

"I thought of that myself, Andy, but I hope not. We will find out in the next twenty-four hours if we begin to see some more patients with Mr. Villalobos' presentation. But let's not get ahead of ourselves. We have to disprove or prove that Villalobos has smallpox. If this is smallpox, then timing is of the essence, because there is only a short window of opportunity of about four days for us to get vaccinated to be protected against this virus.

"Why do you think that, Dr. Kroose?" Andy asked.

"Because if the virus has an incubation period of about twelve days, then we have to be vaccinated within the first four days of being exposed to the virus to give our bodies enough time to respond to the vaccine and be protected against the bastard. Beyond that time, our bodies may not respond to the vaccine, and we may not be protected."

"Holy shit!" Matt exclaimed. "Well, let's find out one way or the other. Let's get this done!"

"If it's a more virulent form of smallpox, is the incubation period going to be any shorter?" Andy asked.

"No, Andy, I don't think so," I said, but the question bothered me on some primal level. I was guessing now based on my existing knowledge. "I think the incubation periods are about the same. The range is between four and seventeen days but, on the average, it's about twelve days. So I think we're pretty safe with that number."

"Well, in that case, it's not only us at stake. It's the rest of this community. Or, for that matter, the rest of this country," Andy said.

"You're right, Andy. That's why timing is of the essence. If we can establish that this is a case of smallpox, they will begin vaccinating the entire American public."

I was giving my friends a lot of information, life-changing information.

And hard to digest.

"What can we do?" Andy asked at length.

"Andy, you understand my dilemma," I said. "It's important that you do."

"Dilemma?" Matt hissed. "Fuck the dilemma. Just talk to them. Make 'em understand what's going on here."

"Matt, it's not that easy. I have to *convince* them, and I don't have much to convince them with right now other than a hunch. And who's gonna believe my hunch?"

"So what are we going to do?" Matt eased up.

"I'm going to talk to Kilgorn. If I can get him to approve the appropriate studies, we can confirm or rule out the diagnosis. If that fails, I have to talk to an infectious diseases doctor and convince him that this is a possible case of smallpox and get *him* to order the appropriate studies. Then we can nip this in the bud."

Andy and Matt considered the options, and both nodded. "I guess that's it then," Andy said. "Boy, did I pick a day to hang out with you, Max."

"What happened to 'sir' and 'Dr. Kroose?'" I smiled.

However, Andy's thoughts had turned inward. I knew he was disturbed. He'd be stupid not to be.

"Andy," I said, "if you can buy me some time—see whatever problems come to the emergency room. I'm going to get a hold of the administrator and talk to him. If there are any cases that are complicated, just leave them for me. I'll take care of those. But until we're sure, I don't want you guys to talk to anybody about this. We really don't want to create a panic. There is nothing anybody else can do until we're sure what the diagnosis is. Then we can tell everyone."

I looked to each man. Matt nodded. "Fuckin' A. Smallpox. Cock-sucking smallpox."

Amen to that, I thought.

$$*\qquad*\qquad*\qquad*$$

Andy, Matt, and myself descended down the stairs into the emergency room. Andy continued to see patients, while Matt assisted the nurses. Norma was wondering what had taken us so long. I explained to her the gravity of Mr. Villalobos' condition. I asked Jamie to get a hold of Kilgorn for me and to pass the call back to the doctors' room where I could have a private conversation with him.

I then went back to the doctors' room to think about how I would approach Kilgorn about this dilemma given our current warm and fuzzy relationship of kill, kill, kill. I remembered thinking had I not had that conversation with Jack earlier that morning, discussing smallpox with him now wouldn't seem so strained. I didn't really think he'd believe me, and I was sure he would tell me to go blow myself; he would look at it as my paranoia about smallpox continuing, and he'd enjoy the moment of having me by the balls. That was the probable best-case scenario. However, the cards already had been dealt that I had to work with. I would just have to tell him what I thought and *why* I thought it and rely on the fact that he knew what my expertise was. That should be enough to raise a level of concern in his mind to allow me to perform the appropriate studies. If it didn't, fuck him. I would go find my ID man.

The intercom buzzer blared out, disrupting my thoughts. I picked up the phone. It was Jamie. "Dr. Kroose, the administrator left early today. He had an important dinner engagement. Would you like me to page him?"

"Yeah. I need to talk to him now. Do you have his pager?"

"No, Dr. Kroose. I'm talking to Katy. I have her on the other line."

"Just tell Katy I need to talk to him. It's an emergency. Use those words. She'll page him for me."

"Okay, Dr. Kroose, I'll try."

I hung up the phone and watched the light, which was the line Jamie was using to talk to Katy. A few seconds later, it turned off.

I leaned back in the chair and closed my eyes. I found something wet on my cheek. I realized it was a tear.

My God, I thought. *I'm so afraid.*

I thought of my children. Their play tonight. I might not be able to keep my promise and see them later—or see them at all, if this thing got to the quarantine stage.

Worse, I might not see them forever.

"No," I said to myself. "No, it's not going down that way. It can't happen."

I embraced the big picture impossibility of our little hospital having a verifiable case of smallpox…something that hasn't existed on the planet in nature for twentysome-odd years. This would all go away, have to. I had wrapped myself up into a stupor on the subject, what with happened this morning, my talk with Glen, my own silly conviction that I had a gut hunch, a Voice.

"Nonsense," I chuckled. Yeah, this was a good case of Dr. Kroose temporarily goes nutszoid paranoid. It happens to good doctors all the time. Hell, most of us are closet alcoholics. My vice of choice was smallpox under the bed, lurking, ready to strike.

The buzzer on my phone pulled me out of my private reverie.

"Dr. Kroose, I have Mr. Kilgorn on the line," Jamie said.

I picked up the phone.

"Called to apologize, Max?" Kilgorn said before I even had a chance to utter one word. "Or called to try to save your career by cutting a deal?"

What was the word Matt used for smallpox earlier? *Cock sucker.*

I sucked in a breath. "Jack, how are you doing?"

"Well, fine, Max, until you had Katy shove a foot up my ass by way of a page to call the high and mighty Kroose with an emergency. Boy, this better be good. I have a dinner engagement in about twenty minutes, and I'm not ready yet."

"I have a serious problem here."

"What kind of problem?"

"I have this patient that I admitted earlier. He came in with a fever and a rash. I admitted him to the ICU a few hours ago, but he has deteriorated. He has developed respiratory failure, and I had to intubate him just a few minutes ago. I talked to Dr. Schwartz and recommended an infectious diseases consult."

"What's the problem?" Kilgorn asked obtusely. This was my fault—Kilgorn wasn't an MD, he couldn't grasp the details I was throwing at him.

"I think this patient has smallpox."

There was a pause on the other side of the phone, then a contemptuous laugh. "Boy, you are a piece of work, Max."

"No. I'm serious. I think this patient has smallpox."

"I don't believe you, but I'll bite. Forget about the coincidence of our talk and the meeting tonight with the committee. Why do you believe he has smallpox?"

"Because of his presentation."

"Does he have the pustular rash that you described this morning?"

I had to give Kilgorn credit on this. He must have listened to something I said regarding rashes and such.

"No, he doesn't."

"He doesn't."

"No. He doesn't have the pustular rash. That's the dilemma. If he had this, I could get the infectious diseases doctor down to verify the diagnosis and order the appropriate studies to get the Public Health Services involved. But…"

Kilgorn cut me off. "Well then, why do you think he has smallpox, Max?"

"Because of his presentation."

"You said that. What do you mean, his presentation?"

"Because this patient presents as a flu-like syndrome with a rash that only appears over his upper extremities as well as his face. It's not the typical pustular rash, but it is a distribution that is characteristic of smallpox."

"Yeah, Max. I thought it was the pustular rash that was characteristic."

Give a little bit of knowledge to someone ignorant on a particular subject, and you've got a real mess on your hands. I would always follow my gut on this in the future.

If I had a future, that is.

However, I pushed on.

"That is a classic presentation of smallpox. This would be an atypical presentation of smallpox."

"I don't know, Max. It sounds like you're on thin ice here. Have you talked to the ID doctor?"

"No. I'm following protocol and chain of command by calling you first."

"That's who I think you need to talk to. If you can convince him that it's smallpox, then we need to alert the hospital and Public Health."

"Yeah, Jack, but I was wondering whether you'd allow me to order the appropriate laboratory studies?"

"Max, even if I didn't think you were full of shit on this, and I do, by the way…I can't do that. We have a strict protocol. You know that. All these bioterrorist infectious agents need to be handled by the infectious diseases doctor who will then communicate with Public Health."

Kilgorn was good. Policy protocol mantra.

Fucker.

"Well, there may be a problem."

"What would that be, Max?"

"Convincing him."

"Max, you're not suggesting that I should put everybody on alert, call Public Health, and have the hospital quarantined on a hunch, do you?"

"Yeah, Jack, that's exactly what needs to be done, and fast."

"Based on your hunch?" He let that hang for a second. "Now you listen to me, doctor. I don't want you to tell anyone else in the hospital that you have a possible smallpox case unless the ID doc concurs with your opinion."

"Jack," I pleaded, "time is of the essence. Don't fuck me on this. Fuck my job if you want, but…"

"Time is of the essence," Jack said easily, sensing the desperation in my voice. "So you better get on the phone and talk to the ID guy and have him call me if he feels it's a smallpox case."

My heart sank, and time was slipping away from me.

Jack's tone shifted; the consummate politician as always. "Max, I don't mean to be rude, really. Although we had a bad day, I think you're a great doc, and I know you know your stuff. But if there is one thing I took away from our meeting this morning, it is that you're passionate about this disease and its prevention. You work long hours, perhaps you're under some kind of duress."

Mentally fatigued was the implication. Kilgorn, you unbelievably arrogant bastard. You're playing with fire here…

"Give yourself a break, Max. Call the ID doctor and have him go over the case with you. Now I gotta get goin.'"

Mother Fucker.

"Okay, Jack. I'll call the ID doc."

I hung up the phone. Then, instantaneously, I suddenly felt drained of anger or despair, even terror.

For the moment, I only thought of Leana.

5:30 PM

After my conversation with Kilgorn, I momentarily began to feel a little reticent about the diagnosis I had made. Perhaps I was overreacting, and Mr. Villalobos did not have smallpox, but rather a case of influenza, and was one of those individuals who unfortunately dies from the disease. He was right. I was walking on thin ice, and there was no reason to create panic and community hysteria about the presence of smallpox. But, on the other hand, I felt uneasy about not doing anything. I needed more convincing classical lesions to make my case. Otherwise, it would take an act of faith on anyone's part to believe that, in fact, this was a case of smallpox. And classical lesions I didn't have.

The emergency room begins to get busy as it usually does at 5:30 with people getting off work, rushing home and, in their haste, involving themselves in motor vehicle accidents. I would get a rash of those by 5:30, 6 o'clock. Then there are all those individuals with lingering illnesses who want to be taken care of Friday evenings so that they can enjoy the recreation on the weekend. It is as though all that is required is a visit to the doctor, an injection, and, poof, you're well and ready to enjoy a sunny day in California.

Andy was being a great help. He had seen most of the cases, which were flu-like syndromes—some with a rash, some without. With each new case of influenza, we wondered if it was truly influenza and not smallpox, but we couldn't do anything else other than treat them as influenza cases. If we only had a rapid screen like urinalysis that could be done in thirty minutes to identify those individuals with smallpox, this would be but a trivial task. Although this was recommended several years ago, not one of the appropriate institutions—the CDC or the NIH—developed a quick assay for smallpox. So our anxiety about smallpox grew with every case we saw with flu-like syndrome.

Matt was obviously affected by our conversation earlier. He seemed to be very quiet. The nurses noticed that. His head hung down somewhat. He was probably thinking of his family and whether he was exposed, as was Andy. He talked to me at the bedside of one of the patients I was seeing. "So, Dr. Kroose, is anything new?"

"No, Matt, not yet. I'm workin' on it."

He only nodded and closed his eyes.

I took care of some of the more complicated motor vehicle accidents, while Andy took care of the influenza cases, minor cuts, and bruises. Luckily, most of the cases were simple, easy to disposition. I hesitated to ask Jamie to call Dr. Jenner. I wanted to think about how far to take this.

Matt, Andy, and I met in the nurses' lounge to have a cup of coffee. The nurses found it a little peculiar that the three of us were congregating so often.

Andy inquired about my conversation with the administrator as he was drinking his coffee. "How did it go with the administrator? Did you get him to order the studies?"

"No. He didn't believe me."

"What? What do you mean he didn't believe you?"

Matt was intently listening.

"He thinks I'm on thin ice. He says he won't do anything unless the infectious diseases doctor concurs with my diagnosis."

"Dr. Kroose, this doesn't sound good. I'm as nervous as a long-tailed cat in a room full of rocking chairs. I feel like crying every other minute. What the fuck do we do next?"

"I have to talk to the infectious diseases doctor now."

Betty walked into the nurses' lounge, and so our conversation ceased. She walked over to the coffeepot to grab a cup and then looked at all of us. "So what are the boys doing? Why are you guys meeting so often? Are you planning a military takeover of the hospital?"

At that point, we heard over the intercom, "Code Blue, ICU. Code Blue, ICU. Code Blue, ICU."

*   *   *   *

All three of us suddenly stood up. I looked over at Andy. "Andy, take care of the emergency room while I go see what's going on. Betty, Matt, come with me. I need your help."

As the emergency room physician, I am responsible for all Code Blues. We have a routine in responding to these codes. We have our own paraphernalia that we take up with us, knowing that most of the wards and the ICU do not have the paraphernalia that we may need. Betty instinctively bolted for the crash cart and grabbed a tackle box, which had all the equipment I would need. She, Matt, and I began to move quickly for the ICU on the fourth floor. The security guard had the elevator waiting for us on the first floor as we came out of the rear door of the emergency room.

While on the elevator, I was trying to recall what cases were in the ICU and what I may have to do. I had not gotten any calls from any of the admitting physicians telling me about their patients, so I had to presume this was an unexpected deterioration of a patient in the ICU. Who could it be? The only one that was moribund was Mr. Villalobos.

We got up to the fourth floor and headed to the ICU. We could see through the glass windows and doors all the nurses hurrying and busy around one of the beds. Sergio was there already. All the nurses and Sergio were wearing caps, face-masks, gloves, gowns, and shoe covers. It was Mr. Villalobos. He had taken a turn for the worse.

I looked at the charge nurse. "What's going on?"

"Mr. Villalobos, the patient you intubated earlier. I can't get a blood pressure on him. He's got a rhythm but no pulse."

Sergio was taking him off the respirator and was bagging him to make sure that he was adequately ventilating. What the nurse was telling me in certain terms was that Mr. Villalobos was dying or dead. Even though the cardiac monitor revealed a rhythm of cardiac electrical activity, the heart was not pumping. His infection was overwhelming him, and this is what happens when your body is overwhelmed by an infection.

I went up to Mr. Villalobos and felt for a carotid pulse. I placed my index finger on his neck. Zip, nada. I placed my index finger on his groin area, and there was no femoral pulse.

I looked at Matt. "Start CPR."

Sergio looked to me, "Well, doc, you can't win them all."

He was right. I had not lost a case in I don't know how long. However, no one could understand the consequences of this one. His death may have been the beginning of a bio-Hiroshima. It wasn't just Mr. Villalobos' death we were trying to prevent; it was the deaths of many more that were at stake.

I looked at Betty. "Let's give him a milligram of epinephrine and then rig him for IV fluids wide open."

I could see the apprehension in Matt's eyes as he gave vigorous external cardiac massage. He did not want Mr. Villalobos to die. He was hanging on to the possibility that I was wrong, and I shared that hope.

Something wicked this way comes...so speaks the Voice...so speaks the Gut.

We were losing the battle.

In the ensuing twenty minutes, he not only was breathless and had no pulse, but he also had no cardiac electrical activity. We pronounced him dead at five to six.

I looked at Villalobos, his eyes wide open, the intubation tube in his mouth. That goddamned rash was still all over his face and upper extremities. Nothing had developed over the torso or the lower extremities. However, as I closely looked at the rash, I could see small vesiculations over the red-based spots. If there were any doubt or reticence about what I should do, it all dissipated at that very second.

For now, I was sure that this was smallpox. The hunch-factor was now bona fide. It was bad, bad news. The vesiculations were the little blisters that developed before the pustules appear in smallpox. Unfortunately, Villalobos did not live long enough to manifest the classic pustular skin lesion. I asked the charge nurse for an ophthalmoscope to take a better look. With the magnifying lens and the light that is provided in the ophthalmoscope, it was possible to see the lesions better.

Yeah, I said to myself, *vesiculation blisters, no doubt about it.* Small, but larger than a dewdrop, there were only a few.

"Hey, doc," Sergio said. "Interesting skin rash, huh? It seems like everybody has it. Is this an influenza thing?"

"No, Sergio," I said softly, hearing my voice crack.

He looked at me, puzzled. Matt, who was standing next to us, began to hyper-ventilate. I've never seen Matt do this before. He was a pretty rugged individual, but the thought of contracting smallpox—well, I couldn't blame him.

Sergio looked up at Matt, patted him on the back. "Hey, big guy, you did your best. Sometimes this happens."

"Fuck you...you don't have a clue...not a fuckin'..."

I pulled Matt aside as he began to gain his composure again and looked straight into his eyes. "Matt, we're going to be okay. We'll take care of this."

Matt hissed back at me. "We haven't taken care of shit, man. We're screwed. Game over, fucked. Tell me I'm wrong, doc. Go ahead, tell me."

Sergio overheard us but didn't say anything.

"Matt," I said slowly, "please take the tackle box back down to the emergency room and help the other nurses. Tell Andy what happened."

I held his gaze. Matt took a few deep breaths and then looked at Sergio, who was looking immensely uncomfortable with this little scene. Matt nodded, and I released him.

I went back to the charge nurse to sign off on the Code Blue sheet, which we are required to do, per procedure. I then tried communicating with Dr. Schwartz to inform him of Mr. Villalobos' condition. He was apparently out having dinner and didn't want to be bothered. And now, with Villalobos' death, he wouldn't worry about being bothered throughout the night about an unstable patient. As she was talking to Dr. Schwartz, the nurse was filling out the paperwork. She needed to send the body to the morgue. I could hear her ask what the cause of death was, and I saw as she wrote down on the line labeled "immediate cause of death." She wrote down "*staphylococcal auerus* infection," and on the line labeled "due to," she wrote "influenza."

And this is how Mr. Villalobos' death would be recorded; no mention of smallpox.

Yet, if he did indeed have the disease, the most horrifying question inevitably rose its ugly head.

How many individuals, aside from my staff and those personnel in ICU, had he already infected?

✳   ✳   ✳   ✳

I felt chills pass through my body—a mind-numbingly cold, vice-like flush course through me as I realized that I was most likely infected and so were all my nurses. I had to get back down to the emergency room and talk to the ID doc.

Betty and I took off our gowns, facemasks, hair caps, and shoe covers and headed back down to the emergency room. As we got to the elevator, Betty asked, "Why was Matt so anxious? What was wrong with him? He's not normally this way. Did he know Mr. Villalobos personally?"

"No, Betty. He's just had a hard day. Who knows what goes on in an individual's life?"

We got onto the elevator and descended down to the emergency room while she continued the conversation with me. "Dr. Kroose, what have you three been up to?"

"Just taking care of patients, Betty."

"Why all those private conversations?"

"What private conversations?" I bluffed.

"Doctor, I'm a pretty observant girl."

"I could tell you it's none of your business."

Betty gave me a strange look. Of course, she'd never heard me talk like this before. I felt instantly dreadful.

"Sorry. I'm just being a little nosy," she said at last.

I looked to her and sighed. "Look, I'll tell you what, Betty. I *will* tell you before the end of your shift. And…it's very much your business."

She looked up at me and smiled, but there was a frightened tint in her eyes. I couldn't return the smile.

I could only turn away in shame.

*   *   *   *

Andy was taking care of business down in the emergency room. When I got there, there were only a couple of cases that hadn't been seen. I signed off on all his charts and went directly to Jamie and asked her to call Dr. Jenner. Matt seemed to calm down quite a bit by this time. Betty seemed to be appeased by what I told her in the elevator and didn't raise the issue again. I helped Andy take care of the last few cases that came in.

Luckily, the pace of the ER had slowed, and I was able to head back to the doctors' room. I laid down on the bed. I was only an arm's length away from the phone on the desk and wondered about how I would convince Bill Jenner that Villalobos had smallpox.

The buzzer sounded off.

It was Jamie telling me that the flashing light on line one was Dr. Jenner returning my call. I punched a button down and picked up the phone.

"Bill, thanks for getting back to me."

"Max. How ya doin'? It's good to hear from you. Got any good stock tips?" He and I would often talk about investments we had made. We were always ready to give each other advice on which stocks to buy, which to sell, and stocks from which to stay away. Not that it made any difference in our portfolios. We all lost quite a bit at the end of the day.

And we were about to lose everything unless a lot of things went very right, very, very soon.

"Bill. I have a case here that I want to chat with you about."

"Well, I'm in the middle of..."

"I'm sorry for any interruption, but this can't wait."

"Okay, Max, shoot."

"It's a patient that I admitted earlier; a young man in his thirties who came in with a flu-like syndrome. He had a fever of about 105. Pulse oximetry was low. It turned out that he had pneumonia, but he developed a peculiar rash and that's why I'm callin' ya."

"It sounds like influenza. You typically get infections. And the most common cause of pneumonia in these patients is probably staphylococcal aureus."

"I know that, but he died."

"Jesus, Max. Pretty aggressive virus."

"We put him on antibiotics, Bill, but he didn't improve. I intubated him a few hours ago, and he continued to deteriorate. I just pronounced him a few minutes ago."

"Okay. So it sounds like a simple open-and-shut case."

"Bill," I said, taking a huge breath. "I don't think he had the influenza virus."

"What do you think he had?"

I took another measured breath.

"I think he had smallpox."

Bill didn't immediately respond.

"Let me tell you why, Bill," I said softly.

I then described the presentations, the rash—not pustular but macular—and finally the vesiculations.

"Max," he said, "maybe it was the chicken pox."

"Bill, how many patients die from the chicken pox? Unless he was immuno-suppressed, it's not something you find."

"Look, everything you've told me smacks of influenza. There can be atypical presentations of the influenza virus." He sounded a bit defensive.

"Yeah, but this rash was over his face and upper extremities. He had none over his legs or torso. And this is typically where variola, or smallpox, initially begins. Perhaps he died before he could manifest the classic pustular rash in the classic distribution."

This gave Jenner a pause. I could hear him sigh on the other end.

"Yeah, Max. It's possible, but so far-fetched."

I expected this response at some point. Smallpox, the "dead disease" for two decades, now risen from the grave to eat once again from the living. Right.

"Bill, I would like you to see the patient. Or rather, I'd like you to examine the corpse."

"Right now, Max?"

"I think it is important to determine whether, in fact, you agree with me or not."

"Can you hold for a minute, Max?"

"Sure."

I could hear some bickering on the other end. A few seconds passed, maybe ten, maybe twenty. To me, whole planetary systems could have formed out of the void in that time. Bill finally got back on the line.

"Sorry."

"It's okay. So?"

"Well, I can tell you Max that I don't have any reasons to suspect smallpox from what you've told me. It sounds like the influenza virus or some other type of viral exanthema. Many viruses cause rashes. Smallpox hasn't been seen in more than twenty-five years. In this country, more than fifty years, so I think it's a little far-fetched to contemplate the diagnosis. And I'm sure not gonna go out on the limb even writing it down in my differential diagnosis. From what you've told me, it's not a plausible diagnosis."

"Bill, I'd just like you to take a look at the lesions, the rash. I think you'd be more convinced."

"I don't think so, Max. Besides, I'm having dinner, and if I do this to my wife—I've done it on three other occasions—I'll never hear the end of it. But I'll tell you what I'll do. Out of courtesy to you, I'll drop by in the morning and take a look at the body."

"Bill, the body may not be here by morning time. The morgue has already been called."

"That's the best I can do, Max."

"Bill, Jesus Christ, listen to me. Only you can order the appropriate studies."

"You mean the viral cultures and electron microscopy? I'll have to call the Public Health for that—the CDC. With what you've told me, there's no way I'm gonna convince them to do that. It requires special procedures to obtain the samples, and then they have to be sent down to Atlanta for processing. And do you know what kind of panic that would create? I mean, the news media would probably get a hold of this before the samples were obtained. No, no, I can't give those orders."

I could not fucking believe what I was hearing. I suddenly thought the whole world was conspiring against me on this.

"Bill, please."

"No, Max. I'll see the patient in the morning. I'll talk to you tomorrow."

And then he was gone.

*   *   *   *

I felt utterly defeated.

I felt my last chance for avoiding a catastrophe had slipped away. Sure, I could go to the Public Health, but their response would probably be no better than Bill's. They would probably be just as dismissive. They might even call Kilgorn and say that he had an ER doctor who should be knitting baby booties in a pretty room for about six months due to fatigue rather than practicing medicine.

Still, I had nothing to lose.

I called the CDC.

Some young girl answered. "Hello, CDC Physicians' Hot Line." I told her the story and the physical findings. As I described the case, I could hear her rustle through the papers.

"Sir, let me put you on hold while I confer with my colleagues."

A few seconds later, she was back on the line.

"I can give you the Rash Line number."

They have a Rash Line number? Was she joking?

I called that number, and there was a recording. So much for homeland defense. I felt helpless. Who would believe me? Who would believe that this was a case of smallpox? Who would believe that Mr. Villalobos had died from anything other than the influenza virus?

I tried Glen Hamilton one last time.

6:15 PM

I glanced at my watch as I waited for Jamie to patch me through to Glen's various numbers.

The kids were going to be so disappointed in dad, I thought. Clearly, there was no way I was going to get to their play. I made a mental note to call Esmerelda after my talk with Glen and then realized that by the time that happened, they would already be off to the school theater.

Someone knocked on the door. Andy popped his head into the room. "Dr. Kroose, can we talk to you?"

He and Matt didn't wait for my reply. They both walked in, closing the door behind them.

"Andy, do you think it's wise for you guys to be back here? What are the other nurses going to think?"

"Don't worry about that Dr. Kroose," Andy said. "They're all in the nurses' lounge, having a little coffee or watching the tube or getting ready for the end of the shift at 7:30."

"So they don't know that the two of you are back here?"

"No, they think I'm in the library."

"Yeah, I told them I was going to take a piss. What's the word, doc?"

I looked at Matt, then to Andy. I shook my head.

"No word."

"Did you talk to the infectious diseases doctor?" Andy asked.

"Yes, I did. And he wouldn't buy the story."

"What do you mean he wouldn't buy the story?"

"He feels that Mr. Villalobos had the influenza virus and probably died from that."

"Oh, fuck me," Matt groaned.

"Look, guys, I know this sounds like some kind of Greek tragedy, but Bill didn't even want to come in. And he won't order the studies."

"Aw, man," Matt continued to moan to himself.

"And," I added, "more bad news. They declared COD as influenza, with a secondary *staphylococcal aureus* infection."

"Jesus Christ," Matt whispered. "This guy will be buried and will be the inception of an impending smallpox epidemic, and the first clue will be buried with him."

"Okay, okay," Matt said, trying to rally. "This is smallpox. We're all exposed. What are we going to tell the other nurses? I mean, they have to know."

"Matt, I haven't established a diagnosis."

"Fuck diagnosis. Let's just tell everybody it's smallpox."

"If we do that, what do you think the response is going to be? They're gonna think I'm crazy. They're not going to order the studies, they'll trivialize what we have said, and nothing will be done. We will be right where we are right now, and any attempts we make to establish the diagnosis will be met with a lot of resistance. There is a reason why smallpox was misdiagnosed during the Aral Sea Seaport outbreak. Smallpox didn't present typically. In many cases, it presented like the measles or an allergic reaction. And there was obviously some reticence in committing to the diagnosis with an atypical presentation of smallpox. So what happened is the epidemic progressed until either there was a case of the typical smallpox rash or patients were dying unexpectedly from a virus."

"What outbreak are you referring to, Dr. Kroose?" Andy asked, curiosity momentarily replacing fear.

"In 1971, the Russians divulged that there was an outbreak of smallpox. It was thought to be an outbreak beginning from an accidental exposure of a shipmate in the Aral Sea to the release of a weaponized form of smallpox from one of their bioweapons laboratories. That epidemic progressed undetected and misdiagnosed for thirty days, killing everyone it infected who was not immunized. The only way it was contained at that point was with the military, in essence, laying siege to the city or the countryside. They quarantined the entire area and then subsequently vaccinated the entire population. If this is one of the first cases of smallpox, we will be lucky to convince anyone that it is smallpox given its atypical presentation. That's what we're up against. If we don't make the diagnosis, it may be several days before the diagnosis is made. And, if that is the case, many more patients, many more individuals, may die."

"Yeah, like us," Matt said with disgust.

"Guys, I have a call into Glen Hamilton. I'm waiting for a return."

"Right, Hamilton," Andy said with renewed hope. "He's our only chance now."

I explained to Matt who Glen was, and he also brightened.

"But, Matt, you're right about the nurses," I said. "We need to tell them. The question is when. Let me talk to Glen first. Then we'll decide."

Andy and Matt left the room with the understanding that we would talk after I had spoke to my friend…in essence, our only hope for immediate salvation.

I lay back down, turned the light off, and began to think about Villalobos. He came in coughing. I was sure he was infectious. How many people had he infected? With the bouts of coughing and the viral particles expelled with each cough, I was sure this entire emergency room was contaminated or, for that matter, a good part of the hospital, if not the entire hospital. We know how the smallpox virus is passed on from floor to floor through the air duct system. There was a good chance that many in the hospital were already exposed. And how many *outside* of the hospital were exposed? Anyone who came into contact with Mr. Villalobos in the sphere of exposure as he coughed was obviously contaminated. Who knows what the ratio of exposure is, one to four, one to ten, one to fourteen. The studies of past smallpox epidemics indicated different ratios. In the worst-case scenario, it was one to fourteen. That was in one of the last European epidemics. However, here in the hospital, it could be much greater, with one individual contaminating the ambient air. With the air conditioning system we have, you could conceivably contaminate many, if not most, of us. If this was day one, we would have a chance if the diagnosis was established, and we got the vaccine within four days. Our bodies would then have a chance to develop immunity before the virus caused havoc in our own bodies. There was some consolation in that thought, some but not much.

I also pondered on the obviously more chilling ramifications of Villalobos' illness and subsequent death. If he was indeed a terrorist (and I had little doubt that he was), had he been aware of his infection? Or had he simply been a tool—a killing device—sent out by his fellows, *unaware* of his purpose as a peripatetic kind of Typhoid Mary? Was he a human bomb capable of conceivably killing thousands simply by moving about in public, among other human beings, until eventually succumbing to the hideous contagion within.

Just then, my phone rang.

*   *   *   *

"Glen, how are you?"

"Max. Two calls in one day? Must be important."

"Glen, it's a goddamn wildfire, and you're my last hope. If you have a seat, sit down."

I then summed up the events of the day and finished with my suspicion that this was sledgehammer smallpox.

There was a sigh on the other side of the line. Then Glen spoke. "Sledgehammer smallpox. I thought we shelved that several years ago."

I was stunned by his comment. "What do you mean, Glen?"

"Max, what I'm about to tell you is top secret but, at this point, it doesn't matter. I know the disease you're talking about, and it is very lethal. And it presents exactly as you described. It's not a description you can make up."

"I'm listening." I fought back the urge to simultaneously vomit and cry at the same time.

"There is a virus that causes this disease. It *is* smallpox. It is a very virulent form of smallpox. We labeled it "sledgehammer smallpox," but it's different from the smallpox described by C. W. Dixon. It was something we made or, should I say, nature helped us make. You remember our discussion earlier this morning?"

"Yeah. What about it?"

"About two decades ago, we began our research on smallpox. I know it was against the bioweapons convention agreement that both the Russians and we signed. That's why it was top secret. However, we knew they were doing something, and we didn't want to be left behind. It was our national defense at stake, so we began to do research. We finally sequenced the variola virus. We began to do extensive analysis on its various genes, which you know is a very complex DNA virus. It has a gene to deal with almost every environmental condition and various alleles from which to select. The virus knew how to survive. It had developed a symbiosis with man for thousands of years, killing only enough of us to propagate, however leaving enough of us alive to continue the epidemics.

"We wanted to make the virus more virulent than any natural occurring strain. One way of doing this was to accelerate the replication of the virus once it got into the human cell. This involved identifying the genes that were responsible for the transcription. You know—the transcriptase enzymes—and other naturally occurring catalysts or cofactors that could accelerate the virus replication. We thought that if we could do this, we could reduce the incubation period of the naturally occurring variola virus, thus making it more infectious so that it would spread more rapidly. Since the variola virus was a DNA virus and able to circumvent the human cell nucleus, then all we had to do was manipulate the virus, and we would have a more rapidly replicating strain. As simple as it sounds, this is a very complex bug, and it was a very complex ordeal. We spent millions of dollars. We couldn't get anywhere with it.

"However, I had an idea in 1985 that perhaps there was already a naturally occurring strain of variola that replicated more rapidly and had a shorter incubation period. Now I thought if we could take this naturally occurring strain of variola and, if you will, splice it with a more *virulent* form of smallpox variola—such as, sledgehammer variola—that we would have a more lethal form of the smallpox virus. Much to our surprise, there it was in our own arsenal of various variola strains. There was a strain of variola that had an incubation period of three days. However, the interesting thing about it is that it caused a mild form of small-pox—alastrim—with mortality rates of less than one percent. We theorized that this was the case because if it was as virulent as sledgehammer smallpox, but with a shorter incubation period, this strain of variola would not have left anybody alive. Thus, it would have signed its own death warrant.

"So we began to try to alter the virus. We took a strain of the variola virus that gave rise to sledgehammer smallpox and, using recombinant DNA technology over the ensuing year, we were able to take these two strains of variola, and what we came up with was what we labeled sledgehammer smallpox. This strain had a mortality rate of nearly a hundred percent in the unvaccinated individual, with an incubation period of only about three days."

"Good God," I heard myself say, despair creeping through my entire being.

"Hang on, Max. It gets worse. We decided to table it when we realized that our present vaccine would protect us and others from it. So we shelved it and stopped doing research on it. As far as I know, the only samples of this strain exist in Fort Dietrick. I don't know how that would have ever gotten out unless we did something stupid like we did with the anthrax in Iraq. Sometimes these idiot bureaucrats' perspectives on national defense is a perversion of reason."

I listened, horrified. I thought we had twelve days—plenty of time to get vaccinated. However, by his measure, we had no time.

Something wicked this way comes.

"Glen, this strain actually exists?"

"Yes, Max, it does. By your description, that's probably what this gentleman had. You are absolutely right. In his age group, he shouldn't have succumbed to the influenza virus. It's very rare unless he had some underlying illness."

"No. He had a clean history. He was a healthy-appearing individual in his thirties."

"Max, have you spoken to anyone about this yet?"

"They don't believe me. They don't believe this is smallpox."

"I can understand that. Nobody knows that this variola strain exists. They don't know that it presents atypically and that it kills before the rash can fully develop. I find it fascinating that the virus seems to know what it's doing. It causes an infection but allows the individual to ambulate, to get around, while he is coughing, spreading the disease, and then suddenly kills him before the identity of the virus is made. It's the perfect killer, the perfect survivor."

"Glen, what are we going to do?"

"You have to make a diagnosis. You're absolutely right, Max. I don't think anybody else will believe you. We need to get samples—throat, nose, and samples of the vesicles that you saw. They have to be collected in the appropriate containers. I have a contact here in Los Angeles. He is a CIA agent. He is also an ex-SEAL. I'm sure he can commandeer an F14-A to bring the samples back to Fort Dietrick. You know they can make Mach 2.4. At that speed, we should get the samples down here in a couple of hours. I'm heading out there myself within the hour."

"Glen, why do we have to fly him down to the East Coast?"

"Because nobody will touch the samples of variola. Typically, they would be flown to the CDC in Atlanta, but the labs at Fort Dietrick can get things processed more quickly."

I felt a resurgence of hope.

"What about the vaccine?"

"If you're right, you *need* the vaccine. And I know it works."

Those were further words of consolation for me. I thought that maybe we had a fighting chance. With Glen behind us, things were going to get done.

"Max, I have to go. I've got to get a hold of that friend of mine so he can get down there as soon as possible and pick up those samples. I should get him there within an hour. Take care of yourself. Remember, this is a lethal virus. Don't take any risk."

"I'm afraid that risk is an afterthought, Glen, but I really appreciate all this."

"Max, I only wish you were out here and not there."

No shit. Me, too.

"Yeah," was all I could muster.

With that, our conversation ended. I hung up the phone and prepared to get the samples Glen would need.

*   *   *   *

It would have been bad enough if the naturally occurring smallpox had reappeared, finding humanity vulnerable. But men would not have it this way. Using DNA recombinant technology and gene reassortment, the virus was altered and engineered to be more virulent. It was made hardier to allow it to be airborne for longer distances, thus increasing its infectiousness. Its incubation period was shortened without variation to three days, making containment of an epidemic more difficult, and it was made to present in stealth (that is without the typical pustular rash, so its identification was made almost impossible). As a result, the virus was made more lethal, killing its victims in as short a time as thirty-six hours.

How were we to know all this?

We were led to believe that the reappearance of smallpox would be typical, easy to identify, giving the public health agencies ample time to identify it and contain it and giving us ample time to receive the vaccine once exposed to it. However, there was no warning, and there was no time for the vaccine.

There were only us and the virus.

There would be no time for the public health agencies to put into action their plan of homeland defense—the surveillance, the quarantine, the ring vaccination. All were well-thought-out plans to confront the reappearance of the naturally occurring variola. However, this was not a naturally occurring virus. This was manmade—manmade to circumvent man's best efforts to contain it. All we were left with was chance—chance that someone with a hunch and all the unusual resources it would take to carry through with that hunch. A feat so improbable that one could only think of it as providence, for we were not in a Mecca of medicine, a center of research with a full array of consultants and specialists with unlimited resources. No, we were just a small community hospital with all the shortcomings of those small facilities. Yet, this task was given to us for some reason.

Correction: given to me.

6:30 PM

I was about to leave the room to look for Andy and Matt to discuss what I had learned from Glen when the door opened and Andy and Matt walked in. They were apparently watching the telephone in the nurses' station and, when they noticed the light on the telephone indicating I was on the line turned off, they realized I had finished my conversation with Glen.

I told them the gist of our conversation.

"So the reason it presents atypically is because it was man-made, man-engineered? Is that the only characteristic that's different?"

"No, Andy. It gets worse. This strain of variola gives rise to smallpox that's almost a hundred percent fatal in the unvaccinated person."

The color washed out of both their faces. Even as I spoke, I found it difficult to believe what I myself was saying.

"So we're all dead," Matt said, eerily calm.

"No, Matt. That's not what I'm saying. First, we're not sure whether we're infected. Two, the virus is also sensitive to the vaccine we have for smallpox, so there's a good chance we're going to be okay as long as we get vaccinated."

"And when is that going to happen exactly?" Matt asked.

"Our original problem hasn't gone away. We still have to *prove* that this is smallpox, and then we can get the vaccine."

"Dr. Kroose. Kilgorn won't help, and even your friend in ID just blew you off. That leaves us little recourse in any direction," Andy said.

"Let me finish. Glen has made arrangements for someone, a friend of his from the CIA, to come by the hospital and pick up samples that we're to collect for him. He will take these samples to Fort Dietrick, where they will do the analysis to confirm the diagnosis. I need to get samples of the oral secretions, as well as nasal secretions, and a sample of the vesicle. Time is our biggest enemy right now. The sooner we confirm the diagnosis, the sooner we get the vaccine. The sooner we get the vaccine, the more likely our bodies will have sufficient time to respond to it and render us immune to this son of a bitch."

"How long will that take? A day, two, three? We could still all end up dead if your pals at Fort Dietrick don't move at fucking light speed," Matt said angrily.

"No, no, Matt. I think if we can collect the samples within an hour, we'll probably get someone here within that period of time. It's possible to get these samples to the East Coast within a couple of hours. That means by midnight we should have results."

"And how long would it take to get the vaccine after that?" Andy asked.

"The vaccine is here in Los Angeles, so it shouldn't take long after a confirmation that it's variola to get it to us. So I think, by the latest, tomorrow morning we should have the groceries."

"We have plenty of time then. We have twelve days to contain this epidemic," Andy concluded optimistically.

"How do you come to that conclusion?" Matt asked.

"What Andy means is that from the time the virus infects someone to the time the individual becomes symptomatic and infectious is about twelve to seventeen days. Now, that's important, because at that point, those individuals that were initially infected could begin to infect the second-generation of individuals. And if the epidemic were unimpeded, twelve days thereafter, there would be another generation of infections. The rate of infection is about one to ten. One individual who may be infected could infect ten others, so it would be important to begin the vaccination program as soon as possible so as to prevent others from getting infected. The problem, Andy, is the incubation period is not twelve days. Glen tells me this virus has an incubation period of three days, so that every three days, potentially, there is a second generation of infections from the initial infected. Now, if our public officials are correct in that it would take ten days to vaccinate the entire American public, then the simple math is before the entire American public was vaccinated, it is conceivable there would be three generations of infections from the inception of the epidemic. Now, if there were only one individual infected, then in ten days, conceivably, the first infected individual would infect ten. Those ten would infect ten others, which would be a hundred individuals infected. And those hundred would infect ten others, which would be a thousand individuals infected. So very quickly, in ten days, an epidemic could get out of hand given the incubation period of this virus."

Andy began to pace. He understood the ramifications of what I was saying. "Dr. Kroose, that's if it's one individual. What if Villalobos, through the course of his wanderings, had infected thousands of individuals? The first indexed cases would number ten thousand. The second generation of infections would number a hundred thousand. The third generation of infections would number a million if the epidemic were not stopped or impeded, and this would all happen in ten days."

Something wicked this way comes.

"Yeah, Andy," I sighed. "You get my point. And that's if we presume that the public health officials are correct in estimating that it would take us *only* ten days to vaccinate the entire American public. But what if it would take thirty days as it did in the last epidemic in this country in 1947? That was in New York. It took

New York a month to vaccinate six million people, and that was during a time when they *had* vaccination programs up and running with individuals experienced in giving the vaccinations, quite in contrast to today."

Andy continued to pace. I continued my line of reasoning.

"You can further extrapolate that if, in fact, it takes thirty days to vaccinate the American public, there would be several more generations of infections giving rise to probably millions of individuals being infected. Now, if these individuals don't receive the vaccine in a timely way, this virus, having a mortality rate close to a hundred percent, I don't even want to fathom how many individuals would succumb to this illness."

"Mother of God," Matt muttered.

"Jesus, Dr. Kroose," Andy said, "it just dawned on me. If the incubation period is only *three* days, are *we* going to have enough time to be vaccinated? I mean, the common experience in the past indicated that an individual exposed to smallpox had to be vaccinated within four days of being exposed. And, mind you, this would be with a strain of smallpox that has an incubation of about twelve days and a prodrome of about four or five days. So does the three days of incubation of this virus give us enough time to be vaccinated so our bodies will respond to the vaccine and render us immune to the virus?

I was afraid Andy would ask that question. I didn't know the answer to it. I was not sure at all whether, in fact, we *had* enough time. However, I couldn't tell Matt and Andy that now. If, in fact, Andy was right, Matt's concerns about dying were justified. There was a chance that the vaccine would work in that short of time with the three days of incubation the virus would give us. Perhaps the vaccine would take just enough to protect us from death. Perhaps it would attenuate or lessen the disease so we would suffer a milder, moderate amount of symptoms without ending up dead.

That was my hope, but I wasn't going to tell them this.

I looked at both Matt and Andy. "Guys, in my way of thinking, if we receive the vaccine within the next twenty-four hours, we should be protected. We'll be okay." And I left it at that.

"Are we going to tell the nurses?" Matt asked.

"Matt, I don't think we have any choice. I think we *have* to tell them. I think we have to tell everyone in the department so they can make up their own mind about what to do."

"What do you mean, Dr. Kroose?" Andy asked.

"If anybody else comes into this emergency room, any of the staff members, they can conceivably be exposed, and I think we should prevent that from happening if we can. But I can't make that decision for them. I can't tell the nurses to stay. I think that's their choice."

"I agree with you," Andy said. He had stopped pacing, now leaning against the door, suddenly looking like a little boy, troubled and lost. "I think you should tell the nurses and let me collect the samples. I've had a lot of experience at Fort Dietrick when I was doing research there."

"That's a good idea, Andy. Make sure you protect yourself. Make sure that you wear the gown, the gloves, the hair cap, the facemask, and the shoe covers. Don't take any unnecessary risks. And, if anybody asks you what you're doing, tell them you're collecting routine cultures, surveillance cultures."

Andy nodded, as he looked at the floor and began to pace once more.

"And don't forget, Andy, that the body is in the morgue. After you have finished collecting the samples, double bag them in *HazMat* bags."

"I know that, Dr. Kroose," Andy replied, almost petulantly.

"Sorry. Just want to make sure we do it right. And bring them back up here. Or hold them in my room until they're picked up."

With that, Andy left the room as well as Matt.

I had one last duty to perform before I spoke with my staff.

I had to call my kids.

I also had forgotten that I had put Villalobos' gun on the table…and now it was gone.

I would notice this only too late.

6:45 PM

"Esmerelda, it's me," I said into the phone.

"Hello, Doctor," Es said. "We are here at the theater. Are you on your way?"

"No, Es, and I won't be coming at all."

There was a moment of silence.

"Señor Doctor, the little ones, they will be very disappointed," she said.

"I know. Do me a favor, can I speak to them?"

"They are backstage right now, doctor," Es said. "I think maybe it is better if you speak to them after?"

It was good advice. They would be heartbroken now if they knew I was not out in the audience. It was better to wait and suffer the wrath of disappointed children after their performance.

"Yeah, sure. You're right," I said.

"Is everything okay, Dr. Kroose?" Es asked. "You sound funny. No like usual."

No, Es, everything presently sucks on every level right now here at the old farmstead. I'm staring my own death in the face and, by the way, if things don't go well in the big picture, you may very well be dead within a week or two—you...and my babies.

I closed my eyes and screwed what little courage I had remaining against the wall.

"Yeah, just busy," I said. "A couple of bad accidents. Listen, I'll call later. What time does the show end?"

"I think maybe an hour," Es said.

"Good. I'll call then."

"Bye, Doctor," Es said.

"Bye," I said and hung up the phone.

Just in time, too, because then the tears came in earnest.

*   *   *   *

The evening continued to be slow. It was unusual for a Friday. It usually tended to be a little busier during this period of time. The last few cases that presented to the emergency room had come in about forty-five minutes ago and were seen by Andy before we had our conversation.

I slowly made my way to lounge where all the nurses seemed to be having light conversations. Cynthia suddenly broke into laughter. They were talking about how busy it was earlier and about how many influenza patients had been seen. They would probably all call in sick the following day after being exposed to the virus. I wasn't sure how I was going to break the news to them or whether they would believe me. I had worked with them several years, and they had grown to trust me and my clinical judgment about the various diseases we had encountered over the years, so I knew they would take me seriously. However, the presence of smallpox in our emergency room was incredible, an event almost impossible to fathom. So far-fetched in their minds, it would probably not be considered a plausible event.

I had no proof, but my strong convictions compelled me to tell them.

Norma was sitting in the middle of the couch. On each side of her sat Betty and Linda. Matt was not in the lounge. Martha and Cynthia were standing next to the coffeepot, each pouring a cup as I entered.

Betty looked at me, and her smile disappeared. It was probably because of our prior conversation in the elevator…and the news that I promised to share with her and the rest of the staff.

"Hey, Dr. Kroose," Cynthia said. "Did you get any sleep? If not, you probably should get some rest before the rest of the evening begins. It may get a little busier later."

"You looked a little tired, Dr. Kroose," Linda observed. I only hoped my bloodshot eyes gave rise to the supposition that the old head sawbones was taking a nip or two from the brandy flask during breaks. Now that would really hurt my reputation.

"We have to talk," I said flatly.

The tone of my voice instantly wiped every smile off every face.

I began to tell them about Mr. Villalobos and the fact that he died a little earlier. I then unraveled the details of his death, as well as the implications overall. Five minutes later, I finished.

No one said a word. Finally, I heard a few sniffles from Betty and Cynthia. Linda looked at me imploringly. "But Dr. Kroose, I thought you said that smallpox was eradicated in 1980. There hasn't been a case in decades. That's what you said earlier this morning."

Yes, that's what I had said. It felt like a century ago when all was right with the world.

"I know, Linda, but the variola virus has existed since that time in what we thought were controlled laboratories—well secured, and that no one with errant intents would obtain it. But it's believed that terrorists may have obtained samples of the variola virus."

"Oh, God," Betty said, and she was unable to control her tears. "You mean, if this is a smallpox case, it's…it's a biological weapon?"

I could only nod.

"Oh, God," Betty said once more, shaking her head.

It was Norma who seemed calmest of all. "Well, have you done any studies to prove that this is smallpox?"

"No, Norma."

"Then how can you be sure, Dr. Kroose?" Norma drilled me.

"Personally, I am sure, given the cadence of Mr. Villalobos' illness and the distribution of the rash, as well as the characteristics of the rash. But I can't do the studies until I get the okay from Public Health, and they're not willing to give it to me right now."

"So then how are you going to prove it one way or the other?" Linda asked.

"I have a friend who is a very influential infectious diseases doctor who, as we speak, is trying to help make the diagnosis."

"How long will that take?" Norma asked.

"If everything works out well, we could probably get a confirmation as early as by midnight, and then we'll be sure."

Norma came forward, holding my gaze. "Dr. Kroose, we trust you, and I know you wouldn't be saying this unless you had strong feelings about Mr. Villalobos having smallpox. I know you not to be wrong when it comes to life and death problems, but what if you're wrong this time?"

"Norma, I'm praying I've never been so wrong in my life."

I could see a tear beginning to develop in Martha's eyes as she analyzed every word I said.

"How soon can we hope for the vaccine?" Norma asked quietly.

"If we have confirmed the diagnosis by midnight, we should probably be able to get the vaccine in the morning."

"Are we infectious?" Linda asked.

"No, Linda."

Though with this new, monstrous form of sledgehammer shit we were dealing with, who could be sure?

Linda must have been reading my mind. "How can you be absolutely sure?"

"Unless you're symptomatic, you're probably not infectious."

Everyone with children began to shake their heads in disbelief. Those weren't assuring words from me. As far as they were concerned, they *had* been exposed, and they could conceivably expose their children. They weren't willing to accept a scientific explanation of why they weren't infectious. When it came to their children, they wanted absolute certainty. They began to talk amongst themselves.

"No way I'm gonna expose my children," Martha said, blowing her nose.

Cynthia nodded in agreement.

Matt had just entered the room, having overheard part of the conversation and shaking his head. "My boys are too important to me. No way I'm gonna expose 'em. I would never be able to forgive myself. As a matter of fact, I think we should stay here tonight until we're sure whether Villalobos has smallpox or not."

Then Norma spoke. "You have a point, Matt. Where else can we go? I don't want to believe Dr. Kroose that we're probably not infectious. How do we know Mr. Villalobos wasn't the first case that we've come into contact with? How do we know that we haven't been exposed before? And how do we know that over the next twelve to twenty-four hours we're not gonna develop symptoms and begin to cough and then expose someone? How would we feel if we go somewhere—a motel or hotel—and expose someone?"

I let this all go in stride. My staff had now become a collective hive of analysis and dissemination. I remained silent as I listened to them ruminate.

"Well, I don't need much. I'll just grab my bags and stay in the car until we find out for sure," Martha said.

"What about the night staff?" Linda said. "If they come into this emergency room, they may also be exposed."

It was Norma, again, who made the outstanding point of the night. "And what about further cases we admit. If they're exposed, too, and then released…they could infect others."

"That's beyond our immediate control," I said. "I can't unilaterally shut this ER down. We can only act on our own convictions and hope to reduce exposure of risk from ourselves."

"Seems it doesn't fuckin' matter whether we stay here or not," Matt said.

"Maybe not," I said.

There was silence again in the room. No one said anything. I could only imagine the torment that was going through their minds: The thought of whether they would ever see their children again, their families; the torment that if they were to see their children exposed to the variola virus—would they be able to live with that guilt? Or whether if, in fact, this was variola, and they knew about it beforehand, if they allowed their colleagues to become infected, what torment would that bring to them? What guilt?

Betty broke the silence. "I think we should get on the phone and talk to who-ever is coming in tonight, and let's just encourage them not to come in."

Matt said, "I know Norm was coming in tonight. He wanted the night off. He tried to get me to switch earlier today. I can just call him and tell him I'll stay and cover his shift."

Betty followed by saying, "Well, I know Sheila wanted the night off, too. She wanted to spend some time with her kids and her husband. I don't think it'll take too much encouraging to keep her home. I'll give her a call."

Jamie, who had been quiet throughout all this while listening to the conversa-tion, broke her silence. "My husband is not in town tonight. He's on a business trip, and my children are not home. I know we've had trouble trying to fill the night shift tonight. My supervisor asked me to stay over tonight, which I politely refused, but I agree with all of you, and I think we should stay. I'll give her a call and tell her I'll take the shift tonight."

I looked at my staff and fought back the lump in my throat. A twelve-hour shift was long enough, even exhausting; to consider working beyond this…it was a simple act of courage, especially in light of developing circumstances. This reminded me that I also had to make arrangements and encourage Dr. Green not to relieve me this evening.

It was a consensus. They would stay in the emergency room to work the night shift and, by so doing, they would eliminate the risk of others being exposed to the variola virus—not only their families, but also their colleagues. Curiously, they didn't ask me about smallpox, about the specific risk, about the mortality, about their individual risk if they were infected, their risk of being debilitated, or succumbing to the illness. However, I am sure this was part of their psychological defense. All they could accept now was that they were in danger. Yet, there was still hope.

Andy entered the lounge while the nurses were making their way to phones to call colleagues. He seemed to be winded as he came up to me. "Dr. Kroose, I got it all. It's in your room."

We both walked back to the doctors' room to review the samples that he had obtained. It was a little after seven o'clock, about one hour after I had talked to Glen.

The buzzer in the doctors' room went off. I picked it up. It was Jamie on the intercom. "Dr. Kroose, there's a gentleman out here. He says he's a friend of Glen Hamilton's."

"Jamie, let him in. Send him back to the doctors' room."

I went out to the hall to meet him. We shook hands. "I'm Dr. Kroose. This is Dr. Goodman." He was a man in his early forties with slightly graying brown hair, sporting a thick beard and mustache, wearing a T-shirt, jeans, leather jacket, and tennis shoes—New Balance. He was about six foot, a hundred and eighty pounds.

"Dr. Kroose. Tim Fairoaks. I've heard a lot about you from Glen. Do you have the package I'm supposed to pick up?"

The three of us walked into the doctors' room. He was carrying a black briefcase large enough to accept the samples. He opened the briefcase and pulled out a large *HazMat* bag.

"Are those the samples, Dr. Kroose?" he asked, pointing at the items Andy had collected.

"Yes. There's three samples here. One of the oral secretions, one of the nasal secretions, and one of the rash."

As he placed the bags into his larger HazMat bag, he asked, "Did you follow protocol in collecting these samples?"

"Yes, Dr. Goodman collected them, and he's well aware of the protocols in collecting these types of samples."

"Good. I'd hate to expose anybody. I've been vaccinated so I'm not worried about myself." Envy and anger loomed into my psyche. Had our hospital accepted the vaccination program, we all would have been vaccinated at this point, and we wouldn't be in this dilemma. However, that wasn't the case. Now we were hoping that we'd get the vaccine on time, early enough to prevent the disease that could conceivably cause our deaths.

Fairoaks placed the HazMat bag into the briefcase, closed the lid, and locked the latch.

"Mr. Fairoaks, how long do you think it'll take for these samples to get to Glen?" I asked.

"I have a chopper waiting for me at the heliport about a mile down from here. That'll take me down to the Edwards Air Force Base. I've got an F-14-A, one that's been stripped down, waiting for me there. Glen will be flying with me; he's probably at Edwards already. At Mach 2, 2.4, it should take us two, maybe three hours to get to base. The ride to Edwards will probably take us only about thirty, forty minutes. So we should get this down to Fort Dietrick by, oh, let's say, three, three-and-a-half hours. Once Glen has it, it won't take him long to identify if, in fact, it is smallpox."

I truly was amazed at the ability of Glen to orchestrate this entire venture. It probably was fortunate that no one believed that this, in fact, was smallpox. Had anyone other than Glen orchestrated the analysis of these samples, it probably would have been a slower process. Instead, Glen, in the matter of a few hours, would have an answer for us and truly may have an impact on whether we were to survive or not.

"Thank you, Mr. Fairoaks," I said.

He gave me a look that could only be described as regretful.

"Good luck, doctor," he said at last and then turned and left ER.

7:30 PM

True to their word and intent, my staff remained beyond their scheduled shift end. It was easy to convince Dr. Green from coming in; though he lived only a mile from the ER, he had better things to do on a Friday night.

The emergency room line picked up somewhat. A few of the patients with the flu—some with the rash, others without—as well as a few cuts and burns and headaches came into the emergency room. Although they were relatively simple cases, it was difficult to focus on them given our distraction with the potential presence of smallpox. There was no longer a jovial mood in the emergency mood as there was before our discussion. Everyone seemed to be quiet. There was very little conversation among the nurses. All of our patient care seemed to be very mechanical.

I had a wild, fleeting thought that perhaps I could kidnap and hold every patient that came to us for the next few days—to minimize their reintroduction back to the world...now possibly infected. Though I had assured my staff they were not infectious at this time, it begged the question: What the hell did we *really* know about this new sledgehammer smallpox?

Damn little, and you can take that to the bank courtesy of the Voice.

My gut and Voice were right on the money there. Even Glen Hamilton expressed ignorance in some areas of this new, horrible contagion. Sure, if smallpox changed too much it would stop being smallpox...but since so many things about it could be defined as atypical, could not the degree of infection, or latent infectiousness, also be called into question?

I looked at my watch; I would call the kids around eight-thirty. Billy was going to lay into me, I just knew it.

Andy was busy seeing most of the patients coming into the emergency room. He had grown quite a bit over the few hours that he had been with us. He had seemed to take charge of ER while I was not there, and the nurses seemed to respect his posture, bolstered by his fund of knowledge and clinical acumen. He gave the nurses the right orders and the right answers to their questions, engendering their trust and confidence. *A natural*, I thought.

I hoped he would live to see his potential realized.

Nothing too complicated or serious had come into the emergency room after that batch of patients we had earlier, so I decided to head for the doctors' room for a little rest and to catch up with the day's news, not that it made any difference to me given the peril we were confronting. However, it would serve to distract me from a sense of doom. We had about five hours to wait for Glen's call confirming or disproving that Mr. Villalobos had smallpox. If I could only sleep until then, it would allow me to escape this reality, and I hoped that when I awoke, it would have only been a bad dream. In this state of pensiveness, I ran into Andy. He was at the nurses' station.

"Hey, Andy, I'm wondering if you could take care of things while I get some rest?"

"Not a problem. You've had a hard day, and who knows how it's gonna be later?"

"Andy, you know, the nurses are telling me that you're doing very well. You know, this is like a practice run for your internship. You're doing basically everything you would do as an intern."

"If I live so long, I think I'll take up ER as my focus. You sure do run into some strange shit on this shift. Heck, imagine smallpox."

I laughed, and so did he. It was the kind of laughter men must experience just before going into battle—or coming out of combat with their skins.

As we calmed, Andy mused, "I can't imagine that many people sick with one disease and dying of one disease. It's incomprehensible."

"It's hard to fathom that," I said. "I remember reading about smallpox when it was brought over from Europe and Africa to the Americas, initially to what is now called the Caribbean. It was brought over by slaves who were infected with smallpox. This was in the 1500s. Those communities had no immunity to smallpox. The mortality rates of smallpox in that setting was reportedly fifty percent and above.

"In the 1700s, there were accounts by the individuals involved in the exploration of our West Coast. The counts described villages that were deserted along the West Coast. These were Indian villages. The explorers found the skeletal remains of these villagers. It was concluded later that what gave rise to these ghost villages was probably smallpox, which was introduced into these villages by earlier Spanish explorations. This they gathered from stories told by natives who survived the disease. These were communities that also were not immune to smallpox. One can surmise that in these communities, the mortality rate of smallpox was close to a hundred percent. My theory would be that since we find ourselves in similar circumstances—that is, with no immunity in our communities—that we are exposed to the same risks. Granted, this country has an infrastructure to deal with it."

Andy gave me an expression that could only be described as cynical. "Do you believe that?"

"Yes, I do, but such an epidemic could conceivably inundate our emergency medical services. And, as a result, perhaps the mortality rate of smallpox would be higher."

During my discourse, most of my nursing staff had moved closer to listen in. I thought to myself, *I should have just not said anything and dodged the question.* However, I said what I said, and I thought they heard what they allowed themselves to. Nonetheless, I wanted to end it with a positive note, so I continued.

"I think the importance of what we're doing here is that this is one of the first cases of smallpox, and if we can identify it early, we have, in fact, prevented a greater catastrophe. And you, individually, by not allowing your colleagues to take their shift tonight, have prevented them from being exposed to this same risk."

They seemed to be anxious to grasp that last thought, and, with that, I left the nursing station and went to the doctors' room.

I looked at the clock on the wall and then remembered that there was an executive committee meeting tonight in the adjacent annex to the hospital. I knew the number to that conference room. It was time to tell Jack Kilgorn that I would, regrettably, not have time to attend. He was sure to ask questions as to why; had I obtained what I needed from my infectious diseases doctor? My answer would be "no." My reasons for not attending would have to be more prosaic in nature. Fine. It would appease the bastard and, if truth be known, he'd probably be delighted I wouldn't be around to contest his quashing of the vaccination issue. Further, Maynard Schwartz, since his complaint was on the table for tonight, could have free reign to accuse me of every goddamn thing in the book—most of which was personally directed at him.

I had to stay here, though. I couldn't risk that I was *not* infectious at this stage.

I punched in the extension to the exec committee's conference room. Jack Kilgorn actually picked up himself.

"Kilgorn here," he said.

"Jack, it's Max."

"Ah, Max. Are you joining us this evening?"

"No, no can do. I'm swamped here in ER. We're having our asses kicked from here to Tuesday. Give my regrets to the board, would you?"

"That's a shame, Max," Jack said, dripping sarcasm. "I would like to have had you participate."

"I'm as devastated as you, Jack."

"I'm sure. Say, about your smallpox fears, did your ID guy ever come down there and make any kind of determinations on your suspect?"

"No, Bill Jenner was on-call, but he was busy."

"Ah. Well, I'm sorry. Perhaps tomorrow will yield further information."

"Perhaps."

"Okay, gotta go. We're about to start. Later, Max."

He hung up without further preamble.

And I could only look at my watch for the thousandth time and wait anxiously for some word from Glen and Fort Dietrick.

11:30 PM

I was awakened by a loud buzz from the phone.

I remember getting into bed and turning on the tube to watch CNN. I must have fallen asleep shortly after that. I was dreaming about a summer day, having a picnic at a lake near a town where I grew up with my sister and mother. I remember feeling safe with my family on this warm summer day under a shady tree. I could feel the warm breeze coming off the lake. This image segued into moments of my honeymoon with Leana…and then the birth of our children. Such pleasant memories and not one nightmare; surprisingly, given my present set of circumstances.

Another buzz. I picked up the phone. It was Jamie, telling me that Glen Hamilton was on the line. His voice came through a moment later.

"Max."

"Glen. So what's the verdict?"

There was a pause. "Max. You have never been wrong before."

Oh, Jesus. My heart sank. This was one time I wanted to be wrong.

"It's a large block-shaped virus by electron microscopy, so we know it's a pox virus. But, as you know, the chick embryo cultures and the serologies will take a little longer to do."

He was referring to more specific studies which help identify the specific species this pox virus was. These studies help distinguish the other pox viruses from smallpox, such as monkey pox, buffalo pox, or cow pox. Unfortunately, these studies take between twenty-four and forty hours to perform. I was hoping this would not delay the administration of the vaccine we needed.

"But, Max, given the historical and clinical signs that you described Mr. Villalobos having, I am absolutely sure this is smallpox. And it is very probable that it is the sledgehammer strain that we discussed earlier."

I wanted to throw up. I felt like I was going insane, but I had to hold on.

"Are we going to get the vaccine now?" I asked hoarsely.

"Yeah. I think you should get it as soon as possible, Max, but you know these bureaucrats. Because of the litigious nature of our society, they want to be absolutely sure before they expose anyone to it."

"But we can't wait to confirm it's smallpox with these other studies. That would be two days down the line. We need to receive the vaccine now."

"I know, and I'm going to see if I can get it to your facility by tomorrow morning."

"If this was anything other than sledgehammer smallpox, then we would have some time to spare. But if it *is* sledgehammer smallpox, then we don't have a day to lose."

"I know that, Max. And if it is sledgehammer smallpox, the strain we created, then I'm to blame for your peril, and that does not make me feel like a good friend. You know, I was never into this bio-weapons development. It always seems to me to fly in the face of our Hippocratic oath. However, I thought that as a participant, I could help guide the research and limit what we could use it for. Sometimes some of us have to dirty our hands to keep the rest of us clean." He paused at this. "God forgive me."

I could hear the palpable pain in his voice. I tried to sound reassuring, yet, to be honest, there was a deep-rooted anger at his participation in such unholy research. Still…

"Glen, I don't blame you for my predicament. You've always been a good friend, and that goes without saying. I don't think we could have gotten this far without you. I just hope we get that vaccine on time, or, better yet, that it's not sledgehammer smallpox. Are they quarantining the hospital?"

"As we speak, Max, they're on their way. Your administrator is being called. What's his name?"

"Kilgorn. Jack Kilgorn."

"Right. Anyway, I've contacted the CDC, the NIH, the FBI, and the Secretary of Homeland Defense. There will be several meetings over the next twenty-four hours to discuss how we're going to contain this epidemic. I know they're going to want absolute proof before they get anything going, and they're probably going to want to stick to their ring vaccination program. But you'd probably agree with me that if this was bioterrorism perpetrated by a terrorist, then there was a good chance that more than one individual was infected initially. And I'm sure it was done very insidiously.

"We are reviewing various hospital and ER admission diagnoses to see if there has been any unusual illnesses, viruses, or causes of death. And guess what? We've identified three individuals other than Mr. Villalobos who've died from the influenza virus—so they think—but the cases presented very much like Mr. Villalobos'. What's even more worrisome is that these three cases were from different parts of the country. One on the East Coast, one in the Midwest, and one in the South. If this turns out to be sledgehammer smallpox, there is no way they can contain this with ring vaccination."

Holy Jesus, I thought. This was 9/11 all over again, except on the biological level.

And didn't you feel this was going to turn into one shit-turd of a day when you woke up this morning? Yeah, Tiger. How right you were.

Ring vaccination was a program used to contain epidemics of smallpox during the eradication of smallpox in the sixties and seventies. However, these were naturally occurring epidemics of smallpox. They were successful in containing epidemics in most cases, and this is because the spread of the smallpox epidemic was from person to person not by an aerosolized exposure to smallpox. Typically, individuals who are exposed to a known case of smallpox were all vaccinated and quarantined. By so doing, they were able to prevent the spread of smallpox from those individuals who had been infected. Also, they were able to protect those individuals that were vaccinated within four days from the smallpox virus.

However, Glen and I were absolutely sure this was *not* a naturally occurring epidemic. And given what he told me, that there were three other cases, it was very plausible that several individuals were infected at one time, thus making it almost impossible to prevent the infection from spreading in a timely way. If the virus was aerosolized, then there would be more than one index case. There would be many—ten, a hundred, a thousand, conceivably even more than that. How can one identify any or all of those index cases if they were exposed, for example, in a mall, in a theater, or in an airport? If the incubation period of the virus was twelve days, we would have a better chance, albeit small, of containing the epidemic. However, with an incubation period of three days, it would be practically impossible to identify all the index cases in a timely way and use ring vaccination to contain the epidemic. So Glen was right in what he was alluding to: The American public had to be vaccinated immediately and not just this hospital.

"I have to get going now," Glen said. "I have a meeting with the CDC in an hour. We'll talk again tomorrow morning. You should be able to get the vaccine before that time. Take care of yourself, Max."

I could only nod. Words had failed me.

As I hung up, the light on the phone indicating that we were on the line turned off. I knew the staff was watching that and that I had to talk to them to confirm my hunch that Villalobos had smallpox. What I could not have told them was how all this would turn out—which was what they wanted to know.

I then remembered that I had slept through the hour at which I wanted to call my children.

I hoped that Esmerelda tucked them in and told them daddy was fine, just fine.

MIDNIGHT

As I made my way to the nurses' lounge, I met Norma at the nursing station. She had come to tell me that the staff was waiting for me. They were all waiting in the lounge. The TV was on. They were all silent. Most of them were clutching a cup of coffee and sitting on the couch or in a lounge chair, huddling close to each other. As I entered, their eyes turned up to me—hope and fear in every expression; faith that all might turn out well in the end.

I wasn't sure how to tell them, but I had to give them hope, and there *was* hope. After all, the vaccine could immunize us against this smallpox, and we weren't sure if it was sledgehammer smallpox. Maybe the incubation period was longer than three days. Maybe it was twelve. If it was twelve, we had a lot of time. That's what I wanted to believe and that's what I wanted to tell them. Before I could open my mouth, the phone near the lounge rang. It was ER's main line.

I picked it up.

"ER, Dr. Kroose."

"Max." It was Jack Kilgorn.

"Yes, Jack."

"I…I've received…I've been notified by the CDC and other facilities that we are to be quarantined."

"I know, Jack. Glen Hamilton at Fort Dietrick received samples from Villalobos that I sent him. Sorry for going over your head, but I had no choice."

"No…I understand. Good call." There was a pause. "Good Christ, Max…is there anything I can do for you or your people?"

"Not at the moment, Jack. Thanks, though." I was feeling too dejected to rub his arrogance of earlier into his face. He was now as much a potential victim as we were in the big scheme of things.

"I'm sorry," he said. "I should have listened to you. Shit, I should have implemented the…"

"Forget it, Jack. Water under the bridge." I sighed. "Hey, if I wasn't such a paranoid bastard, I might have rolled my eyes at a case of smallpox in our humble little hospital, too."

"You're a goddamned good doctor, Max, and when we get past this, you and I are going to talk. I mean a goddamned good serious, balls-to-the-walls talk, okay?"

"Sure. Listen, I have to go."

"Yes, yes, go. I understand. We'll speak later."

"Uh huh," I said and hung up.

I looked to my staff. They were all wide-eyed with anticipation.

Norma, ever the analyst of human nature, asked first.

"That bad, doc?"

I looked down and shook my head.

"Worse."

*   *   *   *

Martha dropped her cup of coffee and began to cry.

I could hear Matt to the side of me. "Fuck a duck, it had to be on my shift."

I could hear Linda give out a long sigh. Jamie turned away from me as tears rolled from her eyes. Betty stared at the floor quietly.

Cynthia, in a nervous laugh, commented, "Well, aren't we screwed!" Andy, who was standing to my side, began to pace.

In an obvious pensive state, Norma's eyes did not veer away from me. She was obviously studying my facial expressions. What did I really want to tell the staff? I could almost read her mind. She broke her silence.

"Dr. Kroose, from what you had told us before, you were pretty sure this was smallpox, but what does that mean to us now?"

"Well, I'm sure we're not going to be allowed to leave the hospital, since we presumably have been exposed. The hospital will be quarantined shortly. I estimate we'll be here for at least seventeen days."

Martha blurted out, "I can't be away from my family that long."

"You don't want to expose your family to the smallpox virus, do you?" Cynthia said, glaring at Martha.

Martha quietly agreed and seemed to find some resolve in the thought that her isolation would protect her family from this horrific disease. There were no further tears from her throughout the rest of our discussion.

"What do we do now, Dr. Kroose?" Betty asked plaintively.

"We won't be seeing patients anymore," I said. "All patients will be diverted from this facility. Luckily, everybody has been discharged from this emergency room, otherwise we would have to detain any patient here in the emergency room."

"When does all this begin, doctor?" Matt asked.

I looked outside as I heard approaching sirens. From above, two SWAT helicopters circled, floodlights washing over our front exits. Military police and armed Marines filed out of Humvees that rolled into position just beyond our ambulance arrival entrance.

"It begins now," I said.

And I, along with my staff, watched the beginning of our diseased incarceration in frozen horror.

$$* \qquad * \qquad * \qquad *$$

No one tried to enter. Soldiers and police took up positions around a perimeter. News trucks arrived, and a small armada of reporters lined up just beyond a cordoned-off area twenty feet away. So far, aside from Jack Kilgorn, no one had tried to contact us.

Matt approached the ER entrance, and immediately several Marines confronted him; a tacit warning that if he tried to exit, he would be shot, without question, without remorse.

"Oh, fuckin' a," he said loud enough for all of us to hear.

"What about the other patients and staff in the hospital?" Andy asked.

"Anyone in the hospital, be it patient or staff, will not be able to leave the premises. I'll bet every exit and entrance is likewise guarded. We're here for the duration."

Matt then asked, "What about food? And clothing? I mean, what are we gonna eat?"

"Matt, I think there's probably plenty of food within the hospital. And if there isn't enough, I'm sure they'll provide that to us. Clothing, I'm not sure. I'm not sure they'll permit anyone to bring us clothing from the outside. We'll have to ask the Public Health officials that quarantine the hospital when they get here."

"Dr. Kroose," Cynthia said, "I don't understand why we can't just go home once they come and check to see that we're okay. I mean, didn't you say that if we are not symptomatic, the chances are we're not infectious? And if we're not infectious, we're not going to contaminate anybody else."

"Cynthia, that seems to be reasonable, but the problem is twofold. One, because we don't know what strain of smallpox we're dealing with, we don't have a clue as to the probability of our infectious capability. Beyond that, what if you *do* become symptomatic? God forbid. From that point on, there is a possibility you could infect or contaminate someone else. And we just don't know when we're going to get sick if, in fact, we get sick at all."

Cynthia seemed to take my point, but then asked a more daunting question. "What will it be like? Will it be painful?"

The staff's eyes focused on me again. This was the question I hated most of all. Strike that. It was the answer that took first position for the Hate Prize.

"Even if you were to get sick, chances are you would develop an illness, perhaps like a severe case of the flu, and sores, and you would get better after a few weeks."

"Almost like radiation sickness," Andy commented.

"Yes," I agreed. "Radiation sickness is just as insidious as smallpox. You get sick, you recover—gain a sense of false hope—then after this reprieve, you spiral down. More sickness, worsening, and then…" My voice trailed off.

"So a few weeks of this shit?" Matt asked.

"Yes, Matt, a few weeks. It takes a few weeks for the sores to scab and fall off."

"What are the chances we will die from it if we are infected?" Betty asked.

I wanted to be truthful, yet positive about my answer. Still, understanding that in the best-case scenario, the mortality rate of smallpox is as high as the influenza virus…which could be ten percent, or, in the worst-case scenario, in a naturally occurring epidemic of smallpox, it could be forty percent, or…in the hypothetical case scenario, where the infecting strain is a strain like the one described by Glen Hamilton, it is close to a hundred percent in the unvaccinated individual, it was hard to be positive. However, at this point, we only were certain that this was smallpox. My suspicions were that it was plausible that this was an engineered form of smallpox, thus highly virulent and lethal, but I wasn't sure. And I could bank on the hope that it was a more typical strain of smallpox.

That's what I wanted to tell them.

"Betty, in the worst-case scenario, forty out of a hundred die of this infection. In the best-case scenario, ten out of a hundred die of this infection. But, having said that, we're going to get the vaccine. And if we get the vaccine, we're not going to get the disease."

Their fears seemed to be eased by my last definitive statement. I knew I had embellished my reality somewhat, but I thought I had to for all of us to endure the ensuing days. I truly felt that getting the vaccine was salvation, regardless of what strain of smallpox we had been exposed to.

"What about the vaccine?" Norma asked. "When are we going to get it?"

"It is distributed by the CDC—you know, the Center for Disease Control and Prevention in Atlanta. They have to give the order to the local Public Health Department, which, as far as I know, has already been done. We then have to obtain the vaccine from Public Health, so we have to get the okay from Public Health in order to get the vaccine to this hospital. The good news is that the vaccine is here in L.A."

"When, doctor," Linda asked. "When exactly?"

Her voice was soft, mellifluous…and without fear.

"Morning. Morning, I hope."

"I know the Public Health and the Department of Health Services," Linda said, sighing. "They're one slow group of individuals. They seem to hesitate with everything. The last I heard, they did not want to give the vaccine to anyone other than what they consider the first responders, and that was on the voluntary basis. Then it would only be given if the hospital agreed to participate in the vaccination program, and many hospitals, as this one, do not want to participate in this program because of the possible lawsuits that may occur if, in fact, there is a complication from the vaccine."

I was surprised that Linda knew about the administrator's position on the smallpox vaccination program. I thought I was the only one privy to his thoughts. Apparently, she had been making inroads into the circle of nursing administration.

She continued. "Not only has the administrator been an obstacle to the vaccination program, but now we have our unions lobbying us not to receive the vaccine unless the hospital administrators commit to providing workers' compensation for those of us who develop any side effect that will prevent us from working. I can't believe the hypocrisy and the political correctness that exists in this society. Who is going to compensate us for this act of omission? I mean, that's where the paradox is. What if I develop smallpox and die from it because they were not willing to vaccinate me? Mind you, I wanted to be vaccinated. Who's going to compensate me for my illness then? Who's going to compensate me for the suffering from smallpox? Who's going to pay my family if I have the misfortune of dying from smallpox? I was willing to be responsible for whatever consequences from receiving the smallpox vaccination. I wasn't asking for compensation from workers' comp, from the hospital, from the unions. I just wanted to be protected against smallpox. I'm just a little pissed that they didn't give me that opportunity, that they did not allow me to protect myself. And now I find myself in this predicament."

Linda's point resonated with the staff. They all nodded. Many of the expressions were now those of anger rather than fear.

I knew exactly how they felt.

"Linda, you're not going to get smallpox, and you're not going to die. We will get the vaccination, and we will get it by morning."

But would we?

Would we?

SECOND DAY—7 AM

"But why can't you come home, daddy," my daughter asked me over the phone. "Please come home."

"I will, honey," I said, rubbing my eyes. "This is just something that sometimes happens. You know, doctor stuff." My highly technical explanation translated to those of nine years of age…

Billy got on the phone. "Hey, dad, I saw you on TV a couple of minutes ago. Cool." My momentary celebrity had eclipsed my failure to see him lead children to their death in the Pied Piper last night. I smiled to myself.

"Yeah, I should have been a movie star like Harrison Ford."

"Who?"

I tried to recall the movie star of the month that my ten year old might relate to now. I gave up and chose a universal legend. "Like John Wayne."

"Yeah," Billy said. "except you need a horse."

"Okay, I'll work on that. Now you do whatever Es tells you to until I get out of here, all right?"

"Sure, dad."

"And take care of your sister."

"Okay."

I took a deep breath, my eyes watering.

"I love you. Big kisses. Andrea, honey, you still there?"

"Yeah, daddy. Big kisses to you."

Kissing noises came through courtesy of my daughter. I reciprocated.

"Put Es back on the phone, okay?"

"Okay. Bye, dad. Try and get on TV again, okay? Maybe wave at us," Billy said.

"You got it, sport."

Esmerelda finally got hold of the phone once more.

"Hello, Senor doctor. I'm back."

"Es, I'll try to call as often as possible. Sorry for this inconvenience."

"I speak to my husband, he will come and stay here with me in the house for as long as you are there. You no worry, just come home soon."

"Es, you're an angel."

"Sí, I know. And is difficult job."

I got off the phone, looked at my watch. It was seven o'clock in the morning. Still no vaccine.

"This is bullshit," I said aloud.

Bullshit.
My litany.

✳   ✳   ✳   ✳

It had been a long night, and I was still exhausted. With all the activities of the quarantine, we all had been interviewed and asked about whether we had any symptoms consistent with smallpox, whether we had any rash, typical or atypical. We were told that we would be quarantined at least forty-eight hours until they were sure it was smallpox. The experts (as they were called) were still in disbelief. They thought it was more probable that Mr. Villalobos had contracted monkey pox somewhere outside of the States, and that worried me because if they weren't convinced that this was smallpox, they probably weren't willing to vaccinate us. But I was banking on Glen, that he would persuade them not to wait. There was nothing else to do after our interviews, so we all had hit the sack, using the many gurneys in the emergency room as our beds. I was more fortunate; I had the bed in the doctors' room. However, it was hard to sleep with all the activities around us. There was a constant reminder that we were in danger.

As I lie in bed with this insomnia, I reflected on what the Public Health official Dr. Anderson told me earlier last evening. "You know, Dr. Kroose, if this, in fact, is the first case of smallpox, and you've caught it, you may have just prevented a worldwide epidemic. That makes you a hero."

I thought of how naïve he sounded. As I saw it, I had most probably found only one of many first cases of smallpox. And I, as everyone else, was a little too late in preventing this epidemic. I smiled at him as he gave me the compliment. We had seen many flu-like syndromes that day, many with a rash. It was really possible that many of these cases were actually smallpox presenting atypically. And, if this were the case, the epidemic was well on its way. We were categorized as a small- to moderate-sized hospital and emergency room, and we had seen twenty, thirty cases of influenza that day alone. These types of cases were being reported throughout the country. Knowing that there were some fifty-one hundred acute care facilities and hospitals in the country, my calculations were staggering. And if, in fact, this was the first wave of smallpox, then conceivably there could be a hundred thousand, a hundred and fifty thousand index cases throughout the country. It was hard to fathom what that would mean. In the next twenty-four, thirty-six hours, all the emergency rooms in this country would be inundated. The second generation of smallpox infections, if the epidemic was not impeded, would number in the millions, and that would devastate this country if, in fact, this was our reality. I thought had the American public been vaccinated, this would have been averted. This scenario would be quite different. It could conceivably only be an epidemic of a few cases of smallpox, not potentially thousands or hundreds of thousands or even millions of cases. Then I thought that maybe he was right. Maybe this was the first case. Maybe this was a naturally occurring epidemic of smallpox.

Now, this morning, although still tired, I was unable to sleep.

Where was the vaccine?

Something wicked…

I shut the Voice up. Still, surely by now, Public Health would be aware of the impending epidemic, and they would have rushed the vaccine over to our hospital.

But so far, nothing had arrived.

I got out of my bed after I spoke to my kids and walked out into the main area of the emergency room.

Linda was already up, hugging herself, a sweater draped over her shoulders; she was staring at the small army of soldiers, police, and media outside.

"Anyone call, Linda?"

She looked at me, her eyes bloodshot, probably from crying all night.

"You would have been the first to know, Max. Good morning, by the way."

I put a hand on her shoulder. She put her hand on mine and, for a moment, we just stood there, staring out at the world like caged animals eyeing their jailers.

I walked back into my room. Linda followed. I picked up the phone and paged the Public Health official who was in charge of the quarantine. A few minutes later, Dr. Anderson responded.

"Good morning, Dr. Kroose."

"Dr. Anderson, don't take this the wrong way, but where the fuck is that vaccine?"

"Doctor, we need to confirm the diagnosis before we can give you that. You know, this may be monkey pox…"

"Monkey pox doesn't present this way, for Christ's sake."

"The CDC is not quite convinced that this is smallpox."

"Dr. Anderson, we need the vaccine now. If this is, in fact, smallpox, the more time we waste, the greater the risk it is for all of us here."

"Please calm down, sir. I understand. We'll try to do everything to get the vaccine to you. I'll call Atlanta again."

His words were not very reassuring to me, but then I couldn't do anything else. Then I thought I had to get a hold of Glen. He probably wasn't aware that they had not released the vaccine, so I called him. I left a message on his cell phone, and I paged him to our number. We had little recourse now but to wait.

Wait.

Wait to die.

*   *   *   *

CNN was on.

I could see the outside of the hospital that was being projected on the tube. There was a hoard of cameras and news reporters gathered on all sides of the hospital. You could see them run across the street frantically as Public Health officials emerged from the hospital, wanting to get interviews on the impending catastrophe. It was quite a spectacle. A caption at the bottom of the screen read, "A Possible Outbreak of Smallpox."

One of the Public Health officials commented that he was more concerned with the overreaction to this case of possible smallpox which may be, in fact, monkey pox. No one was aware of the virulence, the aggressiveness of this virus, not even myself, but it would play out over the ensuing few days. Media heaven.

I had been interviewed the prior evening through the glass partition of the ER, no less. That clip now was repeated constantly. Captioned beneath my face were the following words: "Hero Doctor Spots Possible Pox."

Catchy, I thought, except completely inaccurate. "Possible," my foot. How about: "Terrified M.D. Shits a Brick When He Discovers Deadly Strain of Weaponized Sledgehammer Smallpox. P.S.—Still Shitting Bricks Because Still No Vaccine For Him and Staff."

I realized I had no sense of media hype.

No, the interviews would run. I'm currently a hero—lightning shot out of my ass, and every word I spoke were pearls of medical genius—so be it.

I would like to see what they'd say after I was dead.

More interviews ensued. Another labor union representative commented why the American public has not been vaccinated against smallpox, and that if this was truly an epidemic of smallpox, heads should roll. I thought of the hypocrisy in his statements. I would say they helped engender the fear of the smallpox vaccine. A poll flashed on the tube indicating there were more Americans afraid of the vaccine than they were of smallpox. What a paradox in reality created by the American media, a misconception the American public was willing to accept. But, then again, these generations that are alive have not experienced the ravages of smallpox, so how were they to know? It was incumbent upon the Public

Health officials to make it clear to the American public that smallpox was a clear and present danger. That if an epidemic perpetrated by terrorists occurred, it would be devastating for this country. For many, it would be too late. They would be the proof, they would be the impetus for the vaccination of the American public. But for those few, or those many, our public health system failed. And who would explain to their family members who survived them that it was for political correctness, all because of the litigious nature of the society that they were not vaccinated. What other explanations would be offered, and who would be blamed for the deaths of those few or those many, for the failure of the system? Or will we be mature enough to accept responsibility for our actions, for our misconceptions, for our derelict behavior, for not paying attention to the harbingers, the dangers of these times?

My thought was suddenly interrupted by a knock on the door. It was Andy. He poked his head in the room. "Dr. Kroose, how ya doin'? Is there anything I can do for you?"

"Yeah, do you mind going across the street to the bar and picking up a bottle of Jack Daniels? Then pick up a pizza on the way back?"

"I'll work on that," he smiled. I knew why he was here.

"No, nothing yet on the vaccine. We've run into a snag."

"What kind of snag?"

"Public Health officials are not quite convinced this is smallpox. They feel it may be monkey pox, but you and I know better. I'm sure Glen will convince them otherwise. Anyway, I'll get back to you as soon as I hear from him."

He took the news in stride. He nodded, sighed, and then smiled wanly at me.

"Do you mind if I go upstairs to the fourth floor? The nurses up there may need some help, and I have nothing else to do."

"That's fine, Andy. I'll give you a call if I need you down here."

With that, he closed the door and left. I looked back at the tube. Again, I saw a picture of the hospital and the spectacle of news reporters running back and forth, chasing down Public Health officials. It would have been somewhat comical if it weren't such a tragedy that they were trying to report on.

"Come on, Glen. Where the hell are you?"

And that's when Linda knocked at my door.

*   *   *   *

She poked her head in.

"Can I talk to you for a minute?"

"Sure. Come on in. Pull up a chair."

She closed the door behind her and walked over to the bed, sitting beside me.

"I just want to tell you that whatever happens, I want you to know that I've enjoyed working with you all these years. And I don't know how to say this, so I'll just be direct, I only regret that I didn't get to know you better."

I could perceive a sense of apprehension and fear as she spoke to me, which drew me closer to her. I reached out for her hand and pulled her into bed with me. It was an instinctive gesture—not wanton. I hugged her.

I wanted to make her feel safe. I wanted to feel her body against mine. I wanted to feel safe myself.

"Linda, I regret the same thing. I confess that I…I've caught myself watching you often. You know, my wife died…"

She clung to me a little tighter, nodding. "I know, Max. I'm so sorry."

"No, it's not…what I mean is, it's been a long time since I've been with anyone. You and she…," I hesitated. "Don't be offended, but you remind me of her. I always found that comforting."

She looked up at me with a tear in her eye. "I'm not offended. I think that's about the nicest thing anyone has ever said to me."

I put my arm around her waist. I could feel her softness, smell her, and it aroused in me something long gone; something I thought was lost forever. She turned her head around and kissed me. It was a good-bye kiss, a kiss I would not have experienced had she not broken our agreement. It reminded me of a quote from the poem of Edgar Allen Poe, "Annabelle Lee."

"She was a child, and I was a child, in this kingdom by the sea.

But we loved with a love that was more than love, and died, my
Annabelle Lee…"

Linda smiled at me and sighed.

"Max, I better go before somebody else comes and sees us here. I don't think it would be right."

"You're right, Linda. But don't worry. I think we have a lot of catching up to do once we get out of this."

She left the room and, for the next several minutes, I felt the tranquility of having been close to someone. Then, as I looked at my watch, it was 7:45, and Glen had not called back.

Time, our sworn enemy, was passing too fast.

*   *   *   *

I found the staff in the lounge drinking coffee. Everybody was wondering the same thing: When was the vaccine coming? I assured them that it was on its way and that we were going to receive it that morning. But I was worried that it would be delayed for twenty-four hours, and that would be disastrous if, in fact, this virus had an incubation period of three days and not the twelve days we see with the naturally occurring variola virus.

The phone rang.

It was Glen Hamilton.

I rushed back to the doctors' room to take the call. Was the vaccine on its way?

SECOND DAY—8 AM

"All good news," Glen said.

Good news?

"Glen, we haven't got the vaccine yet. What's going on?"

And then a prolonged silence on the other end of the line.

"*What*?"

"No, Glen. Public Health is telling us they're waiting for a confirmation according to the cultures and the serologic tests to see whether, in fact, he had smallpox. They think he had monkey pox."

"These idiots! I talked to them about this already. I presented the case. I made them aware of the existing strain of smallpox that created sledgehammer small-pox. They know all of this. I had to argue with them about starting the smallpox vaccination program for the general public. They were supposed to have the vaccine to you already this morning."

My patience was wearing thin, and I know there was an edge in my voice.

"We haven't received a goddamn thing, Glen."

I know he sensed my agitation.

"These fuckin' bureaucrats," he snarled. "The CDC probably hasn't even communicated with the Public Health Department in your area. They should have already received specific instructions to release the vaccine to your hospital. Instead of working with each other, they seem to be working against each other.

"You know, after convincing the CDC that this most likely was smallpox and very likely sledgehammer smallpox—the strain that we created—they agreed to begin the vaccination program, vaccinating the entire American public. By their way of thinking, it would take ten days to vaccinate the entire American public, but I think they are too optimistic. It's probably gonna take thirty days, if not longer.

"And if that's not bad enough, just as I thought we had things rolling, I get a call from the DHHS—the Department of Human Health Services. They refused to go along with the vaccination of the general American public. So I had a sec-ond meeting, and I asked what their rationale was. They told me that they didn't want to put the American public at risk of side effects from the vaccine if, in fact, this was not smallpox. I posed the question to them: 'What if this is smallpox, and you're risking many American lives?' And they responded, 'Well, we can live with that.' To which I said, 'You mean to tell me death as a result of an act of omission is more acceptable than death from an act of commission?' I thought to myself what do they stand to gain from allowing the citizens of this country to die? Were there hidden agendas? I wasn't sure, but there was an inference, or it could be the perception.

"So I threatened 'em. 'If you don't begin,' I said to them, 'the vaccination program, then I will go public and let the American public know that you are willing to accept the death of American citizens from smallpox as acceptable collateral damage, if for no other reason than to bolster the support for the war on terrorism. Let's see how that plays in the media.' They understood the perception or misperception of not acting now.

"But what ultimately convinced them was a report from a CIA agent Teller. This agent apparently had been tracking a terrorist over the last several days. He referred to him as 'Warhead.' Interestingly enough, Warhead was supposed to deliver the sledgehammer. CIA agent Teller did not understand what this was. His initial impression was that it was a type of bomb."

I really had not wanted to listen to a lengthy diatribe from Glen, but I listened with commingled courtesy and horror.

"Fucking unbelievable," I snarled. Glen didn't say anything immediately.

The entire picture was becoming clearer to me. It was a bioterrorist attack, and Mr. Villalobos was a terrorist. My instinct had served me well again. Thanks, Gut and Voice. Thanks for the gift of foresight.

"So Villalobos, was he the 'Warhead'?"

"Max, let me continue. When Teller heard of Mr. Villalobos and the sledgehammer smallpox, he put two and two together. He traced Villalobos back to Mexico, where he had lost Mohammed Haddah. It turns out that Villalobos and Haddah are one and the same. However, Villalobos was not traveling alone. There were a group of ten who made it across the border."

"Glen, you don't think there are ten Mr. Villalobos in this country releasing the virus in various cities?"

"That's the thinking, Max, that these ten individuals were here in this country to do the same thing."

Aw, Christ.

"Glen, the three cases you mentioned in our last conversation presented similarly to Villalobos and died. They also had smallpox, so the epidemic has begun. That means they must have released the virus a few days ago."

"No, Max, those three cases I mentioned before were actually different. They were all older patients. Most were immuno-compromised from cancer, diabetes, and other illnesses. They, in fact, died from the influenza virus. We couldn't identify any smallpox or any pox viruses, so those three were not part of the epidemic."

I was momentarily confused.

"I don't get it. Why is Villalobos the only case thus far? If they all released the virus simultaneously, shouldn't there be any other cases identified?"

"Teller tells me they were able to trace and track three of the terrorists. Three of them were using credit cards, and they were able to trace three of them to separate motels where they were staying. One of them began to talk and told Teller that the virus was released yesterday in ten locations, but he wasn't able to tell us the locations other than the location where he was supposed to disseminate the virus."

I didn't want to ask the next question, but I had no choice.

"Glen…was it aerosolized?"

"Yes, it was, Max. It was aerosolized; it was weaponized smallpox, and it was very similar to the strain that we developed. I surmise they somehow took a sample of the strain we had and improved upon it."

As much as I was terrified by what Glen was telling me, I was also intrigued. It didn't make sense to me.

"If they just released the virus yesterday, then how is it that Villalobos was sick? If the incubation period is three days, he shouldn't have fallen ill until tomorrow."

"You're absolutely right, Max. This one individual that Teller interrogated told him that Haddah was one of the extreme zealots, a hotshot, always pushing the envelope. Do you recall the Chinese pilot that collided with one of our reconnaissance planes near the coast of China, in the process killing himself and forcing our reconnaissance plane into Chinese territory? Well, there's a hot dog in every group, and Haddah was the hot dog. He apparently had infected himself three days before the virus was supposed to be released to ensure that he would not fail. If they found him and confiscated the vial that contained the virus, he thought being infected would allow him to infect several individuals insidiously before his demise. But he miscalculated. He didn't plan on getting sick that quickly. Lucky for us, he did. And lucky for us, you had that hunch, because now maybe we can get ahead of it, get ahead of the epidemic, and begin the vaccination program. We can begin to vaccinate the entire American public before this epidemic spreads."

If it weren't for Teller's report and my insistence, they would have waited another forty-eight hours, and delaying the vaccination program another forty-eight hours would mean many more would die from this virus. Glen's point resonated with my predicament. I didn't want to be one of the casualties.

"Glen, when I intubated Villalobos, he coughed in my face."

There was silence on the other end of the line. I could feel the sense of remorse. I knew Glen understood my predicament with certainty. He must have felt personally responsible. He broke the silence.

"Max, you're getting the vaccine this morning. I'll personally call the Public Health Department in Los Angeles and make sure that they release it." With that last statement of resolve, he said good-bye and hung up.

*   *   *   *

Within the hour, the vaccine was brought to the hospital, and we were all vaccinated. However, in retrospect, it turned out to be no more than a cliché: A little too little, a little too late.

FIFTH DAY—7 PM

Yes, the vaccine was a little too little, a little too late. It was like clockwork. At the end of three days, we began to get sick. Those that were exposed initially were the first to fall ill. It was not that bad initially, however it got exponentially worse as time passed. The pounding headaches, the bone-breaking body aches, the nausea, and the vomiting worsened as the hours ticked away.

It now was thirty-six hours for some of us since the symptoms began.

The virus was true to form—exactly three days of incubation, then on the fourth day the fevers commenced in earnest. We were going be the first statistics, the first casualties of this virus. We had hopes that our vaccine would help prevent this disease, or at least attenuate it.

It seems now it would not come true.

One by one, on that fourth day, we fell sick.

The first was Martha. The virus seemed to hit her hardest.

Next was Betty, then Jamie. My Jamie who would never hesitate to bring me coffee when she thought I needed it most.

Then Norma, my pillar of strength; and then Cynthia. Linda and I were last to begin with the prodrome, I gather because we must have been exposed later. I most probably was exposed when I intubated Mr. Villalobos. We were twelve hours behind every one else. Perhaps there was still time for the vaccine to work for us…a long shot. I felt a little guilty for having these thoughts.

I cried for each one of them when their time came; unabashedly and copiously. This was my family. We had saved so many lives together in the past; ironic, I thought, in the end how helpless we had been in trying to save our own.

Andy and I seemed to be the strongest. We appeared to stay well for a longer period of time and were feeling mild flu-like symptoms initially. He and I were tending to our debilitating staff when we heard a single gunshot from the nearby ER bathroom.

I was the closest to the door. I tried to open it, but it was locked from within. I yelled to Andy.

"Get that swivel chair," I said, pointing at Norma's small chair near the nursing station.

Andy moved quickly and rolled it to me.

I lifted the chair up and slammed it against the lever with one solid blow. The outside handle shattered. I tore open the door, or what remained of it.

There, straddled against the toilet, eyes open, staring at me was Matt.

A single .22-caliber bullet lodged in his temple.

I did not need to feel a pulse to know that he was dead.

Andy rushed over and stared at Matt with horror.

"Oh, Jesus," he muttered.

I lifted Matt off the john, or rather dragged him; he was huge and weighed a ton. I put him prone on the floor and then removed the .22 pistol, still amazingly clenched in his hand.

Christ, I had forgotten all about it. Matt must have removed it on his last office visit to meet with Andy. I was so preoccupied, I hadn't even noticed. I wanted to suddenly blame myself…but why? Matt had simply chosen to move on before his disease ravaged him through hours and days of agony.

From outside, police were knocking on the ER window, wondering what had happened. I glanced back at them, then looked to Andy.

"Tell them."

Andy disappeared to deal with the police, and I stared down at Matt. I nodded in understanding.

"Can't say I blame you, old friend," I said.

Matt had decided not to succumb to smallpox. He had stuck around for as long as he dared.

I have places I must go, and promises to keep,
Before at last I find, a little bit of sleep.

Thank you, Voice, for that little bit of Robert Frost.

I closed Matt's eyes.

"Sleep," I said. "Sleep."

*   *   *   *

I thought my previous vaccinations would protect me. I was having all the constitutional symptoms and severe, but I was able to maintain my strength albeit with moments of confusion. However, in twenty-four hours, that all had changed. My body aches were almost intolerable. The headaches were pounding. It was constant and unrelenting, and the thirst was insatiable.

Andy was the only one spared, but I thought it was due to his youth and late exposure to the virus since he was not in the ER as much earlier in the day. This made sense to me since he was in the library boning up for one of our discussions. However, I thought it would be just a matter of time before he found himself where we were.

There just was not enough time for the vaccine to work. The infection was too rapidly progressing and did not allow our bodies to react to it. Thus, it was useless after being infected. Had we been fortunate and not been prevented by Public Health from receiving the vaccine prior to the infection, we would have probably fared better or maybe not even suffered the prodrome. But this was neither here nor there. This was the hand dealt to us.

And dead men rise up never, and even the weariest river, winds somewhere safe to sea...

My gut, my Voice, were more gentle of late...resigned, perhaps. There was little else to suspect or fear, except death itself. I found myself wandering around in a daze most of the time, mainly staring out at the flotilla of medical, Army, and police personnel outside. I refused to do another interview, though I know that Billy would be disappointed by this. I was simply not up to it. More than that, I guess...I simply wanted to die without becoming a media cornerstone for tragedy.

One by one, the staff was succumbing to the infection. Martha was the first to go. She died earlier in the afternoon, as did Betty. They were followed by Norma, then Jamie, and finally, Cynthia. I thought how tragic. All these individuals had plans. They were to see their families. They had events to go to. It was just supposed to be a routine Friday shift, and then the weekend and family time, but it was not to be.

Smallpox had taken everything from them: Their dreams, their memories, and their hopes for a future, for happiness.

Fucking smallpox.

*   *   *   *

Saying good-bye to my kids was unbearable.

They still had difficulty comprehending the concept of death, inspite of the death of their mother; it was something they could not except easily. What they *did* understand, and this precipitated the same reaction as what an adult would feel with full faculties for the inevitable, was that dad wasn't coming home.

Es was crying nonstop on the phone. Andrea had started crying from the first moment I told her, as gently as I could. What broke my heart more than anything was my son's reaction. He was ten, and he might have had some inkling that death meant a kind of transformation from life (an esoteric concept at best...perhaps not entirely inaccurate); regardless, the implications meant a separation of those we love.

"But dad...no, you have to come home. I have Little League on Saturday," he said. There was almost resentment in his voice.

"I know, sport, I know. Sorry."

"So come on. Get out of there. Stop foolin," he said. He had, of course, been watching CNN and was a smart kid—he understood that the world was turning upside down and in half. He knew things were terribly wrong. However, his mind couldn't accept that such a terrible thing was happening to his father. Oh, sure, maybe for a little while, but not forever.

I thought best not to fight his child-need denial. I would buy into it. I would *encourage* it. No harm, no foul. It would help Billy in the short-term. Later, he would have to deal with the true magnitude of his grief, but that would be for later.

"Okay," I said. "I'll talk to the folks down here at the hospital. See what we can figure out. Fair enough?"

"Yeah," he said. "Okay."

And that was that.

My babies were gone.

And soon I would be, too.

✳   ✳   ✳   ✳

Only Linda and I remained. Andy was still faring surprisingly well even at this late stage.

I was in the doctors' room, lying down and feeling like shit. Andy walked in. He saw that I was struggling to get up, and he eased me back down.

"Andy, how's Linda?"

Andy sighed.

"She was one of the last to develop symptoms, Max, and she's hanging on. We have her on the IV antibiotics." He paused for a moment. "She'd like to speak to you."

"Okay," I said weakly.

"Are you sure you don't want an IV started? What's your temperature now?"

"I don't know." I didn't give a shit, though I suspected my temperature was probably above 102.

"Have you taken any Tylenol or Motrin?" Andy asked.

"Yeah. I just had some. Andy, if you can give me some water to drink and then maybe you can help me to Linda's bedside."

As Andy went out to get the glass of water for me, I noticed the telephone line flashing. I thought it was odd no one had picked it up. Then it dawned on me, Jaime was no longer with us. There was no one to answer the phone.

I picked up the receiver. "Kroose here."

"Dr. Kroose. Just the man I want to talk to. I'm Mr. Teller. Jerry Teller."

Yes, the CIA guy, I remember now. Wonder what the hell he was calling me for...

"How can I help you, Mr. Teller?"

"Dr. Kroose, Glen asked me to call you."

"You're the fellow who was chasing the Warhead"

"Yeah. Yeah, that's what we called him—the Warhead. It was a code name. His real name was Mohammed Haddah—or to you, he was Mr. Villalobos. Glen tells me you were the doctor that identified the first case. If it hadn't been for you, we probably wouldn't have gotten ahead of the epidemic. Although there have been thousands of cases reported, it could have been worse had we not initiated the vaccination program when we did. I thought since you helped us crack this case, you deserve an explanation of what happened and who these perpetrators were."

"You said there were thousands of cases." I really didn't care a damn who the perpetrators were. My continued concern was for the price this caused in terms of human life. It was the doctor in me.

"Yeah, Dr. Kroose. We estimate maybe a hundred thousand indexed cases. There were ten of them."

"Ten who?"

"There were ten terrorists, Villalobos and nine others. Villalobos, however, fell sick and was not able to get to his location and release the virus. We found it in his hotel."

I thought to myself that was the business that he was so intent on not missing. I was glad he was too sick to leave the hospital. Or, rather, I'm glad Matt and I dragged his ass back in. That son of a bitch.

"The other nine, however," Teller continued, "did get to their destinations. From our epidemiological studies, we located the facilities where the viruses were released. There were three sports arenas, three airports, and three malls. The variola virus was aerosolized into the air conditioning system, and that's how they were able to disseminate it so effectively."

"Did you get the terrorists?"

"Yeah, Dr. Kroose. Three we caught before they fell sick; the other six fell sick, as did Mr. Villalobos, and we were able to find them at their deathbeds. They will no longer be with us, but we were able to find out who they were. They belonged to a radical Islamic fundamentalist group based out of Afghanistan. Their ultimate goal was to establish a pan-Islamic state, incorporating most of the Middle East. They figured they weren't able to do that without getting us out of the way, thus the attack on the United States. However, if it's any consolation to you, they won't be bothering anybody. We tracked two head guys in the Pamir Mountains, and our special forces guided a cruise missile straight down their throats. Anyway, Dr. Kroose, I gotta get goin'. If you have any questions, feel free to call me. You can get hold of me through Glen."

I let that digest for a moment.

"Thank you for the update, Mr. Teller."

A moment of silence, and then, "I salute you, sir. Goddamn good piece of work. I'm sorry you're getting the shit-stick end of it all."

"Not half as sorry as me, Mr. Teller, but thanks for the thought."

"Good-bye, Doctor," he said, and then the phone disengaged.

Andy returned with a glass of water as I hung up the phone. I felt some peace of mind that the terrorists were apprehended and their leadership was destroyed. However, I had my own battle to fight, and the outcome was all but certain.

Sure, it's certain, Max, and you know it.

And I did, I guess.

"Andy, help me up." As I rose, I took the glass of water, gulped it down quickly, and looked up at Andy.

"Take me to Linda."

He put one arm around my waist, and I put my left arm around his neck. He helped me to Linda's bedside. As we approached the bed, I could see that she had been ravaged by the virus. She appeared to be bruised from head to toe. There was crusted blood around her mouth and nose. Her fingertips were blue. She was hemorrhaging. She was suffering from hemorrhagic smallpox, one of the presentations of this strain. I knew she had little time and nothing could be done for her. She was breathing rapidly, struggling with every breath. Yet, she was still conscious and competent and had refused any resuscitative measures, but we ultimately convinced her to allow us to try to help her. Much good it did; it only prolonged the inevitable. She had four IV lines running—one to transfuse blood, one to transfuse clotting factors, one for fluids to keep her body hydrated, and one for the IV antibiotics. The nurse who had been vaccinated previously was caring for her. Her temperature was 106. The cooling measures were not working. I knew she couldn't hold out too much longer.

She saw me approaching her, and she raised an unsteady hand. I reached for it as Andy helped me approach the bedside.

"Oh, God...Max..." her small, brown eyes were ravaged with pain and fear. She pulled me a little closer, as her voice was weak, ravaged with the disease consuming her body. "I don't want...to stay on...anymore," she said. She released my hand, then reached out and touched my face with one finger. Then her hand dropped to her side.

With that, she immersed into a comma. At least now she would not feel the pain, but she was still fighting on.

I looked up at the monitor. I could see her rhythm was normal, her blood pressure was good, and her oxygen level was maintaining. I felt for her pulse, it confirmed a good pressure. I could only wish her struggle would not be in vain. If only I could do something, but what?

"Next lifetime," I said softly.

*   *   *   *

Andy helped me back to my room. The body aches and the head pain were unbearable. My daughter used to call headaches "head boo-boos." I had the mother of all head boo-boos right now. I felt my body giving into this suppurating nightmare. Andy again offered to start IVs. I refused. *Why the hell for?* I thought. *To prolong the unbearable? To see another one of my interviews on CNN?*

I think not.

Andy helped me back into bed. As I lied there, I saw on CNN pictures of emergency rooms throughout the country being inundated with patients that had smallpox. Yet, the caption at the bottom of the picture read, "Smallpox Identified in Uganda, South Africa, Buenos Aires, and Chile." This was followed by a news alert. The commentator was reporting on several cases of smallpox identified in Europe. The caption at the bottom of the picture then read, "Smallpox Identified in China and Russia."

So hell on earth had returned, I thought. A new era of demonic biological anarchy.

We should have seen it coming.

God damn,we should have seen it…

It was a global epidemic. With the poor infrastructures found in Africa and South America and the large AIDS populations on both those continents, smallpox would prove even more devastating to those countries. I thought projections by some, that a billion deaths from smallpox would eventually occur, was probably not far from reality.

I began to fall into a deep sleep, a dream state. It was the only refuge I had from this torment. An image of a man came to me. He was suffering from smallpox—the classic form. His body was covered from head to toe, hands and feet, with smallpox lesions—the pustular rash. He had suffered for five days with high fevers, body aches, abdominal pain, and headaches. But as he suffered from the rash covering his entire body so as to provoke pain any time he moved(from the cracking of the crusts covering the lesions), he thought of how more merciful it would have been if he had died in the prodrome. He ultimately survived his illness, blind and disfigured from all his scarring. I thought in my dream that perhaps I was going to be lucky to succumb to the disease and not suffer as he did.

I woke up with a pounding headache, feeling all the more weak, and fell quickly back into the dream state.

I saw Linda smiling at me. She touched my cheek. She appeared the way I saw her every day and especially that day we last spoke. She kissed me, turned, and walked away.

And last…Leana. She was far away in the distance. She was calm, collected. Waiting.

I slowly awakened from my dream as Andy tugged at my shoulder. I could barely open my eyes. My voice was weak. I couldn't catch my breath.

"Max," said Andy. "Glen Hamilton is on the line. He wants to talk to you."

He handed me the phone. Slowly propping myself up with my right shoulder, I grabbed the receiver as my hand fell to the bed. I slowly put it up to my ear.

"Glen?"

"Max," he said. "How are you feeling?"

"How do you think, old friend?"

"Yeah. Okay. Dumb question."

"And you're not a dumb guy."

A moment passed.

"I wanted to let you know…you were right. All the studies are back. They confirm it was smallpox."

"Really. No shit. I never would have guessed."

"I know, Max, a bit after the point. Anyway, the genetic and antigenic studies verify that it was sledgehammer smallpox. The vaccination of the American public has already begun, and I am amazed that at least half of the population is already vaccinated. It's going very well. In the next five to ten days, we should have the entire American public treated, all thanks to you."

And on behalf of Dr. Kroose, we accept this heartfelt acknowledgement. Thank you. The Gut and the Voice, creators of The Hunch.

"Is there anything I can do for you?" Glen asked quietly.

"No, Glen," I said. "Except…make sure something like this *never* happens again. Okay?"

I thought I heard something akin to a choked sob on the other end of the line, but it could just have been my imagination. Glen's voice was ragged when he responded.

"Count on it," he said. "I'm taking names and kick ass from now on."

"Good," I said. "Take care."

The world began to spiral around me; strange, surrealistic colors seemed to coalesce around the periphery of what little clear vision I had; oxygen deprivation to the brain, I surmised.

The phone slipped from my hand, and my shoulder gave way to my weight.

As I fell back into bed, I could feel what little of my remaining strength leave my body.

The world seemed to go terribly bright for just a moment...and then cold without being uncomfortable. Ah, I thought...so here it is. Here it is...

And, at last, the Voice inside my mind...became silent forever.

THE LAST DAY A DREAM

Or so I thought.

Yet what dreams may come in that sleep of death must give us pause...

It was odd that Shakespeare would so evocatively surface as a kind of preamble to more cohesive thoughts to come. Even in this troubled, restless sleep induced by my delirium, there was a thread of logic that was still intact within my fevered mind. I was not, of course, yet dead, though at that last moment before I fell into unconsciousness, I felt the chill of some kind of passage—my erroneous translation that at last the Great Sleep had consumed me. In fact, my subconscious was merging with a strange kind of waking rationale that was both disturbing and fascinating.

Within moments, I was at some point in the distant past. Distant by which I mean a time before my wife's death. I was in ER, and the images that loomed before me assumed a surreal, crystalline quality not usually associated with the diffused and disjointed quality of dreams or hallucinations. This had happened five years earlier. A young boy, around eight years old, had been presented to my ER moribund, unconscious, and slipping rapidly from the effects of a rattlesnake bite. His mother was there also. She was hysterical to the point where we needed to tranquilize her simply to keep her from thrashing about the ER and making my job of trying to save her son more difficult. The boy apparently had been playing in the backyard of his house near Lancaster. The area was on the edge of some foothills known to be a favorite hangout for rattlesnakes in general. They rarely moved out of their brush territory and did not favor the more crowded communities occupied by people. But on occasion, on those hot days when water was scarce and the sun was a merciless tyrant for man and beast alike, an intrepid viper would head for a more liquid environment, braving even an encounter with human beings. This was one of those occasions. The snake had holed up near the lawn sprinkler system of the backyard where the boy lived. He had been playing nearby when he chanced upon the snoozing rattler. The rest, of course, was history. The boy was fortunate because the snake had struck his leg and not his arm or upper body. Had this been the case, given the boy's size and weight, the venom would have worked its ugliness more rapidly, causing paralysis and hemorrhaging in short order. At the time, however, the poison was arrested from its full impact...but time was still against us.

We intubated the child quickly and applied our usual emergency procedures to ameliorate an otherwise deteriorating situation, but what was really needed (and fast!) was antiserum. I knew this would be a bitch to obtain, and even in this dream state, I could viscerally recall my heart sinking so many years back. I remembered calling—more like begging—the county facility for antiserum; requisitioning the stuff from them was like asking France to take back the Statue of Liberty. It just wasn't gonna happen in a hurry. The renewed nightmare of dealing with an officious little bastard who felt that proper channels and paperwork were more important than expeditious action to save a life filled me with anger even now. At the time, I was a raging lunatic, threatening the official with whom I was dealing with loss of life, limb, consortium, spiritual freedom, and every other damn thing in the world I could think of. At last, I was granted the needed antiserum, and it arrived barely in time to administer to the boy, and thus save his life.

I began to awaken from the dream, and my jumbled thoughts of the past, the boy, the rattlesnake, and the antiserum began to coalesce into more immediate thoughts of here and now, of smallpox, and of dying.

Jesus, if we only had the equivalent of viper antiserum for this sledgehammer smallpox.

Yeah, and if I was kinda black and could dance, I'd be Michael Friggin' Jackson. Bottom line, there was nothing we could use to create an antiserum (and thus antibodies) for our Star of the Moment Disease presently killing myself and my staff...or, more accurately, what remained of it. To have had the vaccine while the disease was far from its genesis, and temporally distant to the infection, would have been to give us a fighting chance. By now, they and I would have had time to develop antibodies. Of course, to obtain any kind of serum would mean that someone here, close by, had, by some stretch of the imagination, actually *been* exposed to some form of sledgehammer smallpox in the past. Fat chance. Even myself, a former infectious diseases specialist, had never been blessed with that kind of exposure.

As I woke, I realized Andy had started an IV to hydrate me. I thought for a moment that was probably why I had been dreaming of IV antidotes. I was feeling a little strong and clearer of mind.

I began to get the shakes. *Shit*, I thought. *I hate these.* Andy came in a moment later, carrying a glass of water.

"Max, how are you feeling?" he asked, his voice soft, conciliatory...resigned.

"Oh, fine, Andy. Try to imagine what it feels like to come out of the backside of a baby rhino, and that should give you a pretty good visual," I said, not feeling remotely funny but irritated by the patronizing question. Of course Andy wasn't intentionally trying to sound this way, but I was annoyed by everything in the known universe at the moment.

"Gotcha," he said, then handed me the water.

I took it in trembling hands, my head an anvil of pounding agony. I glanced at Andy and nodded a mumbled "thanks."

Then a thought came to me. I'm surprised it hadn't come to me earlier.

"You look so goddamned healthy," I said to Andy. "How do you feel?"

Andy seemed uncomfortable with the question. He, of course, wasn't sick. In fact, he looked like he might, in a pinch, be able to run the triathlon at the Olympics just for kicks and giggles.

"I'm okay, Max. A little stressed, I guess."

"Can't understand that, Andy. Just because you're witnessing the onset of a disease that was ostensibly eradicated from the face of the Earth over twenty years ago and are currently a part of history in the making...no, stressing out, I just don't get it."

Andy chuckled, and I realized I was sounding like Prince Prick of the Century.

"Sorry," I sighed. "This whole dying thing has me a bit down. Don't mind me."

"Is there anything I can get you, Max?"

I thought, *cyanide, about a gallon of methadone laced with morphine, and just to give things a happy hour feel, how about a case of Jack Daniels?* However, I decided not to go there. I simply nodded no.

Yet, I was staring at Andy again.

Why *wasn't* he sick yet? Surely he would be, if not in the next day, then a few days. Was it his youth? His immune system was clearly a composite of superhuman titanium, the love of Jesus Christ, and God knows what else. Or was it something else...something...

*   *   *   *

I again fell back into what amounted to be a frenzied, restless sleep accompanied by disjointed images of my past. This time, I was back at Fort Dietrick...back with my friend and mentor, Glen Hamilton. We were walking down a corridor, both drinking coffee and talking. We were discussing, of all things, the nature of smallpox, its genesis, its eradication—the possibilities of its recurrence in the world, either naturally or artificially. The conversation, though somewhat muted in my fevered condition, was still startlingly clear.

"Of course, we've all been vaccinated for smallpox," Glen had said.

"Yes, I'm aware of that," I responded matter-of-factly.

"Ah, but you're wondering if there's any possibility of being vaccinated against an altered or artificially manipulated strain?"

"I've wondered that for a long time," I remember saying.

"It's something I've considered," he said, "but you must remember, there could literally be thousands of different mutational strains conceivably created."

"But if a boilerplate, for lack of a better word, strain could be used as a firewall to other as yet unknown strains—wouldn't this be better than nothing at all?"

"Max, you make a very good point," was all Glen said at the time.

I remember him giving me the strangest look.

Because, you see, no one at Fort Dietrick should even be playing with the notion of a sledgehammer-like antigen of smallpox. Why would one, therefore, get inoculated for it?

Why indeed?

Unless…

Then my gut woke me up.

$$*\qquad*\qquad*\qquad*$$

I was standing, barely, and shaking uncontrollably, but, after this last dream, I was agitated…even excited. I waved Andy over from the ER desk twenty feet away.

"Andy," I said. "When you were at Fort Dietrick, you weren't by some small chance inoculated for smallpox? Monkey pox, perhaps, cow pox, anything?"

Andy shrugged. "No, none of those. We were vaccinated for smallpox, of course, but we were given vaccinia."

"You sure?"

"I was vaccinated with vaccinia, but that was standard for the whole staff," Andy said.

I thought about that for a moment. True, Glen would have these mandatory vaccination procedures well in place, at the bare minimum, given the nature of the work at Dietrick.

However, Glen was, for all practical purposes, a medical spy, a spook for infectious disease analysis and investigation.

What was I thinking? Where was I going with all this?

I studied Andy once again.

"You said you never met my friend Glen Hamilton?"

Andy shook his head. "Never. Only knew of him by reputation. That, and he ran the place."

For the first time in a long time, I actually smiled and felt a fleeting moment of hope.

I struggled to a standing position assisted by the irritatingly strong and healthy young Andy.

"I need to call Fort Dietrick," I said.

"I don't understand," Andy said, looking clearly confused.

"You don't need to at the moment," I snapped back, though I was not really even that annoyed. I was more excited, but I fear my response came off churlish. "Just get Glen on the line, Andy, and forget that I'm sounding like a son of a bitch, okay?"

"Sure, Max, anything you say."

Andy left me, and I leaned against the wall, my mind racing.

Oh, for Christ's sake, this is a long shot, but what the hell...

I was probably grasping for straws, a last desperate attempt to cheat the grave.

I prayed that my friend, Glen, at least this once, was one sneaky, clever bastard, all in the name of national security.

I glanced outside of my emergency room. Andy was punching numbers on the phone near the reception desk. Linda was lying on her back with a blanket over her.

Linda, Andy, and myself were scions to oblivion, the last survivors of this nightmare. I walked into the ER and looked down on Linda. Even so sick, so ravaged by this hideous abomination of a disease, she was still beautiful. I reached down and touched her head. I winced as I could feel the near boiling levels of her temperature. I now prayed more than ever that my gut hunch about Glen had some wheels to it, to mix a metaphor.

I stared outside at the police blockade and the television news vans. I conjured up notions of huge, mechanized buzzards, waiting for the unburied dead to finally, courteously, simply die, so that the festivities of a postmortem could begin in earnest. I suddenly thought of my kids and felt a renewed sense of sadness, the likes of which made me sit down on the edge of the sofa near Linda's feet.

I closed my eyes.

Please, God. Please...make this happen...

"Max."

I opened my eyes. Andy was holding out the phone to me.

"I have Glen Hamilton on the line."

I staggered to my feet and hobbled over to Andy and the phone receiver. I took it, my hands shaking uncontrollably.

Please, God...

✳ ✳ ✳ ✳

"Glen," I whispered.

"Max, I'm surprised. I didn't..."

"Expect to hear from me again, I know," I finished Glen's thought for him. "Listen, old friend, I have a few questions for you, and I need you to be dead honest, no pun intended, with me. Fair enough?"

"Of course, Max. My God..."

I didn't have time for small talk. "Do you remember a young student named Andy Goodman? He worked with you at Dietrick a while back."

"No, can't say that I do. I've had so many students move through there. I may have crossed paths, but that's all I can tell you."

"Well, he knows you," I pushed on. "He worked with your team."

There was a gaping silence at that.

"Glen, did you ever utilize any form of sledgehammer smallpox in that facility, simply for observational purposes, obviously."

Again, Glen was quiet.

"Glen...please. Did you?"

At last, Glen sighed on the other end of the phone. "This isn't a secured line, Max. You have to understand that."

"Fuck security," I said softly. "Talk to me."

Glen covered the phone for a moment, this much I could tell. It sounded like he was asking someone to excuse himself. I waited an eternity. It seemed that continents could have risen and fallen in the span of time I last heard his voice, yet Glen was only off the line for a few seconds.

"Sorry, Max. Okay. Yes."

"Yes, what?"

"Yes.... we did use an attenuated form of sledgehammer. It was top secret, experimental stuff contained to the max on bio-levels."

I closed my eyes and nodded. "Glen, you marvelous bastard," I said softly. "My boy Andy. He's a young doctor on my staff. He's the only one of us not sick. He was probably inoculated at Dietrick and for stuff other than just vaccinia." *no informed consent !?*

Glen was again silent. Then, "I had everyone inoculated against the existing sledgehammer. I didn't take chances."

"I knew you wouldn't. Glen, you know where I'm going with this?"

"I sure do, Max," Glen said, and he chuckled. "If you have to chain your young doctor to a pole, do it. I'm sending in a team to steal his blood."

He didn't wait for my answer and simply hung up the phone. I didn't mind a bit.

I looked over to Linda and put my hand on her face.

"Don't give up yet, beautiful. We just may have a cure for a rainy day."

✳   ✳   ✳   ✳

Glen and his team arrived within five hours. They descended on young Andy like jackals on a hapless gazelle in the Serengeti. He was phlebotomized—a sexy medical term for bled—right there in the ER, so quickly and so efficiently that your basic vampire would have thrown in the towel and taken up needlework as an alternate profession.

Though, of course, all of us (the perennial victims in this drama) were kept quarantined in ER, the team exited posthaste to an outside lab two miles away, wherein Andy's blood was just as immediately processed through centrifuge. Centrifuging the blood was critical, of course, to separate the various blood components, such as the cellular products and the immunoglobulins—the stuff that was intrinsically lethal to disease and/or otherwise would annihilate the stuff killing yours truly—was needed for the ultimate antiserum. Various proteins would then be separated and identified (and no doubt catalogued) through immunodiffusion and immunoelectrophoretic techniques.

This took, fortunately, only a matter of hours.

A day would be too late.

And so we waited.

We had little choice in the matter.

Linda remained in coma, although her vital signs remained stable. I again felt her head, and instinctively, from the previous touch, I could tell her fever had kicked up half a point.

Thank God, however, we were only twenty-eight hours into this disease…more or less. Perhaps the vaccine had bought us who were infected later a little time. Any longer and I might as well consider an eternal career in harp playing along with my unfortunate staff.

The wait was interminable, and I found myself feeling more irritable with every passing quarter hour.

Jesus, hurry.

My rational mind knew that we were in the best of hands. There was no one better out there then Glen Hamilton. Still, the mind, when it feels like it's cooking next to a few frying eggs, does funny thing to emotion and spirit.

Andy watched us silently and offered me a small smile. He, of course, could not be taken off the premises until everything was checked and rechecked by Glen's team. It wouldn't have mattered.

"I'm not leaving these people," Andy said to Glen, even while being bled. "Understand, Dr. Hamilton?"

Glen had looked at him and given him a small smile that didn't need any verbal translation. Andy nodded just to confirm his conviction.

I could have kissed the kid at that point.

If I lived, I still might do so and take him as my adopted son, make him play Furry Furry Rabbit with my kids, or leave him my vast fortune. Something.

I looked at the clock on the wall.

Glen had been gone an hour.

I remembered a poem by William Blake.

To hold the world in a grain of sand,
heaven in a wild flower,
infinity in the palm of your hand,
eternity in an hour.

It was the longest hour of my life.

*   *   *   *

The second hour was tortuous, but it passed, and finally Glen and his team returned. He almost jogged up to me and took me by the shoulders.

"We're going to harvest the antiserum right here in the lab. I've brought some equipment that we'll need. We'll save time working on-site and possibly find other donors—there were several on staff when we were working on sledgehammer who were vaccinated with the attenuated virus."

I couldn't reply. I just nodded.

I then turned and walked over to Linda and kissed her on the lips. She was unusually tranquil, as if she had total confidence in what we were doing.

"We just might get through this, my dear."

I sighed, nodded, and thought maybe we should pray.

Not the best technical or medical advice, I thought to myself, *but, Jesus Christ—it sure couldn't hurt.*

*   *   *   *

Glen and company had returned in twenty minutes, syringes loaded with what we assumed was the serum manna from heaven. So we hoped.

We were not disappointed.

Linda was injected first, myself a few minutes later by Glen himself.

"What now?" I asked him.

He didn't even blink.

"We wait."

*   *   *   *

And wait we did.

To kill the hobgoblins of panic within my brain, I attempted to construct an image of what was taking place in my body. I could feel the antibodies attach themselves to this vicious virus triggering billions of explosions as each virion exposed itself, giving time for my own immune system to generate its own antibodies and rendering me immune to it.

A few hours passed…and then I was keenly aware of how I was feeling. I first realized that I was no longer in pain. I had begun to defervesce, as well. I had been sitting next to Linda the entire time, holding her hand, but now I stood up and looked to Andy.

"Andy, come here, would you?"

Andy approached me.

"Take my BP, would you?"

He nodded.

"Okay, last time we did this you were 80 over 40."

"How can I forget?" I quipped.

He smiled at that, then pumped me up.

I tried not to hold my breath as he studied the gauge. He then looked to me, and a very slow smile crossed his face. "130 over 88."

"Coming up," I whispered. "Coming up."

"Damn right it's coming up," he chuckled.

I pointed at Linda, and he moved over and performed the same BP procedure on her. He looked back to me after he had finished. "Ten points higher, as well." As he did this, Linda began to awaken. "The serum is kicking in."

I leaned against the wall and closed my eyes.

"Thank you," I said, staring at the ceiling.

*   *   *   *

Another hour passed, and it became obvious that the secondary infections that Linda and I were both infected with had been somewhat controlled and, in gestalt, we both looked a hell of a lot better.

Four hours later, it was apparent that we were going to survive.

We drank water constantly and continued to improve, as Glen fussed over us like a mother hen. We didn't mind a bit. I looked at him at one point and shook my head.

"Disaster averted. Western civilization as we know it saved."

He nodded and stared at me with clear respect.

"Thanks to you, my friend. You saw the signs, the demon trying to take over. If it had been someone else—someone without your instinct…"

"But it wasn't."

"This time," he said softly.

I couldn't disagree on that point.

"There can't be another time, Glen. Not after this…"

"Yeah," he said.

Not ever!

*   *   *   *

I took a week off and did nothing more exertion-filled than play with my children. It was the most profoundly happy period in my life. The press continued to be intrusive, but this was to be expected. I was a survivor to the unsurvivable, myself and Linda, of course. We were earmarked for a special place in medical history. I smiled once and awhile at the thought. I was not, nor ever would be, a Louis Pasteur or Alexander Fleming—medical giants who were responsible for the preservation of millions of lives. No, I was just plain damn lucky. That would be my footnote for posterity in the chronicles of biological posterity.

Glen, of course, would tell me otherwise. He would say that I single-handedly saved (or conceivably saved) the world—with my gut, my hunch-hatching guy. Flattering…but I think exaggerated.

Or was it?

Alexander Fleming was cleaning out petrie dishes of bacteria when he noticed some mold surrounding one of his specimens. That mold was killing the bacteria.

His exact words at the time were not unlike mine a few weeks back. They were, quite simply, "That's funny." His gut, his curiosity, helped developed penicillin, and he had been working from a gut hunch as well.

Maybe Glen was right.

Maybe one man—one woman—one individual with a feeling, or with a certain diagnostic instinct, could make the difference between life and death for millions...or billions, on a planetary scale.

These thoughts continued to cogitated as I sat behind my desk ten days later, taking a break from the renewed activity in my ER. Behind closed doors, I had my feet up on a chair, thinking about what had happened to me. I thought about the future more than anything else: Could this, *would* this, happen again? Though I had gently admonished Glen that a sledgehammer scenario could never be allowed to manifest itself again on American soil—nay, anywhere on the planet, I asked myself if I was being totally realistic? Even with additional safeguards in place, a renewed, vigorous biological antiterrorism forum even now being implemented and fortified due to the events of a mere two weeks ago...was this enough, I wondered? Was there really any deterrent to such an obscene utility of mutated smallpox by a determined force, such as Al Queda, or some other well-motivated extremist group?

I shuddered as I recalled my near miss with death. Glen had suggested that I return to my initial field of calling—infectious diseases. Hell, it was more than a suggestion, it was a tacit plea. He felt that with my close encounter with the sledgehammer kind, I could be invaluable to the cause, as it were, and contribute greatly to the growing awareness of the very real dangers of bioterrorism. I can't say it wasn't tempting.

Yet, after the recent events and with the self-knowledge that I possessed some gift, some preternatural instinct for disease detection...I decided that my place should and always would be here in the emergency room. I had been the first line of defense in detecting the sledgehammer a few weeks back. Perhaps...perhaps, I would be called upon again, should such terrible circumstances again rear the ugly head of apocalyptic proportions. If not myself, I could guide others—like Andy—who had determined after his experience in ER to become an ER doctor himself—to keep vigil, like a medical Cerebrus at the gates of hell, for the signs and symptomatology of a worse-case scenario.

And in a blinding, crystalline moment of clarity, I realized that another bioterrorist attack was not only a possibility...but a certainty.

We must be ready. All of us.

For it is not a matter of *if* an attack should come, but merely a matter of *when*.

Will we be ready?
Will we?

THE END

0-977-13870-4